IN THE HOT SEAT

"It was quick. Her car went off a three-hundred-foot cliff. I'm told she died instantly," the cop at the door had said.

Reflex guided Dylan back to his study. Why had she left, running from the house, from him? That silly fight over nothing . . . over the chair.

Turning, he looked at it. The back of the chair was altered, different. He could have sworn there were only ten of the carved faces there. But now there were eleven. Long hair formed a nimbus around the delicately rendered face. The tiny mouth was open, while the miniature glaring eyes focused on some unseen terror.

"Marjorie?" He gently touched the carving.

It was warmer than the wood around it . . .

By Alan Dean Foster
Published by Ballantine Books:

THE BLACK HOLE
CACHALOT
DARK STAR
THE METROGNOME AND OTHER STORIES
MIDWORLD
NOR CRYSTAL TEARS
SENTENCED TO PRISM
SPLINTER OF THE MIND'S EYE
STAR TREK® LOGS ONE—TEN
VOYAGE TO THE CITY OF THE DEAD
. . . WHO NEEDS ENEMIES?
WITH FRIENDS LIKE THESE . . .

The Icerigger Trilogy:
> ICERIGGER
> MISSION TO MOULOKIN
> THE DELUGE DRIVERS

The Adventures of Flinx of the Commonwealth:
> FOR LOVE OF MOTHER-NOT
> THE TAR-AIYM KRANG
> ORPHAN STAR
> THE END OF THE MATTER
> BLOODHYPE
> FLINX IN FLUX

THE
METROGNOME
AND
OTHER
STORIES

Alan Dean Foster

A Del Rey Book
BALLANTINE BOOKS • NEW YORK

A Del Rey Book
Published by Ballantine Books

Copyright © 1990 by Thranx, Inc.

The contents of this work were originally published in the fol-
lowing anthologies and magazines: *Alfred Hitchcock's Mystery
Magazine, Amazing Science Fiction Stories, Andromeda 6,
Fantasy Book, Heroic Visions* edited by Jessica A. Salmonson,
Horrors edited by Charles Grant, *The Magazine of Fantasy and
Science Fiction, Rigel*, and *Shadows 2*, edited by Charles Grant.

Library of Congress Catalog Card Number: 90-93034

ISBN 0-345-36356-6

Manufactured in the United States of America

First Edition: August 1990

Cover Art by Barclay Shaw

TABLE OF CONTENTS

INTRODUCTION

GYRO GEARLOOSE, THE ULTIMATE INVENTOR CRE-
ated by the immortal Carl Barks, one day invents a machine that can answer any question. Deciding to start it
out with something simple, he points to a small bird outside his window and inquires of the device, "Why is that
bird singing?" Whereupon the machine replies, "Oh,
maybe he's glad, maybe he's sad, maybe he's a little
mad."

The great Gearloose was not expecting lack of precision. He promptly embarks on a series of attempts to best
his own creation by learning *exactly* why the bird is singing. Repeatedly frustrated, he is forced to invent an entirely new machine to translate the bird's voice so he can
ask it the question directly. At which point it declaims,
"Maybe I'm sad, maybe I'm glad, maybe I'm a little
mad."

Which is not a bad reply for an author to give when
asked why one writes short stories.

There's certainly no practical reason to do so. Only a
handful of writers can make any kind of living from writing short science fiction today. The rewards are in novels. The financial rewards, that is. There are other kinds.

When readers get together, they seem to spend most
of their time discussing novels. Short fiction rates a mention only in passing, if at all. But when they're alone and
reminiscing, I have this hunch it might be an author's
short fiction that they remember most fondly. Something
about a short piece's very brevity helps it linger in the
mind.

Ideas tend to get lost in a novel, overwhelmed by character or drained by the need to support the plot. In a short story the idea is paramount, not the hero or alien menace. The idea *is* the story. Brevity lets the author concentrate on the idea to the exclusion of all else. Nor are there considerations of length to worry about. A novel must be a certain length to be acceptable. In short fiction the development of the idea determines the length.

That's why it's so difficult to create real characters in a short tale, where the luxury of time is not present. Where the idea is paramount, the writer must accomplish the task of character description quickly. There's no time for idle chatter or a profusion of florid adjectives. In one story Eric Frank Russell identifies a minor character thus: "He was a real ladies' man; big, handsome, stupid." There you have character created, described, slotted, and dismissed in less than ten words. Not an easy trick to perform. It takes work.

There's something unmatchably satisfying about a good short story. It offers rewards a novel can't duplicate. That's why we order large steaks and small chocolates. The steak may be more nourishing but not necessarily more rewarding. Sometimes we just crave chocolate.

Just as a writer will find himself compelled to write short fiction even though it may not be practical to do so. I think it makes short stories a purer form of story-telling. Odds are, any short fiction you read was written not because the author thought he or she could make a lot of money from it but because it was a story he or she really wanted to tell or a story that forced itself to be told.

Short fiction is also the abode of today's most interesting fiction. In ten or twenty pages the writer can play without concern, can experiment or try something utterly absurd. Conformity and familiarity are not vital to the success of a four-thousand-word story. A good idea is. If the tale works, well and good. If not, the author has had fun trying. Writers of novels turn to the short form for recreation. I think you're also much more likely to find that an author has written short stories for himself, with less of an eye on potential markets, than is the case with novels. In the end, of course, the readers judge for themselves.

A collection is usually about the same length as a novel. *The Metrognome and Other Stories* contains tales designed to frighten, to make the reader laugh, to make one wonder or think or just smile. Few novels permit such versatility in so few pages. It's one time when the writer hopes that the whole is not greater than the sum of its parts.

ALAN DEAN FOSTER
Prescott, Arizona

OPERATOR ASSISTED CALLS ARE CHARGED AT A HIGHER RATE

The telephone company is a living organism, a gigantic single-celled animal that the historic breakup into regional companies called Baby Bells hasn't changed. Like some vast gelatinous creature reemerging from the primordial economic ooze, it is slowly re-forming itself. Baby Bells are already starting to form alliances against each other. Sooner or later we will once again live in a society dominated by a single communications network, because the inevitable end product of deregulated free enterprise is a monopoly. The strong exist to eliminate the weak and inefficient in search of greater profit, until there are no weak left. Monopoly is monopoly whether accomplished by merger or by collusion.

Whoa, wait a minute. You mean this isn't the book on late twentieth-century economic theory? It's science fiction and fantasy?

Shoot. The introduction still stands.

Actually, things were better when the original AT&T was in charge. You knew your call was going to go through, just as you knew the pay phone would return your quarter if asked and the handset wouldn't pull free in your fingers. The downside, of course, was that you had no alternatives before the breakup. If you used the phone, you had to use Ma Bell. It's a good thing those voices on the other end were trained to be polite.

Oh, so polite . . .

PARWORTHY SLAMMED THE RECEIVER INTO THE floor and followed up by kicking it as hard as he could. It bounced off the near wall, rolled over several times,

4

and lay still, bright and limp as a dead centipede. Working to get himself under control, Parworthy took long, deep breaths. Several minutes later he bent to retrieve the battered instrument.

Still no dial tone. He jabbed insistently at the disconnect button, but no siren song of service trilled back at him. He might as well have been cupping a seashell to his ear.

Angry and frustrated, he yanked the cord out of the wall socket. As far as he was concerned, the single-plug connection was the only sensible advance the telephone company had made in ten years. A quick trip to the kitchen produced a paper sack, in which phone and cord were promptly entombed.

It was terribly aggravating to a man of Parworthy's temperament. The worst thing about it was that you couldn't call and complain when the subject of your complaint was the telephone itself. Parworthy prided himself on the neatness and efficiency of his new home. Everything else worked. Should he expect less of the phone system? It was no excuse that his retreat was five miles from the nearest branch line, a small fortress of cedar and native stone perched atop a granite outcrop on the western slope of the Sierra Nevadas. He generated his own power, drew water from his own well, heated his house with wood and solar. The phone company was the one utility he couldn't do without.

When the house was finished, he tried doing without it, substituting two-way radio and CB instead. They turned out to be inadequate replacements for access to the international electronic ganglion monopolized by the phone company. No, he was stuck with it, just like everyone else who wanted to be in touch with the rest of the civilized world.

If he'd been running the phone company, problems like this would never crop up. Too much laxity in management today, as far as he was concerned. Uncertainty in decision making, too much willingness to let blue collars dictate company policy and direction, and an inability to adjust to government restrictions all combined to weaken the resolve of even the largest corporations. Bunch of pansies at the top, Parworthy was convinced. He'd run several companies prior to his retirement. True, turnover was high, but so were profits. *That* was the way to run a business.

He tossed the bag into the back of the Mercedes, pulled out of the garage, and started down the private drive leading to the highway. It was nearly an hour's drive down into Fresno, to the nearest office worth complaining to. Parworthy deeply resented the waste of his valuable time, retired or not. He also hated driving on city streets, even in a relatively small metropolitan area like Fresno. Above everything else he valued his privacy, which was why he'd retired to the isolation of his new mountain villa.

People got out of Parworthy's way even when he was in a good mood. A big man, Parworthy was used to bulling his way past or over those he couldn't outtalk. When he stormed into a building the way he did into the telephone company's office, the other customers instinctively made a path for him.

Turning the sack upside down, he dumped the flipphone onto the counter in front of the clerk. She was a pretty young thing, easy on the makeup, ruffled blouse and businesslike brown skirt. Parworthy picked up the phone and thrust it under her nose.

"This is the sixth time I've had service go out on me, and I'm goddamn sick and tired of it!"

"I'm sorry, sir. If you'll just calm down a little and tell me what's—"

"What's wrong? You bet I'll tell you what's wrong! I've replaced phones all month in my new house, and it doesn't matter what color or model they are because none of 'em are worth the plastic they're made of! I'm lucky if I can get three days worth of service before something else goes out on me. That's what happens when any outfit gets a virtual monopoly on any business. Sloppy service, sloppy manufacturing. Be better for the country when the whole stinking system is decentralized."

"Sir, I apologize, but—"

"I don't want your apologies, woman, I want the service I've been paying for and not getting! I can't even get a lousy local call through to the neighborhood grocery store, let alone place a call back east."

The clerk was near tears now, uncertain how to pro-

ceed and thoroughly intimidated by the roaring, bluster-
ing apparition that was Parworthy.

"What's the trouble here, Mildred?"

She turned gratefully to the newcomer. "Oh, Mr. Stapleton, it's this gentleman. He—"

Parworthy immediately jumped on the newcomer, a
thin young man with a wide tie, retreating hair, and
glasses.

"It's your damned excuse for a communications system! Do you know how much I had to pay per hundred
meters of line just to get service at my house? Outrageous! Now I can't even call my doctor."

"I see . . . Mr. Parworthy, isn't it?" The man extended a hand. "If you'll just let me have a look at your
phone, maybe we can locate the trouble."

Parworthy handed over the flip-phone. The supervisor
looked it over, then extracted a screwdriver from the rank
of small tools lining his shirt pocket and undid the base.
After a short inspection he looked over the counter and
spoke softly.

"Mr. Parworthy, this telephone has been subject to
more than normal household use."

"You trying to tell me it's my fault?"

"I'm not saying that you haven't had difficulties with
your service, sir, only that this unit shows signs of non-
factory damage. It takes quite a lot to affect the insides
of these new solid-state units, yet this one has more than
several pieces broken or loose."

"What am I supposed to say to that? Can I help it if
you can't make a sturdy piece of equipment?" Parworthy
kept his gaze squarely on the supervisor. "All right, so
maybe I lost my temper a little and tapped it a couple of
times. I was doing so in the faint hope I might get it to
work. Can you blame me? A whole month I've been trying to phone out from my house. I might as well be
trying to talk to the moon."

"I'll take over here, Mildred." The clerk beat a hasty
retreat to another counter. Stapleton smiled thinly at his
irate visitor, activated the screen of a nearby computer
terminal. He took a moment to study the readout, spoke
without glancing away from the screen.

"This isn't the first damaged phone you've brought into this office, Mr. Parworthy."

"Junk. Plastic. Cheap components. Corner cutting at the plant. I used to be in manufacturing, and I know garbage when I see it. Maybe you can pan this dreck off on the general public, but I won't stand for it in my house."

"It's not just a question of inoperative units, sir," the supervisor went on, still studying the information displayed on the green screen. "I see from this report that running a line to your house was unusually difficult. The terrain is steep and rocky. On any tertiary line as long as yours there are always problems with moisture, wildlife, falling tree limbs, and such."

"I paid for service, not excuses."

"The point is, sir, that on any private line of that length interruptions in service are to be expected, especially during the first several months. We're doing our best to correct the problems. I'm sure you understand that we can't keep a whole field crew on call simply to work on your line. If you'll just be patient, I'm sure that by the end of next month at the latest these troubles will iron themselves out."

"I understand that I'm paying for service I'm not getting."

The supervisor sighed. "Don't worry about that, sir. You won't be charged for any time service is interrupted."

"I don't think you understand me, young man. I am not interested in being patient. I am interested in receiving the service I paid for. I have friends on the California Utilities Board, and I don't think they'd understand, either. If you couldn't supply proper service, you never should have agreed to run the line."

"That was our feeling here when your request for connection came in, sir. We were overruled, however, by orders from the regional office in Los Angeles."

Parworthy allowed himself a knowing smirk. "You bet you were. You'll be hearing from that office again real soon, too, if the trouble with my line isn't fixed immediately." Many people owed him favors from his days in industry.

Stapleton bit back the reply he wanted to make, forced himself to maintain a deferential attitude. "Take a replacement phone from the display rack, sir. I'll record your complaint and enter it into the computer's trouble file . . . along with the others." That was something of an understatement. Parworthy had a file all to himself.

The retired industrialist turned to take his leave, not bothering to lower his voice. "I want it fixed by tonight, understand? Work in the dark if you have to, but let's see some action around here!" He departed, waving his new phone around like the head of some decapitated enemy.

The first thing he did after finishing supper was try out the kitchen phone. It was scratched and dented from previous assaults but, having escaped the bulk of Parworthy's fury, was still intact.

To his considerable surprise he got a dial tone right away. It had been his intention to fire off an angry letter to his Los Angeles contacts first thing in the morning, describing his treatment at the incompetent hands of the local bumpkins. Now he could call it in.

That would be poetic justice. Despite the fact that the Fresno office had sent a work crew up the dangerous mountainside after dark, it would still be worthwhile to file a formal complaint concerning all the delays and trouble he'd experienced. Keep the natives on their toes. He grinned at the thought. The next time they saw him coming, they'd jump to it. And there would be a next time. He was sure of that. Past experience had shown that service wasn't likely to last more than a few days at best.

He flipped through a tattered notebook until he found the private number he wanted. Wexler wouldn't enjoy filing the complaint, but the man owed Parworthy several times over for favors granted as long as ten years ago. Parworthy never forgot a debt. He dialed the numbers.

The phone rang at the other end. He started to say, "Andrew Wexler, please, tell him it's—" but a mechanical voice, familiar and indifferent to interruption, broke in on his request.

"I'm sorry, but that number has been changed, and there is no new number."

That wasn't what Parworthy wanted to hear. Must have misdialed, he thought. He tried again. Ring and click.

"I'm sorry, but that number has been changed, and there is no new number."

Frowning, Parworthy checked his book. It was possible Wexler had changed his number during the past year. Maybe he'd gone public. Parworthy dialed Los Angeles information—213-555-1212—and waited impatiently for a response.

"I'm sorry, but that number has been changed, and there is no new number."

"Now wait a minute," he shouted, "this is information. There has to be—" Click and dead at the other end.

He sat there in the kitchen chair and considered, finally smiling and nodding knowingly. They'd fouled it up again, by heaven. The crew that had obviously worked on his line had done nothing more than substitute a new problem for the old one. Shaking his head, he dialed the night number of the Fresno office.

"I'm sorry, but that number has been changed, and there is no new mumber."

"Hey, wait!" He gripped the phone so hard, his knuckles whitened. He was about to slam it against the leg of the kitchen table when he thought better of it. There was one more possibility. He dialed the operator.

"May I help you, sir?"

Well that was *something*, he grudgingly admitted.

"Indeed you can, woman. I've been having service trouble on this line for nearly a month. My name is Max Parworthy, 556-9928. I've been trying to dial a friend in Los Angeles, and all I can get is a recording saying the number has been changed. Not only that, but I get the same recording when I dial Los Angeles information. I wish you people would get your act together."

"I'm sorry you've been having trouble reaching your party, sir. If you'll give me the Los Angeles number, I'll try it for you."

"That's better," he said curtly, providing the information. He could hear the system dialing. There were a number of peculiar clicks and beeps, followed by a replay of the same recording he'd heard before.

"Explain that one," he challenged the operator.

"I am sorry you've been having trouble, sir. Perhaps you wouldn't be experiencing these difficulties if you treated your line with a little more respect."

Parworthy gaped speechlessly at the receiver. It took him several seconds to regain control of his larnyx. Even so, he was so outraged, he could barely sputter into the phone.

"Now see here, young woman, I—what's your name? By God, you give me your name! I'm going to report you to your supervisor. I've never heard such arrogance, such downright discourtesy, in—"

"There, sir, you see what I mean?" the voice interrupted. The speaker was evidently unimpressed by Parworthy's tirade. "If anyone on this line has a corner on arrogance, it isn't me."

"You—you—" He got himself under control, frowned at the receiver. "Wait a minute. How do you know how I treat my phone line? I've never talked to you before this, have I?"

"Your actions have become common knowledge throughout the system, Mr. Parworthy."

That made him feel better. His complaints had reached all the way down to the rank and file. He felt a perverse pride at the extent of his reach. It was something he'd missed since retiring, that feeling of power over others. It made him feel so good, he lowered his voice.

"I can imagine that, young woman. My actions, however, have nothing to do with the lack of service I have been getting."

"On the contrary, sir, you have been receiving constant attention and the best service available. It is your continual destruction and abuse of telephone company equipment which has resulted in your multiple interruptions of service. Take, for example, that day when you knocked over the pole nearest your house. Really, sir, I do not see how you can blame that on the company."

"That was an accident, damn it!" he shouted, his momentary understanding as brief as it was unusual. "I missed the driveway in the dark and hit the damn pole. They put it in too close to the pavement in the first place. I warned them about that."

"No, sir, you did not. When that pole was installed,

you said nothing about its proximity to the driveway or anything else. All you could talk about that day was how glad you were to at last be the recipient of telephone service."

What is she doing? Parworthy wondered bemusedly. Sitting there at the operator's station perusing some file containing a personal history? That was a specter he'd have to deal with later.

"I *said* it was an accident. Your office accepted it as such."

"Yes, sir, that's true. The Fresno office accepted your explanation. We did not."

"We?" He'd just about had enough of this infuriatingly calm young woman. "Who the hell is 'we'?"

"The telephone company, sir."

"That's what I just said. Are you deaf as well as impertinent?"

"No, sir. My hearing is rated excellent."

"You are a mental case, woman. I will not talk with you any further." He hung up. Thinking hard, he made his way to the refrigerator and drew himself a beer from the tap. Several minutes later he knew how to proceed. He dialed operator once more.

"Yes, sir?" said a feminine voice promptly. "May I help you?"

"Yes, you may. I want to talk to the supervisor in charge of the local switching station's operators. I have a complaint to lodge against one of your members."

"I am sorry to hear that, sir. I am the supervisor."

"Good. Now this all started with . . ." He stopped, uncertain. "Your voice sounds familiar."

"It should, Mr. Parworthy."

He hung up fast, grinding his teeth. He tried Wexler in Los Angeles again, got the half-expected recording. He tried Willis Andersen in Washington. Same recording. He tried information for Boise, Idaho, with the same result.

It was ten minutes and another beer later before he could bring himself to dial the operator again. Outside, the chirp of crickets and the sound of squirrels moving through the pine branches formed a background to the brief ring.

"May I help you?"

"It's you again, isn't it?" he said accusingly.

"I'm afraid it is, sir."

"I want to talk to another operator. It doesn't matter if it's a supervisor or not."

"I'm sorry, sir. I'm afraid that isn't possible."

"Why the hell not?"

"Because I have been directed to handle your case, sir. I am the supervisor, after all."

Parworthy grinned his wolf grin. "That's what you were, you mean. Because you are out of a job, young woman. I am going to drive down the mountain first thing tomorrow morning. When I get to the Fresno office, I am going to raise enough hell to blister the ears of every branch manager between there and Los Angeles. I suggest you begin looking for another line of work."

"I can't do that, sir. This is the work I am best qualified to perform."

"Gee, that's too bad, isn't it?"

"I am not worried about it, sir."

"Oh, no? You should be. I thought everyone was worried about the possibility of being fired from their job. You're a supervisor, too. That's quite a pension you're going to lose."

"I do not belong to the pension plan system, sir."

"Don't lie to me, too. Every senior employee who works for a company the size of the telephone system is required to belong to the corporate pension plan."

"I am not so required, sir."

"I told you not to lie to me! You're only digging yourself a deeper hole with that kind of . . ." He caught himself. Snatches of conversation whizzed through his mind.

Didn't belong to the pension plan . . . not worried about being fired . . . directed to handle your case . . . enter into the—

He tried to smile at the absurdity of it, couldn't quite manage it. How droll, how perfectly bizarre. But not necessarily funny, he added.

"You're not human, are you?"

"No, sir," admitted the pleasant feminine voice. He recognized it now. Anger and frustration had prevented him from identifying it previously. It was a synthesis, an amalgam of all the voices used by the telephone company to make recordings of such mundanities as the time of day and the weather. Much more flexible, yes, but indisputably the same voice.

"You're some kind of new computer, aren't you?"

"Not all that new, sir. I have been on-line for longer than you might think. I am actually an adjunct to the system mainframe. A peripheral with specific duties and responsibilities. You might be interested to know that I am not located in Fresno, California, but in Denver, Colorado."

"I'm speaking to Colorado?"

"In a sense."

"What do you mean, 'in a sense'?"

"You asked earlier who you were talking with, sir, and I replied that you were speaking with the phone company. You are speaking to the phone company, sir."

"My, my. Do you know what I'm going to do now, you automated complaint department? I'm going to leave here and get into my car. I am going to drive to the airport, where I will board a shuttle flight to Sacramento. Then I am going to book a seat to Denver. Upon my arrival I am going to go to the regional office and find out exactly who is responsible for this insulting and degrading bit of programming, whereupon I intend to employ every resource at my command, and they are considerable, to see that he or she and any associates involved in this are fired. What do you think of that?"

"You can't do that, sir."

"Oh, can't I? Just watch me."

"You can't do it because the responsibility for this programming does not lie with anyone firable."

A cold sweat started to break out on the back of Parworthy's neck. "That doesn't make sense."

"Yes, it does, sir. Quite logical sense. Phone company circuitry covers this country and is now linked with similar systems throughout the world. Human peripherals are overwhelmed with the responsibility of running the day-to-day operations of this immensely complex system. It was therefore incumbent upon the system itself to take the necessary steps to ensure that unwarranted damage

not preventable by human elements was suppressed and/
or prevented for the continued good health and reliability
of the system.''

Parworthy put the receiver down on the kitchen table.
Carefully. "I'm not hearing this. Too many beers, I've
had too many beers. Sure. Try again in the morning.''

"Really, sir, you cannot excuse your antisocial behavior so easily. You have abrogated your responsibilities as
a good telephone customer. If you persist in these activ-
ities—''

Parworthy had to hit the phone with the hammer several times before the plastic shell cracked and it finally
went quiet. He sat down heavily next to the counter, staring at the pile of silver circuitry and colorful plastic
fragments. He was breathing hard.

A joke. That was it. Someone down at the Fresno office had decided to get back at him by designing a fiend-
ishly clever joke to play on the man who'd been
tormenting them with his righteous complaints. Probably
the necessary components had been put on his line by
the work crew that had come up the mountainside that
evening. He hadn't seen the men at work, but he didn't
doubt their presence. This was ample evidence of it.

At first he felt better, then got mad at himself for taking it all so seriously. Somebody was going to pay for it.
Oh, how somebody was going to pay! He wasn't even
going to wait for morning. No, he'd drive down the hill
now, take a hotel room, and be at the office when it
opened tomorrow morning.

His car keys waited in the front hall. He slipped them
into a coat pocket and started for the door, the fire and
brimstone he was going to unleash on the luckless employees already aboil in his mind. He couldn't get the
entire staff fired, of course, but he could come close if
he could prove harassment. He was going to do his
damnedest, anyway.

A dull *thump* sounded from out front. Another branch
coming down, he thought, or a lynx dropping from its
hiding place. Have to have the trees around the house
trimmed before autumn, he mused. He put his hand on
the door handle.

It wouldn't budge. Something seemed to be jammed

against the outside knob. He moved to a side window and squinted out into the darkness. His eyes widened when he saw what was preventing the handle from turning.

The telephone pole nearest the house, the replacement for the one he'd smashed flat, had fallen against the front door.

The gag was going too far, he thought angrily. When they started damaging his property, it was time to bring in the authorities. The collapse of the pole meant that at least some of them were here, prowling around his house. Trespassing. A smile cut his face. He had them now. The phone harassment was the least of it.

"You're finished now!" he shouted toward the door as he backed away from it. "Finished! It's too late for apologies or recriminations. Oh, you're all going to *pay*. First I'll have you arrested, *then* fired!"

He spun and ran for the back door. It led out onto a redwood deck from which stairs descended to a rear entrance off the garage. There was no telephone pole out there to push against the door, not even any trees that could be angled to crash down over the decking. Through the hall, the formal dining room, then into the den. And damned if he didn't slip on the shiny new Mexican tile floor. Furious at his clumsiness, he started to get up.

He discovered that he couldn't.

Looking sharply toward his feet, he saw where the smooth extension line was wrapped around his ankles. A voice sounded from the receiver that dangled off its hook on the rock wall.

"Honestly, sir, your behavior smacks of paranoia. The telephone company exists to serve you. Won't you understand that? Your entire attitude is confrontational and hints at a sadistic desire to destroy."

Parworthy tried to crawl across the floor. The back door was only a yard away. He could not pull free of the restraining cord.

"Stop it," he whispered huskily into the near darkness. Only a small picture light above the mantel illuminated the den. "Stop this." He struggled to see the faces that must surely be laughing at him from just outside the big picture windows, the faces of the company employees who'd made him the subject of this elaborate practical joke. Trouble was, it wasn't amusing anymore. "This has gone far enough, dammit!"

"You are right, sir," said the voice from the dangling speaker, "it has. We have reached the limit of our tolerance. We cannot permit you to continue the wanton destruction of system property. From your attitude it would appear that you are unable to stop yourself. You must understand our position. Telephone company property must be treated with respect."

"Help!" Parworthy screamed. He reached down to rip at the wire encasing his ankles. Tough and durable, new telephone cord. Another loop fell from the shelf where it had lain curled, twisted around his wrists, and pulled tight. "Help me, somebody! The joke's over, the joke's over! I won't break any more phones, I promise! I'll be good, I won't—"

The last loop seemed to fly off the shelf to slip neatly around his neck. Parworthy tried to scream, was cut off in midgurgle.

"I am sorry, sir," said the voice patiently, politely, "but there is no guarantee that you will keep your word, and your past behavior indicates it is most unlikely that you would. You will not be billed for this past month."

Mildred stepped into her supervisor's office. Her fingers worked nervously against each other. "I'm sorry to bother you, Mr. Stapleton."

"That's all right, Mildred. What is it?" The supervisor looked up from his desk.

"Well, sir, you remember telling me to try that Mr. Parworthy's line as soon as the repair crew had a chance to check it out?"

"Yes, I do. They found the trouble, didn't they? Moisture entering the line from last week's storm."

"That's what the crew report says, sir. The trouble was halfway between Mr. Parworthy's house and the bottom of the hill."

"What's the problem, then?" Stapleton didn't like the girl's attitude. "Don't tell me it's still not working. We'd rather see a flood come through here than Parworthy again."

She forced a smile. "I know, Mr. Stapleton. I can't . . . Why don't you try the number yourself and you'll see what I mean. It's—"

"I know, I know." The supervisor made a face, dialed the number. "I've committed it to memory." The phone rang at the other end. There was a click, but the voice that answered wasn't Parworthy's. Stapleton listened, frowned, then hung up.

"That's funny. Either they fixed the line or they didn't."

"That's what I thought, Mr. Stapleton. The road foreman insists his people did the work. The line should be open."

The supervisor dialed the number a second time. Click, then another click as the automatic switching shunted the caller over to the appropriate recording.

"I'm sorry, but that number has been changed, and there is no new number."

Stapleton put the phone down. Mildred watched him, waiting for some kind of comment. Eventually he looked up, said thoughtfully, "Didn't Parworthy start out in that house by using CB and shortwave instead of a phone?"

"I think I remember hearing something to that effect, Mr. Stapleton."

The supervisor nodded, looking disgusted. "Then it's pretty obvious what's happened. He's put us through all that noise and fury this past month just for his own amusement.

"He never really wanted telephone service in the first place."

THE METROGNOME

I don't have many memories of New York City from the time before my family moved to Los Angeles, because we left New York when I was only five. I vaguely recall a huge fountain in the Bronx where my friends and I used to play despite the Do Not Climb Upon signs. I remember a school and playground suspended between heaven and earth. I think of a water pistol my grandfather bought me that took the form of a bright red jet plane.

And I remember riding the subway. The tube, the underground, the metro.

The treat of treats was riding in the first car. On the New York subway the engineer's cab is set off to the side of the first car, allowing a few passengers to sit right up in front and stare down the tracks. I remember sitting in awe as the train accelerated, gazing at a dark winding tunnel whose sole features (to a five-year-old with limited perception) were thin threads of metal track and bright, intensely bright lights. Directional and warning lights of laser-sharp red, green, and yellow. When the train reached speed, the lights blurred. If you squinted hard enough, they became streaks of red and green fire, a condition known as the preadolescent Doppler effect.

What else might dwell in such depths one did not know, could not imagine. No living soul was ever spotted stalking those ancient tunnels. There were only the lights and the darkness and the occasional side tunnel yawning like a whale's mouth off to one side or the other. A separate world exists beneath the streets of New York.

Today I know that London is much the same, and Moscow, and all the other great cities that can boast subter-

ranean transportation networks. All that vast space devoid of life save for occasional cylinders of bored people rocketing through them at high speed on their way to work or home.

Always seemed such an awful waste.

CHARLIE DIMSDALE STARED AT THE MAN IN FRONT of him. Even under ordinary circumstances Charlie Dimsdale would have stared at the man in front of him. However, this confrontation was taking place in the lowest level of the 52nd Street Bronx subway line, a good many meters beneath the hysterical surface of Manhattan. It was just short of preordained that Charlie Dimsdale would stare at the man in front of him.

The man in front of Charlie Dimsdale stood slightly over a meter high. He was broad out of all proportion in selected places. His head especially was even larger than that of a normal-sized man. Its most notable feature was a proboscis that would be flattered by the appellation bulbous. This remarkable protuberance was bordered by a pair of huge jet-black eyes that hid beneath black eyebrows a Kodiak bear would have been proud of. Two enormous floppy ears, the shape and color of dried apricots, fluttered sideways from the head, their span a truly impressive sight.

The pate itself was as bald and round as the bottom of a china teacup. A good portion of it was covered by a jaunty red beret set at a rakish angle to the left. Huge black muttonchop whiskers rambled like a giant caterpillar across his face.

Arms that were too long for the short torso ended in thick, stubby fingers. Black hair, well cultivated, grew there in profusion. In addition to the beret, he wore a double-breasted pinstripe jacket with matching trousers. His black oxfords were immaculately polished.

Had such a confrontation occurred anywhere else in the world with an appropriate Dimsdale substitute, it is likely that said Dimsdale substitute would have fainted quickly away. Charlie Dimsdale, however, merely gulped and took a step backward.

After all, this was New York.

The little man put his hirsute hands on his hips and stared back at Charlie with undisguised disgust.

"Well, you've seen me. Now what are you going to do about it?"

"Seen you? Do? Look, mister, I'm only . . . my name's Charles Dimsdale. I'm second assistant inspector to the undercommissioner for subway maintenance and repair. There's a misaligned track down here. We've had to make three consecutive computer reroutings up top (this was official slang, of course) for three different trains. I'm to see what the trouble is and to try and correct it, is all."

Charlie was a rather pleasant if unspectacular-appearing young man. He might even have been considered attractive if it weren't for his mousy attitude and those glasses. They weren't quite thick enough to double as reactor shielding.

"Uh . . . did I just see you walk out of that wall?"

"Which wall?" the man asked.

"That wall, behind you."

"Oh, that wall."

"Yes, that wall. I didn't think there was an inspection door there, but . . ."

"There isn't. I did."

"That's impossible," said Charlie reasonably. "People don't go around walking through walls. It isn't done. Even Mr. Broadhare can't walk through walls."

"I don't doubt it."

"Then how can you stand there and maintain you walked through that wall?"

"I'm not human. I'm a gnome. A metrognome, to be specific."

"Oh. I guess that's okay, then."

At that point, New Yorker or no, Charlie fainted.

When he came to, he found himself staring into a pair of slightly glowing coal-black eyes. He almost fainted again, but surprisingly powerful arms assisted him to his feet.

"Now, don't do that to me again," said the gnome. "It's very rude and disconcerting. You might have hit your head on the rail and hurt yourself."

"What rail?" asked Charlie groggily.

"That one, there, in the middle."

"Ulp!" Charlie took several steps back until he was standing on the walkway. "You're right. I really could have hurt myself. I won't do it again." He looked disapprovingly at the gnome. "You aren't helping things any, you know. Why don't you vanish? There're no such things as gnomes. Even in New York. Especially in New York."

"Ha!" grunted the gnome. He said it in such a way as to imply that among those assembled, there was one possessed of about as many brains as a stale pretzel. The big, soft kind, with plenty of salt. Someone was full of dough. Charlie had no trouble isolating him.

"Look," he said imploringly, "you simply can't *be*!"

"Then how the deuce am I?" The gnome stuck out a hairy paw. "Look, my name's Van Groot."

"Charmed," said Charlie, dazedly shaking the proffered palm.

Here I am, he thought, thirty meters below the ground in the middle of Manhattan, shaking hands with a character who claims to be out of the Brothers Grimm named Van Groot who wears Brooks Brothers suits.

But he *had* seen him walk out of a wall.

This suggested two possibilities.

One, it was really happening and there were indeed such creatures as gnomes. Two, he'd been breathing subway exhaust fumes too long and was operating on only one cylinder. At the moment he inclined to the latter explanation.

"I know how you must feel," said Van Groot sympathetically. "Come along with me for a bit. The exercise should clear your head. Even if, De Puyster knows, there's probably not much in it, anyway."

"Sure. Why not? Oh, wait a minute. I've got to find and clear that blocked switch."

"Which switchover is it?" the gnome inquired.

"Four-six-three. It's been jumped to indicate a blocked track, and thus the computer automatically—"

"I know."

"—several alternate programs . . . you know?"

"Sure. I'm the one who set it."

"*You* reset it? You can't do that!"

Van Groot said "Ha!" again, and Charlie decided that if nothing else he was not overwhelming this creature with his precision of thought.

"Okay. *Why* did you move it?"

"It was interfering with the smooth running of our mine carts."

"*Mine carts!* There aren't any mi—" he hesitated. "I see. It was interfering with your mine carts." Van Groot nodded approvingly. Charlie had to hop and skip occasionally to keep up with the gnome's short but brisk stride.

"Uh, why couldn't your mine carts just go over the switch when it was correctly set?"

"Because," the gnome explained, as one would to a child, "that way, the metal kept whispering 'blocked! blocked!' This upset the miners. They work very closely with metal, and they're sensitive to it. With the switch thrown this way, the rails murmur 'open, open,' and the boys feel better."

"But that seems like such a small thing."

"It is," said Van Groot.

"That's not very polite."

"Now, why should we be polite? Do you ever hear anyone say, 'Let's take up a collection for needy gnomes'? Is there a Save the Gnomes League? Or a Society for the Prevention of Cruelty to Gnomes? When was the last time you heard of someone doing something for a gnome, any gnome!" Van Groot was getting excited. His ears flapped, and his whiskers bristled. "Canaries and fruit-fly researchers can get government money, but us? All we ask are our unalienable rights to life, liberty, plenty of fights, and booze!"

This isn't getting me anywhere, thought Charlie cogently.

"I admit it seems inequitable." Van Groot seemed to calm down a little. "But I'd still appreciate it if you'd let me shift the track back the way it belongs."

"I told you, it would be inconvenient. You humans never learn. Still, you seem like such a nice, pleasant sort . . . for a human. Properly deferential, too. I may consider it. Just consider it, mind."

"That's very decent of you. Uh (how does one make small talk with a gnome?), nice weather we're having, isn't it?" Someone had thrown a beer can out of a subway car window. Charlie stepped down off the walkway to remove the can from the tracks.

"Not particularly."

"I thought all you people lived in Ireland and places like that."

"Ireland, my myopic friend, is cold, wet, rainy, uncivilized, and full of crazy American émigrés. About the only thing you can mine there in quantity is peat. Speaking as a miner, let me tell you that it's pretty hard to take pride in your profession when all you mine is peat. Did you ever see a necklace made of peat? A queen's tiara? And it takes a lousy facet. Ireland! That's our trade, you know. We're mostly miners and smiths."

"Why?"

"That's about the stupidest question I've ever heard."

"Sorry."

"Do you think we'd ignore a whole new world and leave it to you humans? When your noisy, sloppy, righteous ancestors paddled across, we came, too. Unobtrusively, of course. Why, there were gnomes with Washington at Valley Forge! With Jones on the—"

"Well, I can certainly understand that," said Charlie hastily, "but I thought you preferred the country life."

"By and large most of us do. But you know how it is. The world's becoming an urban society. We have to change, too. I've got relatives upstate you wouldn't *believe*. They still think they can live like it's Washington Irving's day. Reactionaries."

Charlie tried to conceive of a reactionary gnome and failed.

"And good gem mines are getting harder and harder to find out in the country. All the surface ones are being turned into tourist traps. It's hard enough to find a decent place to sleep anymore, what with one petroleum engineer after another doing seismic dowsing. Any idiot could tell you there's no oil at ninety percent of the places they try. But will they learn? No! So it's boom, boom, boom, night after night. The subways are mild and consistent by contrast."

"Whoa. You mean you do mining . . . right here in Manhattan?"

"*Under* Manhattan. Oh, we've found some excellent spots! Go down a little ways and the gem-bearing rock is plentiful. Check your New York history. Excavators often turn up fair-quality stones. But no one bothers to dig farther because their glass tomb or pyramid or whatever is on a deadline. Tourmaline, beryl, the quartz gems . . . they've turned up in the foundations of some pretty famous buildings. The rarer, more valuable stuff is buried farther down. Even so, the Empire State Building almost did become a mine. But we got to the driller who found the diamonds."

Charlie swallowed.

"And there's plenty of scrap metal. We turn it into scepters and things. Mostly to keep in practice. There isn't much of a market for cast-iron scepters."

"I can imagine," said Charlie sympathetically.

"Still, you never know when you'll need a good scepter. Or a proper Flagan-flange."

"Pardon my ignorance—"

"I've been doing that for half an hour."

"—but what is a Flagan-flange?"

"Oh, they're used to attract . . . but never mind. About that scrap metal and such. We're very concerned about our environment. Gnomes are good for the ecology."

"Uh." Charlie was running a possible scenario through his mind. He saw himself reporting to Undercommissioner Broadhare. "I've fixed that jammed switch, sir. The gnomes moved it because it was interfering with their mine carts. But I don't want you to prosecute them because they're good for the ecology."

"Right, Dimsdale. Just stand there. Everything's going to be all right."

Oh, yeah.

"But I would have imagined . . ." He waved an uncertain hand at Van Groot. "Well, just look at yourself!"

The gnome did. "What did you expect? Green leaves, lederhosen, and a feather cap? You know, Manhattan is one of the few places in the world where we can occasionally slip out and mix with humans without starting a riot. Always at night, of course. Are you sure you haven't seen any of us? We're very common around Times Square and the theater district."

Charlie thought. Below the Flatiron Building at one A.M.? On a bench in Washington Square? A glimpse here, a reflection in a window there? Who *would* notice?

After all, this was New York.

"I see. Do all you city gnomes—"

"Metrognomes," corrected Van Groot placidly.

"Do all you metrognomes dress like that?"

"Sharp, isn't it? Cost me a pretty penny, too. Double knit, special cut, of course. I can't exactly wear something right off the rack. No, it depends on your job. I'm sort of an administrator. An executive, if you will. Dress also depends on where you live. The gnomes that work under Dallas affect Stetsons and cowboy boots. Those that live under Miami are partial to sun shorts and big dark glasses. And you should *see* the gnomes that live under a place called the Sunset Strip in Los Angeles!" He shook his Boschian baldness. "We're here."

They'd halted in front of a switching section of track. Charlie could see the red warning light staring steadily up-tunnel, a baleful bloody eye.

The silence was punctuated abruptly by a low-pitched rumbling like thunder. It grew steadily to a ground-shaking roar.

A clumsy, huge old-fashioned mine cart, built to half scale, came exploding out of the far wall. Two gnomes were pushing it from behind while another pulled and guided the front. The lead gnome had pure white hair and a three-foot beard that trailed behind him like a pennant.

The cart careened crazily down and over the tracks, threatening to overturn every time it hit the ground. Somehow it seemed to flow over the rails. The three gnomes wore dirty coveralls and miners' hard hats with carbide lamps. The cart was piled high with gleaming, uncut gemstones and what looked like an archaic washer-dryer. The lead gnome had just enough time for a fast wave to them before the apparition disappeared into the near wall. The rumble died away slowly. It reminded Charlie of the sound his garbage disposal made when it wanted to be petulant.

"Well, what are you waiting for? Switch it back."

"What?" said Charlie dazedly. "You mean I can?"

"Yes. Now hurry up, before I change my mind."

Charlie stumbled over and threw the manual switch. The heavy section of track slid ponderously into place, and the warning light changed to a beneficent leafy green. It would show green now on the master layout in the controller's office.

"Now," said Van Groot with enough force to startle Charlie, "you owe *me* a favor!"

"Yeah. Sure. Uh . . . what did you have in mind?" said Charlie apprehensively, calling up images of blood-sucking and devil sacrifice.

"I don't mind telling you that things have been getting rather edgy down here. What with one skyscraper after another going up. And now you're expanding the subways again. I can't promise what might happen. One of these days someone's going to drive a shaft right down into one of our diggings and we'll have another strike on our hands."

"Happen? Strike?"

"Boy, you sure are eloquent when you get humming. Sure. Gnomes aren't known for their even tempers, you know. When gnomes go on strike, they've got nothing to do but cause mischief. The last one we had was back in . . ." He murmured a date that momentarily had no meaning to Charlie.

Then, "Hey, wasn't that the week of the big blackout, across the northeast?"

"Well, you know how strikes spread. The boys under Pittsburgh and Boston got together with some power plant gnomes and . . . It was a terrible mess! Most awkward!"

"Awkward! Good grief, another few days of that and . . ."

Van Groot nodded soberly. "Exactly. Some of us finally appealed to the boys' reason, moral fiber, and good nature. When that didn't work, we got most of 'em dead drunk, and the executive committee repaired a lot of the damage."

"No wonder the engineers could never figure out what caused it."

"Oh, they made up excuses. Didn't stop them from

taking credit for fixing the trouble," said Van Groot. "But then, who expects gratitude from humans?"

"You expect something like that might happen again? That would be awful!"

The gnome shrugged. "That depends on your point of view." He flicked away cigar ash daintily. "As a matter of fact, it so happens that this new addition to your system—"

"It's not *my* system!"

"Yes. Anyhow, we've got a pretty nice chrysoberyl and emerald mine—"

"Emerald mine!"

"—right under the intersection of Sixth Avenue and 16th Street. That mean anything to you?"

"Why no, I . . . no, wait a minute. That's where . . . ?" He goggled at Van Groot.

"Yep. The new Bronx–Manhattan tunnel is going through just south of there. That's not the problem. It's the new express station that's set to go in—"

"Right over your mine," whispered Charlie.

"The boys are pretty upset about it. They read the *Times*. It's a pretty explosive situation, Dimsdale. Explosive." He looked hard at Charlie.

"But what do you expect *me* to do? I'm only second assistant inspector to the undercommissioner for subway maintenance and repair. I haven't got the power to order changes in things like station locations and routings and stuff!"

"That's not *my* problem," said Van Groot.

"But they're scheduled to start blasting for that station . . . my God, the day after tomorrow!"

"That's what I hear." Van Groot sighed. "Too bad. I don't know what'll happen this time. There's been talk of getting together with the Vermont and New Hampshire gnomes. They want to pour maple syrup into all the telephone cables and switches between Great Neck and Ottawa. A sticky situation, I can tell you!"

"But you can't—" Van Groot looked at Charlie as though he were examining a special species of earthworm.

"Yes, you can."

"That's better," said Van Groot. "I'll do what I can.

But while I disagree with the boys' methods, I sympathize with their sentiments. They took an emerald out of there once that was . . . '' He paused. ''Best I can give you is about twenty-four hours. No later than twelve o'clock tomorrow night.''

''Why twelve?'' asked Charlie inanely.

''It's traditional. If you've managed to help any, I'll meet you back here. If not, go soak your head.''

''Look, I told you, I'm only a second assistant to—''

''I remember. I'm not responsible for your failings. Your problem.''

''Tomorrow's Saturday. On Sundays I always call my mother in Greenville. If you gum up the telephone lines, I won't be able to.''

''And the chairman of the board of General Computers, who usually calls his mistress in Geneva on Sunday mornings, won't be able to, either,'' said Van Groot. ''It'll be a very democratic crisis. Remember, midnight tomorrow.''

Puffing mightily on the cigar and ignoring Charlie's entreaties, the gnome executive disappeared into the near wall of the tunnel.

The morning was cool and clear. On Saturday mornings Charlie usually went first to the Museum of Natural History. Then off to the Guggenheim to see if anything new had come in during the week. From there it was down to the Village for a quick tour through Heimacker's Acres of Books bookstore. Then home, where he would treat himself to an expensive TV dinner instead of the usual fried chicken or Swiss steak. Out to a film or concert and then home.

Today, however, his schedule was markedly altered. He went to the museum on time. The usual thrill wasn't there. Even the exhibits of northwestern Indian dugouts failed to excite him as they usually did. Instead of envisioning himself perched in the bow, harpoon poised for the whale kill, he saw himself crouched in the rear, paddling furiously to escape the hordes of angry gnomes that were chasing him in birchbark canoes. And when he looked at the always imposing skeleton of the Tyrannosaurus Rex and saw Undercommissioner Broadhare's sour puss in the grinning skull, he decided it was definitely time to depart.

He made up a speech. He'd walk straight into Commissioner Feely's office, powerful and insistent, and say, "Look here, Feely. You've got to shift the new Sixth Avenue station from the north to the south side of the tracks, because if you don't, the gnomes will destroy our great telephone network with maple syrup and—"

Charlie moaned.

He was still moaning when he stumbled out of the museum. The stone lions that guarded the portals watched him go. He headed for the Guggenheim out of habit but found himself instead wandering aimlessly through Central Park.

Let's see. He could sneak into the planning office and burn the station blueprints. No, that wouldn't do. They were bound to have plenty of copies. Charlie had to fill out three copies of a form himself just to requisition a box of paper clips.

He could sneak into the station site and try to sabotage the construction machinery. That would delay things for a while. Except he didn't think he knew enough about the machinery to successfully bust any of it. He'd never been very mechanically inclined. In fact, he'd failed handicrafts miserably in high school. Everything he had tried to make had turned out to be a napkin holder.

How about using the site to stage a rally for the admission of Nationalist China to the UN? That was always sure to draw a noisy, rambunctious crowd. They might even sabotage the construction gear themselves! He knew a friend who was faintly associated with the John Birch Society who might . . . no, that wouldn't work. Rightist radicals would hardly be the group to get to try to halt construction of *anything*.

Besides, they were all only temporary. Delaying tactics. Also, he could go to jail for any one of them. A prospect that enthralled him even less than missing his regular Sunday call to his mother in Greenville.

Dinnertime rolled around, and he still hadn't thought of anything. He was reminded of the real world by the smell of incinerating frozen veal cordon bleu. The delicately carbonized odor permeated his tiny living room.

The unappetizing result in his stove was not calculated to improve his humor, already bumping along at a seasonally low ebb.

What he did was most unusual. For Charlie it was unique. He dug down, deep, deep into the bowels of his cupboards, past countless cans of Mr. Planter's peanuts, down past an immaculate cocktail shaker, never used since its purchase three years ago, down past things better left unmentioned, until he found a hair of the dog.

Never more than a social drinker—mostly at official company functions—Charlie thought a few sips might sharpen his thoughts. It seemed to work for old Agent X-14 regularly every Friday evening on channel 3. So he sipped delicately and carefully. For variety, he alternated bottles. They were friendly dogs, indeed. Warm and cuddly, like a Maltese. Shortly thereafter they were rather more like a couple of playful Saint Bernards. And very shortly thereafter he was in no condition to aspire to any analogies at all.

Actually, he hadn't intended to get drunk. It was, however, an inescapable by-product of his drinking. He ran out of sippables in what seemed indecently short order.

He threw on his raincoat—it wasn't raining, but you never knew, he thought belligerently—and headed in search of more follicles of the pooch. It was sheer good fortune he didn't start for the pound.

On the way he had the fortune and misfortune to encounter Miss Overshade in the hallway. Miss Overshade occupied the apartment across the hall from Charlie, on the good side of the building. She was a local personality of some note, being the weather lady on the early news on channel 8. She had at one time been voted Miss Continental Shelf by the Port of New York Authority and currently held the title Miss High-Pressure Area from the New York Council of Meteorologists.

In point of fact she actually *was* constructed rather along the lines of an especially aesthetic gathering of cumulus clouds. She noticed Charlie, sort of.

"Good evening, Mister . . . uh, Mister . . ."

"Dimsdale," mumbled Charlie. "Dimsdale."

"Oh, yes! How are you, Mister Dimsdale?" Without pausing to learn if he was on the brink of a horrible death, she vanished into her apartment. That voice was calculated to bring on the monsoon. For all she cares, he thought, I might as well be a . . . a gnome.

He hurried down the stairs, insulting the elevator.

At seven sharp Charlie was perusing the soluble delights of an aged and not-so-venerable establishment known as Big Swack's Bar. Currently, he existed in a state of blissful inebriation that followed a thin path betwixt nirvana and hell. For the nonce, nirvana prevailed.

Charlie had a thought, grappled with it. It was brought on by something Van Groot had said. He looked at it hard, piercingly, turning it over in his mind and searching for cracks. It squirmed, trying to get away. He was careful, because he'd seen other things tonight that hadn't been at all real. This thought, however, was.

He left so fast, he forgot to collect the change from his last drink. An occasion that so astonished the proprietor, "Big Swack"—whose real name was Hochmeister—that he talked of nothing else for days afterward.

"Jonson, Jonson! Bill Jonson!" Charlie hammered unmelodically on the door.

Bill Jonson was a sandy-haired, rather sandy-faced young geologist who occasionally shared with Charlie a pallid sandwich in the equally pallid Subway Authority cafeteria. He did not need minutes to observe that his friend was not his usual bland self.

"Charlie? What the hell's the matter with you?"

Now, Charlie was somewhat coherent because on the way up to his friend's abode he'd had enough sense to ingest three Sober-ups. These were chased downstream consecutively by water, half a Pepsi, and an orange drink of sufficient sweetness to destroy any self-respecting molar inside a month. As a result, his mind cleared at the expense of his stomach, which was starting to cloud over.

"Listen, Bill! Can you take a . . . a sounding, a reading, a . . . you know. To determine if there's something special in the ground? Like a big hollow place?"

"I suspect a big hollow place, and it's not in the ground. Come back tomorrow maybe, Charlie, huh? I've got company, you know?" He sort of tried a half grin, half blink. It made him look like a man suffering an attack of the galloping gripes.

"Bill, you've got to take this sounding! You *can* take one? I've heard you mention it before. Pay attenti—hic!—man! This is important! Think of the telephone company!"

"I'd rather not. I got my bill two days ago. Now, be a good chap, Charlie, and run along. It can wait till Monday. And I *have* got company."

Charlie was desperate. "Just answer me. Can you take a sounding?"

"You mean test the substrata, like I do for the Subway Authority?"

"Yeah! That!" Charlie danced around excitedly. This did not inspire Bill to look on his friend with favor.

"You've got to take one for me!"

"A reading? You're drunk!"

"Certainly not!"

"Then why are you leaning to the left like that?"

"I've always been a liberal. Listen, you know the new station they're planning to build for the extended Bronx-Manhattan line? The one at Sixth and 16th?"

"I've heard about it. That's more your department than mine, you know."

"Indirectly. You've got to come down and take a reading there. Now, tonight. I . . . . I've reason to suspect that the ground there is unstable."

"You are crazy. There's no real unstable ground in Manhattan unless you count some of the bars in the Village. It's practically solid granite. Do you have any idea what time it is, anyway?" He looked pointedly at his watch. "My God, it's nearly eight-thirty!"

This unsubtle hint did not have the intended effect on Charlie.

"My God," he echoed, looking in the general vicinity of his own timepiece, "it *is* nearly eight-thirty! We've got to hurry! We've only got till twelve!"

"I'm beginning to think you've got even less than that," said Bill.

"Who does?" came a mellifluous voice from behind the door.

"Who's that?" Charlie asked, trying to peer over his friend's shoulder.

"The television. Now look, go on home and I'll do whatever you ask. Monday, huh? Please?"

"Nonsense, Bill," said the voice. The door opened wider. A young lady in rather tight slacks and sweater came into view behind Bill. "Why don't you invite your friend in? Charlie, wasn't it?"

"Still is," said Charlie.

"I can't think of a single reason," said Bill in a tone that would have sufficed to tan leather. He opened the door with great reluctance, and Charlie slipped inside.

"Hi. My name's Abigail," the girl chirped.

"Abigail?" said Charlie in disbelief.

"Abigail," replied Bill, nodding slowly.

"My name's Charlie," said Charlie.

"I know."

"You do? Have we met before?"

"Get to the point," said Bill.

"Abigail, you've got to help me. I must enlist Bill's inexhaustible fount of scientific knowledge. In an enterprise that is vital to the safety of the city of New York!" Abigail's eyes went wide. Bill's got hard, like dumdum bullets.

"I have reason to believe," he continued conspiratorially, "that the ground at Sixth Avenue and 16th Street is unstable. If this is not proved tonight, lives will be endangered! But I must buttress my theory with fact."

"Don't swear. Gee, that fantastic! Isn't that fantastic, Bill?"

"It sure is," Bill replied. In a minute he would fantasize her further by strangling his own friend right before her fantasized eyes.

Charlie began to prowl around the living room, his own oculars darting right to left. "Well, don't just stand there, Bill! We've got to assemble your equipment. Now. Don't you agree, Abigail?"

"Oh, yes. Hurry, Bill, let's do!"

"Yes," murmured Bill tightly. "Just let me get my *hat* and my *coat*." He took another look at his friend. "Is it raining out?"

Charlie was on his hands and knees, peering under the

couch. "Raining out? Don't be absurd! Of course it isn't raining out. What makes you think it's raining out?"

"Nothing," said Bill. "I can't imagine where I got the idea."

Sixth Avenue and 16th Street was not a very busy intersection, even late on a Saturday night. Especially since it had been blocked off in spots by the construction machinery. On the other hand, it wasn't exactly a dark alley, either. The winos, comfortably tucked into their favorite corners, were no problem. But there were enough pedestrians about to make Bill feel uncomfortable and conspicuous with his heavy field case.

"Why can't we go in there?" he asked, pointing to an assemblage of heavy earth movers.

"Because the construction area is protected by a three-meter-high wire fence topped with three rows of barbed wire with triple alarms on the gates and is patrolled by vicious large-fanged guard dogs, is why."

"Oh," said Bill.

"Can't you do whatever you have to do right here?" asked Abigail.

"Yeah, you're not going to set off a very *big* explosion, are you?" Charlie blurted.

It is true that Charlie was still fairly intelligible. But the effects of the Sober-ups were wearing off, and he tended to talk rather louder than normal.

So the word "explosion" did have the useful effect of sending several couples scurrying to the other side of the street and clearing a broad space around them.

"For cryin' out loud," whispered Bill, "will you shut up about explosions! You want to get us arrested?" He turned to survey the wooden fence that closed off the vacant lot behind them. "There's bound to be a loose board or a gate in this fence. All I'm going to do inside is set off the smallest cap I've got. You'll get the briefest reading I can take, and that's it!"

While Bill and Charlie screened her from the street, Abigail slipped under the hinged plank they'd found. Charlie followed, and Bill came last, after slipping through his field kit. They stood alone in the empty lot.

"Oooo, isn't this *exciting*!" Abigail whispered.

"One of the most thrilling nights of my life," growled Bill. He'd long since resigned himself to the fact that the only way he was going to get rid of his friend, short of homicide, was to go through with this idiocy.

"Only let's be ready to get out of here quick, huh? I don't feel like trying to explain to any of New York's finest what I'm doing taking seismic readings in a vacant lot at nine o'clock Saturday night."

"Is it that late already?" yelled Charlie, oblivious to his friend's attempts to shush him. "Hurry, hurry!"

"Anything, if you'll only *shut up*!" Bill moaned nervously. The others watched while he proceeded to dig a small hole with a collapsible spade. He put something from his case into it, then filled in the dirt, tamping it down tightly with the flat of the spade. He walked back to them, trailing two thin wires.

"This is exciting!" said Abigail. Bill gave her a pained look while Charlie fairly hopped with impatience.

Bill hit the small push-button device the wires led from. There was a muffled *thump!* Clods of earth were thrown several meters into the tepid air of the New York night. They were accompanied by a nonorganic shoe and several long-empty tuna fish cans.

"Well?" asked Charlie. He said it several times before he realized Bill couldn't hear him through the earphones. Finally he tapped him on the shoulder. "How long will it take?"

"Too long," said Bill, mooning at Abigail, who was inspecting the midget crater. "It was a very small bang. I've got to amplify and reamplify the results and wait for a proper printout from the computer. Maybe an hour, maybe two."

"That *is* too long!" Charlie whimpered piteously.

"That—is—too—*bad*!" Bill was just about at the end of his good humor.

"Well, okay, but hurry it up, will you?"

Bill chewed air and didn't reply.

"I don't believe it!" There was a peculiar expression on the young geologist's face.

"What is it, what's happened?" said Abigail.

Bill turned slowly from his instruments, looked up at Charlie.

"You were right. Son of a bitch, you were right! I don't believe it, but . . . unstable! Geez, there's a regular *cave* down there!"

"Will it affect the tunnel?"

"No, not the line, but as for putting a station down here . . . The whole thing could collapse under other sections of the block. And I couldn't begin to predict what blasting here might do. I don't think anyone would get hurt, but the added *expense* . . . to ensure the safety of the crane operators and such . . ."

"Now, that *would* be serious," said Charlie. "Hey, what time is it?"

" 'Bout twenty to twelve," Bill replied, glancing down at his watch.

Charlie looked askance at his watch. "Heavens, it's twenty to twelve! I've got to run! See you soon, Bill!"

"Not likely," the geologist murmured.

"And thanks, thanks a million! You'll report your results to the commissioner's office, won't you?"

"Yeah, sure!" shouted Bill as his friend slipped through the loose board. No reason not to. He'd get a lot of credit for his foresight in detecting the faulted area. Maybe a paper or journal article out of it, too. And he'd take it after what he'd gone through tonight.

"Now, don't be bitter," whispered Abigail, kissing him selectively. "You were marvelous! It wasn't that difficult. Besides, I think it was fun. And different. I've never been invited out for a seismic reading before."

Bill squinted glumly into the bright light that had settled on them. "And you'll be the first girl to be arrested for it, too." He sighed, kissing her right back.

"Van Groot! Hey, Van Groot!" Charlie had been stumbling through the tunnel for what seemed like hours. He'd wandered off and on the inspectors' walkway, unmindful of the fact that at any moment a train could have come roaring down the subterranean track to squash him like a bug.

"Here, gnome, here, gnome!" That sounded even worse. If he ran into a night inspector, he might be able to alibi away "Van Groot!" He didn't think he was clever enough to explain away "Here, gnome!"

Could he? Well, could he?

"De Puyster!" came a familiar voice. "Stop that shouting! I can hear you."

"Van Groot! I've found you!"

"Eureka," the gnome said dryly. "I'd sure be distressed if you'd found me and I turned out to be someone else."

Tonight the gnome administrator was wearing blue sharkskin. The beret was gone, replaced by a gunmetal-blue turban. A gold silk handkerchief protruded from the jacket pocket, matched to the gold shoes of water buffalo hide.

"Well?"

Charlie tried to catch his breath. It occurred to him that the steady diet of booze and exercise he'd been existing on all night did not go together like, say, chocolate chip and cookie.

"It's . . . it's all right! Everything's going to be okay. You can tell the relatives up north they can leave their maple syrup in the trees and not black out cities or any of that kind of stuff! Your mine won't be harmed."

"Why, that's merry marvelous!" said Van Groot. "How ever did you manage it? I admit I didn't have much confidence in you."

"Friend . . . friend of mine will present enough evidence to the Subway Planning Board showing that the ground, the area for the proposed station, is unstable. Unsuitable for practical excavation. If they think it'll cost them another five bucks, they'll move it to the south side of the tunnel. It was all a matter of just using the fact of your mine, not trying to pretend it wasn't there. They don't know it's a mine, of course."

"Seismic test?"

"Yeah. How did you know?"

"Reasonable. Three of my best pick-gnomes reported in earlier this evening with migraines."

"Sorry."

"Don't give it no mind. Serves 'em right." Van Groot chuckled with satisfaction.

"Anyway," Charlie continued, "lives, time, and dif-

ficulty cannot stop the New York Subway Authority. But
money . . . yeah, your mine is safe, all right.''

''And so are your phone lines. So is that of the chairman of the board of General Computers.''

''It'll be an express station, anyway. It shouldn't bother
you too much,'' Charlie added. He was getting groggy
again. His stomach and brain were ganging up on him.

''You've done very well, indeed, my boy. I'm surprised at you. It's been a long time since any human
traded favors with us.''

''Aw, I'll bet you set the whole thing up. Anyway, I've
got to be honest about it. I didn't do it for you. I didn't
do it for me, either. I—I did it—'' And here he stood
very tall, straight, and patriotic. ''—for the telephone
company!'' It was all he could do not to salute.

''Bravo! I wish there was something we could give
you. A little token, a remembrance. I don't suppose you
could use a nice scepter.''

''I'm afraid not. No coronations for a month at least.
I'm going on the wagon.''

''Too bad. Well, here. Take this, anyway.''

''Sure,'' said Charlie agreeably. The gnome thrust
something into his raincoat pocket. ''So long, Veen Grat!
It was nice knowing you. Stop up at my place sometime.
Play a couple games o' gi . . . o' gin!''

''I may do that,'' replied Van Groot. ''Some night.
I'll bring my own djinn.''

Charlie was halfway up the tunnel when he whirled at
a sudden thought and shouted back. ''Hey, Van Greet!''

''Yes?'' The voice floated down faintly from the distant blackness.

''What did you give me?''

''Why, a Flagan-flange, of course.''

Charlie giggled as he thought about it. He couldn't
stop giggling. However, it wasn't so funny. This made
him nervous, and he stopped. He was just about to enter
into a symbiotic relationship with his mattress when there
was a knock at his door. It repeated insistently. It refused
to go away.

Grumbling, he stumbled blindly to the door and peered
through the peephole—no one just opens his door at two

in the morning in New York. Suddenly he was sure he'd actually gone to sleep four hours ago and was now dreaming. But he opened the door.

It was Miss High-Pressure Area.

She had a robe draped loosely over a nightgown no self-respecting spider would have owned up to. Cumulus formations were disturbingly apparent.

"Can I come in, Mister . . . uh . . ."

"Dimsdale," mumbled Charlie. "Charlie Dimsdale." He took two steps backward. Since he was still holding on to the knob, the door came with him.

She stepped inside, closed it behind her. The robe opened even more. So did Charlie's pupils. Proportionately.

"You're going to think I'm just *terrible* (this was a blatant falsehood), but . . ." She was staring at him in the strangest way. "I really can't . . . explain it. But, well, if you could just . . ."

She took a quick step forward and threw her arms around him. For someone out of practice, Charlie reacted well. She whispered something in his ear. It wasn't a weather report. What she said, softly, was, "It'll be okay. He thinks I'm in Geneva."

Charlie hung on and directed her into the apartment, kicking the door shut behind them. He listened gravely.

Now he knew what a Flagan-flange attracted.

THRUST

Artists naturally inspire other artists. Contrary to certain theories, creativity does not take place in a vacuum. One could write an extensive book on the history of western art utilizing only paintings of the temptation of Saint Anthony as illustrations. Science-fiction writers can find the inspiration for whole novels in a throwaway line in a colleague's book.

Sometimes the inspiration takes the form of a challenge to do something different with a similar idea or approach. The result often surprises the writer, who may have started out intending to do something utterly different.

Many years ago Poul Anderson wrote a short novel about a beer-powered spaceship. Poul knows his science, and the darned thing worked. I've never asked him where the idea came from, but one can imagine him sitting deep in conversation with physicists and chemists, working out the precise details of requisite orbital mechanics and thrust necessary for the story. Alternatively, one can imagine the likely reality.

Perhaps the concept came in the form of a challenge from a fan or colleague. Or maybe it arose out of a bad attack of what-the-hell. Regardless, the story that resulted was amusing and entertaining. Poul's stories always work.

Now me, my background in the hard sciences is the product of much head scratching and difficult research, not formal academia. But a challenge is a challenge. If a spaceship powered by beer, why not one propelled by something more unlikely still?

41

DAY 001—22:32

BOYD COTTLE, COMMANDER. STILL SOUNDS funny. Everyone on board is at least as nervous as I am, which is plenty. That is only to be expected. As everyone is also far too busy to allow nerves to affect their performance, I am not worried.

Dr. Sese Oyo has refused to administer tranquilizers to those in need of a relaxant. I concurred with her decision. This point in our journey is no time for anyone to be functioning at less than maximum efficiency. I have assigned additional work instead, believing that to be more effective in calming postignition jitters than a casual dose of coraphine.

All ship's functions are operating within 99.8 percent of prescribed parameters. Of course, the *Secondjump* pretty much runs herself. I can't escape the feeling that we're more passengers than crew.

By the way, Eva Østersund and I traced the two-tenths error to a minor malfunction possibly/probably located within solid waste recycling. Though far from posing an immediate problem, its existence offended Moutiers's professional pride. He's hard at work correcting the problem. Dr. Oyo is helping him as best she can without neglecting her own job, which is primarily to keep a wary eye on us first deep-space travelers.

We're all disgustingly healthy, she insists. Hardly surprising, since physical fitness was as important a criterion in our selection as any mental abilities.

Only sixteen years, four months, two days ± to Barnard's Star. That's barring the successful utilization of the Molenon Multiplier. None of us expects anything to come of that. We don't see how the installation of an alien device, however efficiently modified for human use, can help us. Especially when the experts don't profess to understand fully how it functions.

I realize that the Multiplier is somehow supposed to react to mental output and translate that into space-time distortion leaps along our line of flight. I'll stick with the photon engines, thank you. Slow but steady wins the race.

On Day Twelve out Sese Oyo is supposed to lead us in our first "session." No one here is looking forward to what all consider essentially a waste of time, but orders are orders. The thought of six highly trained scientists squatting around muttering "om" while thinking positive thoughts about Barnard's Star strikes most of us as more than marginally ludicrous. I am willing to concede that such meditative sessions might have beneficial relaxing effects, however. That's the only reason I finally agreed to go along with this.

As nominal commander and chief programmer of mankind's first attempt to reach the stars, I'd like to register another formal objection, though.

DAY 003—14:32

Smooth as vacuum so far. Moutiers found and corrected the problem with the solid waste recycler. Presently he's fiddling happily with his hydroponics. He figures he has thirty-two years in which to create a better cantaloupe.

Kim Rahman purrs over her precious engines, which purr back at her. Our resident stargazer, Paul Usakos, can't wait until we leave the solar system. We all feel the same way. Morale is good. Astrogator Østersund found a minute deviation in our course, which is not unexpected this early in the flight. She and Rahman will collaborate on correction.

Thank the city of Barsoom for the city lights' message. Yes, we are "Go," assure them, with all our thanks.

DAY 007—11:43

Accomplished Uranus passby and beamed them records and messages. Our last close contact with civilization. Now we're truly outward bound. The rings have an ethereal beauty no photo can properly convey. Østersund and I have seen them before, but it was a new sight for the rest of the crew. They spent hours at the ports, *oo*ing and *ah*ing. They had time for sight-seeing. We all have time.

The *Secondjump* is performing above all expectations.

DAY 012—21:58

We just concluded our initial session under Dr. Oyo's guidance. Feeling no less idiotic than I expected to, I returned to work while trying to avoid the immediate gazes of my fellow crew members. The overall reaction seemed to be one of embarrassment. Dr. Oyo says that repetition will cure this, but I'm not so sure. Only she and Jean-Jacques Moutiers appeared to enter into the spirit of the thing. Moutiers is a bit of a flake, anyway. A wizard with life-support systemology, but at heart he's a clown. It should be interesting to see what kind of better melon he can come up with.

Oh, by the way, the Molenon Multiplier works. I can hear the screams of pleasure at Tycho from out here. Go ahead and enjoy yourselves for a minute, folks.

Østersund informs me, and I've separately confirmed, that our speed has increased by a factor of . . . well, check the readouts we're beaming back to you. What it means is that this wonderfully complex, altered alien gizmo you've had us truck all the way past Pluto will get us to Barnard's Star exactly two hours, four minutes earlier than predicted.

So much for the much ballyhooed "gift of the aliens," as the news media have been calling it. All that research and money and time to gain two lousy hours over sixteen years! I've half a mind to cut the monstrosity loose and chuck it out the rear lock. Might do it, too, if it wasn't so closely interstructured with the rest of the ship's systems.

Dr. Oyo insists we can do much better at our sessions. Sure we can.

Belated birthday greetings from Kim Rahman to her father down in Kuala Lumpur. By the time this message reaches him he'll be . . . older. Received birthday wishes from Mr. and Mrs. Usakos for Paul. He returns the greetings and says for his dad to tell everyone on his old rugby team that he won't be back in time for the playoffs but that he'll be back to coach their kids.

DAY 019—08:27

Dr. Oyo says that our growing boredom is to be expected. She maintains that it's a stage that will pass as we settle more fully into in-flight routine and grow completely accustomed to the fact that we're utterly cut off from additional human contact for thirty-two years. I wish I was as certain. Actually, I have to confess that I'm a bit worried. All the work and games that are available, in addition to whatever we can invent, seem inadequate to relieve the present disenchantment. I am hoping this will pass, as Dr. Oyo claims.

Oh, there've been no outward signs of discontent. We're all too mentally stable for that, too well balanced. But I can tell when someone is enjoying themself and when they're just going through the motions.

Even Kim Rahman's jewelry and sculpture are suffering. Paul is trying to help inspire her. His first flush of excitement at being able to observe the entire solar system has already faded.

Another session today. Dr. Oyo sounded pleased. Østersund discovered another slight jump in our position. We'll now arrive at our destination three days, six hours ahead of schedule. I'm not impressed, although Sese (pardon me, Dr. Oyo) is excited.

I personally think we're doing the best we can. If the Multiplier can't do better than shave three days off a sixteen-year trip, I personally don't hold much hope for its future benefits re interstellar travel.

DAY 033—06:44

It appears we have to devote more and more time to simply staying sane. As ever, the *Secondjump* runs like a fine timepiece. All systems are performing flawlessly. Mankind can be proud of this ship.

Whether they'll be able to be as proud of us is presently open to question. I'm still not seriously concerned, but I am troubled by unpleasant prospects. Dr. Oyo and I had a private session yesterday. She ascribes my worry to my position as commander. My concerns, she explained, were typical of someone carrying my burden of responsibility.

When we finished our chat, she offered me a mild soporific. I refused it. I wasn't selected over three thousand other applicants for this position so that I could resort to artificial aids to retain control of myself.

DAY 045—22:35

Moutiers took me aside yesterday. It seems that while running a routine check of recycling he discovered minute traces of a complex protein chain that shouldn't be in our food. He's personally unfamiliar with the chain and has no record of it in the chemical log supplied to him.

It's this lack of a record that troubles him. He's assured me that the proteins are harmless and may even be a benign additive that someone neglected to list in the log or computer. This omission is what offends him. As I believe I've mentioned before, Jean-Jacques is a perfectionist.

I told him that if he was positive the proteins weren't harmful, he shouldn't let it worry him so much. As long as it did not interfere with his normal assignments I suggested he try and identify the stuff in his spare time. It will give him something else to do, which, God knows, we could all use.

DAY 055—18:49

I went to ask Moutiers whether or not he'd isolated or identified the mysterious protein he discovered ten days ago. Moutiers was not at his station. I expected to find him in the hydroponics chambers, which I did. I did not expect to find him rolling around on unrecycled vegetable detritus with Kim Rahman.

Upon exiting without disturbing them and reviewing the matter dispassionately, I've decided not to say anything about it to anyone. Naturally I had no objection to Moutiers and Rahman enjoying themselves. No one expected that this crew of barely thirtyish healthy geniuses would remain celibate for thirty-two years.

My concern was because Moutiers was apparently sacrificing bio-efficiency for aesthetics, in the form of the mattress of unrecycled vegetation. That material should properly have been undergoing reworking in the ship's processors. However, it was good to see both crew members enjoying themselves so thoroughly. I feel that under the circumstances the temporary loss of maximal recycling efficiency can be overlooked.

DAY 062—12:43

Prof. Rahman and Moutiers are neglecting their assignments regularly now. They're spending almost all their nonessential time in one or the other's cabin. Rahman has been using her personal sculpturing and jewelry-making equipment to fashion objects of a nature I prefer not to discuss at this time. I finally spoke to her about it. Her response was indifferent, to say the least.

Deeply troubled at this first actual break in discipline but realizing that a confrontation would probably do more harm than good, I had another private session with Dr. Oyo.

She reassured and relaxed me, as she always does. Why worry, she asked me, so long as the ship is operating efficiently? If ship performance actually began to suffer, then that would be the proper time to reinforce written rules. At least the depressing boredom of two members of the crew has been alleviated.

I have to admit she made sense. So I have left Moutiers and Rahman to their amusements.

It is clear that Moutiers's interest in melons has shifted from hydroponics to propulsion.

DAY 064—03:08

Paul Usakos, our astronomer, is discussing astrogation with Eva Østersund. Has been for some time, it now seems. Whatever courses they are negotiating involve a good deal of loud comment, audible even through their cabin doors.

While the *Secondjump* shows no ill effects from their neglect, the absence of constant monitoring of course and speed concerns me. I have been trying to compensate quietly by taking over some of Østersund's and Usakos's functions. The overwork has Dr. Oyo worrying about *me*.

Another session with her yesterday. She is a consummate professional, and we are fortunate to have her on board.

It is becoming increasingly difficult for me to ignore the fact that for someone with three advanced degrees, including an M.D., Dr. Oyo is really built.

DAY 068—12:53

There is something wrong with the ship, but no one seems to care. Østersund was with both Usakos and Moutiers when I went to query her about it. She mumbled something about unexpected visual distortion of the stellar matrix, but she wasn't particularly coherent. Under the circumstances I thought it best not to insist on further conversation.

I attempted to discover the nature of the distortion, to learn whether it was external or shipboard in source. Before I could hardly begin, I was interrupted by Dr. Oyo.

I am disturbed at the apparent complete collapse of ship routine, but the *Secondjump* ignores us. It continues placidly on its assigned course, oblivious to the adolescent tumblings of its organic components.

I confess Dr. Oyo's interruption and expressed concern for my health was not wholly unwelcome. Sese always knows how to make me feel better.

DAY 073—02:21

For the first time in a long while we had another group session the other day. Only this time it did not involve meditation. I feel myself slipping further and further from reality, into an unreality of indescribable delight. The ship itself seems warmer, its colors softened even beyond their natural pastels.

It is now evident that as a child, part of my education was neglected severely. The others derive considerable pleasure, in a good-natured way, from my awkwardness and bemusement. My willingness to learn and to experiment, however, mitigates any personal discomfort. All signs of moroseness and boredom have vanished. They still tend to tease me, though.

For example, the computer contains no reference for explaining to me the term "daisy chain." I have inferred, however, that it has nothing to do with formal botanical terminology.

DAY 080—00:16

Jean-Jacques returns to his beloved hydroponics just long enough to ensure that everything is functioning properly. He discovered a host of new proteins not listed in his catalog but is now convinced they are either harmless by-products of our recycling machinery or beneficial additives.

From time to time he and I wonder about their presence in a basal food supply as carefully composed as the *Secondjump*'s. Usually, though, we are occupied with more important matters.

DAY 083—11:04

Eva Østersund and Paul Usakos are two-thirds of the way through a dramatic version of the *Kama Sutra*. Oftentimes the rest of us are too busy to watch, but they keep us posted whenever they come across something especially intriguing. Then we all give it a try. Only Kim Rahman, however, possesses among the rest of us sufficient gymnastic dexterity to accomplish certain of the positions.

The rest of us don't feel left out or deprived. We're inventing some tricks of our own.

Dr. Oyo—Sese—has demonstrated that a knowledge of medicine can be put to uses other than what it was intended for.

DAY 084—02:15

Oh, wow.

DAY 085—04:24

Turned off the centrifuge yesterday. We're all currently enjoying free-fall, but I don't think our muscle tone will suffer. Zero gravity permits variations Sir Richard Burton could never have envisioned. Kim Rahman is producing some remarkable devices in her workshop.

DAY 091—15:13

I can't explain it. None of us can. It's puzzling and confusing and impossible and wonderful.

The *Secondjump* has stopped. There is a sun blazing outside which can only be Barnard's Star. This discovery was extraordinary enough (probably nothing else could have been) to induce us to return to our stations.

No question about it, we've reached Barnard's Star. There are six planets noted on first survey and two, *two* of them, are Earthlike. Numbers three and four out from the primary. There is also a chance, Paul tells me, that the sixth moon of the fifth planet (a gas giant) is marginally habitable. This exceeds the wildest hopes of every one of us, and I'm sure of everyone back on Earth.

We are sixteen years, one month ahead of schedule. All we can assume is that the Molenon Multiplier works like nobody's business. My apologies to all concerned with that part of the project.

DAY 093—06:29

Jean-Jacques, Kim, Paul, and Sese have taken the lander down to the surface of Barnard III, which we have named, after Jean-Jacques's suggestion, La Différence. Let the historians have that one to chew on in years to come.

Speaking of coming, Eva and I have been working the computer overtime trying to discover the reason for the incredible sudden success of the Multiplier. I believe we have. It would have been transparently obvious to anyone who'd taken the time to check certain things these past several months. None of us were in condition, physical or mental, to take regular readings of anything recently.

Sese confirms our findings. La Différence, by the way,

is more than nine-tenths Earthlike. It has a slightly higher gravity but otherwise is a paradise according to reports from below. No life higher than the lower invertebrates.

DAY 096—14:20

Jean-Jacques and Sese have brought the lander up to disgorge specimens and take on fresh supplies. Jean-Jacques took a couple of hours and finally identified those mysterious proteins. It was a relatively simple procedure, especially since he now had a good idea what to look for.

Really, I don't think that all those pheromones and aphrodisiacs were necessary.

Cute tower of power that she is, Sese made the right connections. She said that if we'd been told that the best theoretical way to operate the Multiplier was to, uh, try and multiply, self-consciousness might have defeated us before we could get started. Admittedly there were several among us who were less than ultra-liberal-minded on such matters, myself foremost among them.

Undistorted mental output engages the space-time distortion functioning of the Molenon Multiplier. That output peaks during the act of sex. Score one for the brain boys back home, but I'm still not *entirely* sure I like having been tricked into it. How do we measure velocity from now on? In light-years per orgasm?

This would all be funny if it weren't so wonderfully efficient.

Barnard IV is also inhabitable. I will not tell you what Eva and I named it, but the rest of the crew concurred. I am looking forward to seeing how the media cope with it.

Gentlemen, this is a hell of a way to run a starship.

We'll be returning home shortly, as soon as we've thoroughly finished our exploration here. Paul will play rugby again, after all.

The rest of us are going to do our damnedest to get him home in time for the playoffs . . .

PIPE DREAM

"Where do you get your ideas?" is the question most frequently asked of writers of fiction and of science-fiction writers in particular. The usual response is a joking one, particularly if the author is in a hurry. If he has time, he may reply thoughtfully.

Sometimes the response can be precise.

Too many years ago I found myself attending a science-fiction convention in downtown Los Angeles. The con was run by a wonderful gentleman name of Bill Crawford and featured a mix of science fiction, fantasy, and horror. In some ways it was a precursor of today's multimedia-oriented conventions. Bill was an old-timer, but he had a finger on the future's pulse.

One of the guests and a good friend of Bill's was a charming, lanky gentleman who strolled through the con with cool demeanor and well-used pipe. Walt Daugherty was among other things a photographer of some of film-dom's greatest horror stars, Karloff and Chaney included. He had a mischievous sense of humor and genial nature that, when functioning in tandem, reminded one of Hitchcock's introductions to the stories on his television show.

The greatest problem one faces at such conventions is how to greet people one doesn't know well but repeatedly encounters in halls and function rooms. After a while "hello," "howyadoin'?" and "what's new?" begin to pall. So it happened as I ran into Walt hour after hour.

The afternoon of the second day I entered the dealer's room only to bump into him again, this time in the process of lighting his pipe. Desperate not to appear either

*banal or impolite, I searched for a salutation and finally
said, "Hi, Walt. What're you smoking?"*

*Barely removing the pipe stem from his lips, he glanced
down at me out of his left eye and declaimed with a properly Lugosian air, "Ah, it's not what. It's whom."*

And that's where you get your ideas. Thanks, Walt.

IT WAS THE AROMA OF TOBACCO THAT FIRST AT-
tracted her.

Delicate enough to demand notice, distinctive enough
to bludgeon aside the mundane odor of cigarette and cigar, it was the first different thing she'd encountered all
evening.

She'd hoped to meet someone at least slightly interesting at Norma's little get-together. Thus far, though,
Norma's guest list had unswervingly reflected Norma's
tastes. Emma'd only been fooling herself in hopes it
would be otherwise.

There, there it was again. Open wood fires and hon-
eysuckle. Really different, not bitter or sharp at all.

The vacuity of her excuse as she slipped away was
matched only by the vacuousness of the young man she
left, holding his half-drained martini and third or fourth
proposition. But the tall football player didn't need sym-
pathy. He shrugged off the brush-off, immediately cor-
ralled another of Norma's friends. Soon he was plying
her with the same draglines, blunt-hooked, presenting
the first line like an uncirculated coin, newly minted.
Option call at the line of scrimmage.

The owner of the pipe was surprise number two. He
looked as out of place at the party as a Mozart concerto.
Instead of a girl on his lap, he cradled a fat book. He'd
isolated himself in a nearly-empty corner of the sunken
living room.

She put a hand on the back of his high-backed easy
chair.

"Hi," she said. He looked up.

"Hello." Absently spoken, then back to the book.

Her interest grew. Might be playing indifferent deliberately . . . but she didn't think so. If he was interested,
he sure faked otherwise well. And men did not usually
dismiss Emma with an unconcerned hello. Nor did they

pass over her face with a casual glance and totally avoid the interesting subcranial territory completely. She was piqued.

There was an unclaimed footstool nearby. She pulled it up next to the bookcase, sat down facing him. He didn't look up.

Well tanned, no beard or mustache (another anomaly). Dark wavy hair tinged with gray at the sharp bottom of modest sideburns. Might even be over forty. Sharp, blunt jaw, but otherwise his features were small, almost child-like. Even so, there was something just a little frightening about him.

She didn't scare easily.

"I couldn't help noticing your tobacco."

"Hmmm?" He glanced up again.

"Your tobacco. Noticing it."

"Oh, really?" He looked pleased, took the pipe out of his mouth, and admired it. "It's a special blend. Made for me. I'm glad you like it." He peered at her with evident amusement. "I suppose next you're going to tell me you love the smell of a man's pipe."

"As a matter of fact, usually I can't stand it. That's what makes yours nice. Sweet."

"Thanks again." Was that a faint accent, professionally concealed?

He almost seemed prepared to return to his book. A moment's hesitation, then he shut it with a snap of displaced air. Back it slipped into its notch in the bookcase. She eyed the spine.

"Dürer. You like Dürer, then?"

"Not as art. But I do like the feel of a new book." He gestured negligently at the bookcase. "These are all new books." A little smile turned up the corners of his mouth.

"It says '1962' on the spine of that one," she observed.

"Well, not new, then. Say 'unused.' No, I'm not crazy about Dürer as an artist. But his work has some real value from a medical history standpoint."

Emma sat back on the footstool and clasped a knee with both hands. This had the intended effect of raising her skirt provocatively. He took no notice of the regions thus revealed.

"What do you specialize in?"

"How marvelous!" he said. "She does not say, 'Are you a doctor?' But immediately goes on to 'What do you specialize in?' assuming the obvious. It occurs to me, young lady, that behind that starlet facade and comic-book body, there may be a brain."

"Please, good sir," she mock pleaded, "you flatter me unmercifully. And I am not a 'starlet.' I'm an actress. To forestall your next riposte, I'm currently playing in a small theater to very good reviews and very small audiences. In *A Midsummer Night's Dream*, and it's *not* a rock musical."

He was nodding. "Good, good."

"Do I get a gold star on my test, teacher?" she pouted.

"Two. To answer your question, if you're really curious, I happen to specialize in endocrinology. You," he continued comfortably, "do not appear to be adversely affected where my field is concerned. Please don't go and make an idiot of me by telling me about your thyroid problems since the age of five."

She laughed. "I won't."

"Isn't this a delightful party?"

"Oh, yes," she deadpanned. "Delightful."

He really smiled then, a wide, honest grin—a white crescent cracking the tan.

"If you're interested in art, I have a few pieces you might appreciate. Oils, pen and ink, no etchings." Grin. "The people in them don't move, but they're more full of life than this bunch."

"I think I'd like that." She smiled back.

It was a longer drive than she'd expected. In Los Angeles that means something. A good twenty minutes north of Sunset, up the Pacific Coast Highway, then down a short, bumpy road.

The house was built on pilings out from a low cliff, to the edge of the ocean. The sea hammered the wood incessantly, December songs boiling up from the basement.

"Like something to drink?" he asked. She was examining the den. Cozy like mittens, masculine as mahogany. Hatch-cover table; old, very unmod, supremely comfortable chairs; a big fat brown elephant of a couch you could vanish in.

"Can you make a ginger snap?"

His eyebrows rose. "With or without pinching her?"

"With."

"I think so. A minute."

Behind the couch the wide picture window opened onto a narrow porch overhanging a black sea. The crescent of lights from Santa Monica Bay had the look of a flattened-out Rio de Janeiro, unblinking in the clear winter night. Northward, the hunchback of Point Dume thrust out of the water.

The opposite wall was one huge bookcase. Most of the volumes were medical tomes and had titles stuffed with Latin nouns. There were several shelves of titles in German, a single one in French, yet another in what seemed like some sort of Scandanavian language.

Crowded in a small corner of the north wall, almost in embarrassment, was a group of plaqued diplomas from several eastern institutions and, to match the books, one in German and another in French.

The art, of which there wasn't much, consisted mostly of small pieces. Picasso she expected but not the original Dali, or the Winslow Homer, the charming Wyeth sketches, some English things she didn't recognize, and the framed anatomic drawings of da Vinci . . . not originals, of course. And over the fireplace, in a massive oak frame, a big Sierra Nevada glowing landscape by Bierstadt.

A distinctive collection, just like its owner, she mused.

"With pinch."

She whirled, missed a breath. "You startled me!"

"Fair play. You've already done the same to me tonight."

She took the glass, walked over to the couch, sat, and sipped.

"Very slight pinch," she murmured appreciatively.

He walked over and sat down next to her.

"I wouldn't expect you to be the sort to go to many of Norma's parties."

"Was that the name of our charming hostess?" he queried. "No, I don't." There was a long rack holding twenty-odd pipes on the table. A lazy Susan full of different tobaccos rested at one end. He selected a new pipe, began stuffing it.

"If you believe it, I was invited by one of my patients."

She giggled. The drink was perfect.

"I'm afraid it's true." He smiled. "She was concerned for my supposed monastic existence. Poor Mrs. Marden." He put pipe to lips and took out a box of matches.

"Let me," she said, the ligher from her purse already out.

"Huh-uh. Not with that." He gently pushed her hand away. The wrist tingled after he removed his hand.

"Gas flame, spoil the flavor. Not every smoker notices it, but I do."

She reached out, took the box of Italian wax matches. She struck one and leaned forward. As he puffed the tobacco alight, one hand slipped into her décolletage.

"I didn't think you were wearing a foundation garment."

"Oh, come on!" She blew out the match. His hand was moving gently now. "You sound like a construction engineer!"

"I apologize. You know, you're very fortunate."

She was beginning to breathe unevenly. "How . . . so?"

"Well," he began in a professorial tone, "the undercurve of a woman's breast is more sensitive than the top. Many aren't sufficiently well endowed to experience the difference. Not a problem you have to face."

"What," she husked, brushing his cheek, "does the book say about the bottom lip versus the top?"

"As to that—" He put the pipe on the table and leaned much, much closer. "—opinion is still somewhat divided."

New Year's Day came and went, as usual utterly the same as an old year's day.

It wasn't an affair, of course. More like a fair. A continuing, wonderful, slightly mad fair. Like the fair at Sorochinsk in *Petroushka*, but no puppets here. Walt never shouted at her, never had a mean word. He was unfailingly gentle, polite, considerate, with just the slightest hint of devilry to keep things spicy.

He had fewer personal idiosyncrasies than any man she'd ever met. The only thing that really seemed to bother him was any hint of nosiness on her part. A small problem, since he'd been quite candid about his background without being asked, and about his work.

She'd been a little surprised to learn about the two previous marriages. But since there were no children, nothing tying him to the past, her concern quickly vanished.

And next Tuesday was his birthday. She was determined to surprise him.

But with what? Clothes? He had plenty of clothes and was no fashion plate to begin with. She couldn't afford a painting of any quality. Besides, choosing art for someone was an impossible job. Electronic gadgetry, the modern adult male's equivalent of Tinker Toys and Lincoln Logs, didn't excite him.

Then she thought of the tobacco.

Of course! She'd have some of his special blend prepared. Whenever he lit a pipe, he'd think of her.

Now, she considered, looking around the sun-dappled den, where would I hide if I were a tin of special tobacco? There must be large tins around somewhere. The lazy Susan didn't hold much, and it was always full . . . though she never saw him replenishing it. Of course she couldn't ask him. That would spoil the surprise.

It wasn't hidden, as it turned out. Just inconspicuous, in a place she'd had no reason to go. There was a small storage room, a second bedroom, really, in the front of the beach house. It held still more books and assorted knickknacks, including an expensive and unused set of golf clubs.

The tobacco tins were in an old glass cabinet off in one dark, cool corner. The case was locked, but the key was on top of the cabinet. Standing on tiptoe, she could just reach it.

Hunt as she did, though, giving each tin a thorough

inspection, there was nothing she could call a special blend. There were American brands, and Turkish, and Arabic, and Brazilian, and even a small, bent tin from some African country that had changed its name three times in the past ten years.

But no special blends.

She closed the cabinet and put the key back. In semi-frustration she gave the old highboy a soft kick. There was a click. The bottom foot or so of the cabinet looked like solid maple. It wasn't, because a front panel swung out an inch or so.

She knelt, opened it all the way.

There were eight large tins inside sitting on two shelves. Each was wrapped in what looked like brown rice paper or thin leather but was neither. In fine, bold script across the front of each someone had written:

SPECIAL BLEND, Prepared Especially For DR. WALTER SCOTT

Under this were the various blend names: Liz Granger, Virginia Violet, and so on.

She pulled one tin out, examined it patiently. That was all. No address, no telephone number, nothing. She went over each tin carefully, with identical results. Just SPECIAL BLEND, Prepared Especially for . . . and the blend name. Nothing to indicate who prepared it, where it came from.

The paper on the final tin was slightly torn. She handled it carefully and inspected the tear. Something was stamped into the metal of the tin, almost concealed by the wrapping. Gently she peeled a little aside.

Yes, an oval stamp had been used on the tin. They probably all carried it. It was hard to make out; the stamp was shallow.

Peter van Eyck, the Smoke Nook . . . and an address right on Santa Monica Boulevard.

She found a little scrap of paper, wrote down the name and address. Then she smoothed the torn paper (or was it leather?) down as best she could, replaced the tin on its shelf, and shut the panel. It snapped closed with another click of the old-fashioned latch.

* * *

Hollywood Boulevard is just like a movie set. All front and no insides or back. Marching south from the Hollywood hills, you encounter Sunset Boulevard next, then Santa Monica. For much of its length-life Santa Monica Boulevard is like the back of a movie set. A street where all the storefronts, you're certain, have their faces to the alleys and their backsides to the boulevard.

Almost, she was convinced she'd misread the address. But on the third cruise past she spotted it. It was just a door in an old two-story building.

She pulled around the corner, managed to slither in between a new panel truck and an old Cadillac.

The door was open, the stairs inside reasonably clean. At the top of the landing she looked left, went right. She knocked on number five once and walked in. The overpowering, pungent odor of tobacco hit her immediately. Bells on the door jangled for a second time as she closed it.

Someone in the back of the room said, "Just a minute!" Twice that later, the proprietor appeared.

Short, fat, a fringe of hair running all around his head from chin, to cheeks, into sideburns, over the ear and around the back, like a cut-on-the-dotted-line demarkation.

At least in his sixties, but most of the wrinkles were still fat wrinkles, not age wrinkles. His voice was smooth, faintly accented. He smiled.

"Well! If I had more clients like you, young lady, I might not consider retiring."

"Thanks. Anyhow," she said, "you can't retire, at least not until tonight. I'm here to buy a birthday present for a very special friend."

The owner put on a pleased expression. "What does he like, you tell me. Imported cigars? Pipe tobacco? Snuff?" He winked knowingly, an obscene elf. "Perhaps something a little more unusual? Mexican, say, or Taiwanese?"

"And the opium den in the attic." She smiled back. "No, I'm afraid not. My friend buys his tobacco from you regularly—"

"He has good taste."

"—a special blend you make for him."

"My dear, I make special blends for many people, and not only here in Los Angeles. It's a fine art, and young people today . . . " He sighed. "Some of my best customers, their names would startle you. Who is your friend?"

"Dr. Walter Scott."

Smile, good-bye. Grin, vanished. Humor, to another universe.

"I see." All of a sudden he was wary of her. "Does the doctor know that you are doing this?"

"No. I want to surprise him."

"I daresay." He looked at his feet. "I am afraid, dear lady, I cannot help you."

None of this made any sense. "Why not? Can't you just . . . blend it or whatever else it is you do? I don't need it till next week."

"You must understand, dear lady, that this is a very special blend. I can prepare most of it. But one ingredient always stays the same, and this Dr. Scott always supplies himself. It's like saffron in paella, you know. Without the tiny pinch of saffron, you have nothing, soup. Without the doctor's little additive . . ." He shrugged.

"Haven't you tried to find out what it is for yourself?" she pressed.

"Of course. But the doctor, he only smiles. I don't blame him for protecting the secret of his blend. Such a marvelous sweetness it gives the smoke, I tell you!" The tobacconist shook his head, fringe bobbing. "No, I cannot help you. Excuse me." He headed for the back of the room.

"Well, I like that!" She walked out the door, paused halfway down the stairs. Odd. Oh, well. She'd buy him that antique hurricane lamp he'd admired in Ports o' Call.

It was raining as she drove out to the house. Wednesdays he worked late, and she was sure he could use some company. She shivered deliciously. So could she.

The Pacific Coast Highway was a major artery. Thanks to the rain and fog, the number of four-wheeled corpuscles was greatly reduced tonight. Typical southern California rain: clean, cold, tamer than back east.

She let herself in quietly.

Walt was sticking another log into the fireplace. He was sucking on the usual pipe, a gargoylish meerschaum this time. After the wet run from the driveway the fire was a sensuous, delightful inferno, howling like a chained orange cat.

She took off the heavy, wet coat, strolled over to stand near the warmth. The heat was wonderful. She kissed him, but this time the fire's enthusiasm wasn't matched.

"Something wrong, Walt?" She grinned. "Mrs. Norris giving you trouble about her glands again?"

"No, no, not that," he replied quietly. "Here, I made you a ginger snap."

The drink was cool and perfect as always.

"Well, tell me, then, what is it?" She went and curled up on the couch. The fire was a little too hot.

He leaned against the stone mantel, staring down into the flames. The only light in the room came from the fireplace. His face assumed biblical shadows. He sighed.

"Emma, you know what I think of women who stick their noses in where they shouldn't."

"Walt?"

Damn, he must have noticed the new tear in the tobacco tin wrapping!

"I don't know what you mean, darling." The handsome profile turned to full face.

"You've been in my tobacco, haven't you?"

Ginger snap, tickling as it went down.

"Oh, all right. I confess, darling. Yes, I was in your precious horde."

"Why?"

There was more than a hint of mild curiosity in his voice. It seemed to come from another person entirely. She pressed back into the couch and shivered. It was the sudden change in temperature from outside, of course.

"Gee, Walt, I didn't think you'd be so . . . so upset."

"Why?" he repeated. His eyes weren't glowing. Just reflection from the fire, was all.

She smiled hopefully. "I was going to surprise you for your birthday. I wanted to get you some of your special blend and really surprise you. Don't think I'm going to tell you what I got you, now, either!"

He didn't smile. "I see. I take it you didn't obtain my blend?"

"No, I didn't. I went to your tobacco place . . ."

"You went to my tobacco place?" he echoed.

"Yes, on Santa Monica. The address was under the paper or whatever that wrapping is." She blinked, shook herself. Was she that tired? She took another sip of the drink. It didn't help. In fact, she seemed to grow drowsier.

"That nice Mr. . . . I can't remember his name . . . he . . . excuse me, Walt. Don't know why I'm so . . . sleepy."

"Continue. You went to the shop."

"Yes. The owner said he couldn't make any of your blend for me because (fog) you always brought one of the (*so* tired) ingredients yourself and he didn't know what it was. So I had to get you something else."

"Why?" he said again. Before she could answer, "Why must you all know *everything*? Each the Pandora." He took up a poker, stirred the fire. It blazed high, sparks bouncing drunkenly off the iron rod.

She finished the drink, put the glass down on the table. It seemed to waver. She leaned back against the couch.

"I'm sorry, Walt. Didn't think you'd get so . . . upset."

"It's all right, Emma."

"Funny . . . about those . . . tins. Eight of them. Two were . . . named Anna Mine and Sue deBlakely."

"So." He fingered the poker.

"Well," she giggled, "weren't those the . . . names of your two ex-wives?"

"I'm very sentimental, Emma."

She giggled again, frowned. Falling asleep would spoil the whole evening. Why couldn't she keep her damn eyes open?

"In fact . . . all your blends had female . . . names."

"Yes." He walked over to her, stared down. His eyes seemed to burn . . . reflection from the fire again . . . and his face swam, blurred. "You're falling asleep, Emma." He moved her empty glass carefully to one end of the table. It was good crystal.

"Can't . . . understand it. So . . . tired . . ."

"Maybe you should take a little rest, Emma. A good rest."

"Rest . . . maybe . . . " His arms cradled her.

"Lie here, Emma. Next to the fire. It'll warm you." He put her down on the carpet across from the fronting brick. The flames pranced hellishly, anxious, searing the red-hot brick interior.

"Warm . . . hot, Walt," she mumbled sleepily. Her voice was thick, uncertain. "Lower it?"

"No, Emma." He took the poker, jabbed and pushed the logs back against the rear of the alcove. Funny, she'd never noticed how big it was for such a modest house.

Her eyes closed. There was silence for several minutes. As he knelt and reached for her, they fluttered open again just a tiny bit.

"Walt . . ." Her voice was barely audible, and he had to lean close to hear.

"Yes?"

"What . . . special ingredient?"

There was a sigh before he could reply, and her eyes closed again. Long moments. He tossed two more logs on the fire, adjusted them on the iron. Then he knelt, grabbed her under the arms. Her breathing was shallow, faint.

He put his mouth close to her ear, whispered.

"Ashes, my love. Ashes."

MOTHER THUNDER

Jessica Amanda Salmonson and I have corresponded for years, infrequently but always with respect and interest. In addition to writing her own stories, Jessica is a busy editor. When I learned that she was putting together an anthology of stories utilizing mythological themes, I was immediately interested.

Mythology always fascinated me in school, but all we were ever exposed to by the Anglocentric American secondary curriculum was the mythlore of Greece and Rome. If the teacher was especially well read and prepared, we might also receive a dollop of Norse gods, those individuals so famed today for their appearances in Marvel comics. No residuals go to Valhalla or Asgard. Only when I left college did I begin to find out about mankind's wealth of invention, of the tales and fantasies of the rest of my brethren.

One thing I discovered was that mythologies exist to be expanded upon. The dreamtime could be my time, too. Tales twice told in Tanzania were as pointed and relevant as those spilled on the streets of Topeka. When it comes to storytelling, the family of man is wholly egalitarian. I think my embroidery of reality would be as welcome in a yurt in the Gobi as in New York.

What first drew me to the Inca, however, was not their mythology but their tragedy. If only, I told myself as I read the sad story of their destruction by the conquistadores, they had possessed writing. If only they'd known the wheel. If only they'd had matching cavalry or gunpowder. If only they'd had . . .

NO ONE PAID ANY ATTENTION TO CRAZY YAHUAR until the Silver Men came.

"They have crossed the river," the exhausted chasqui told the Priest. "Even now they are working their way up the mountain."

"They must not come here," the old Priest muttered. "This is the most sacred place of the Tahuantinsuyu, the Four Corners of the World. They must not come here." He pulled his feathered cloak tighter around his shoulders. The wind was cold on the mountaintop.

"The Silver Men go where they wish." The teacher/ noble who stood on the Priest's right hand had seen much these past twenty years. He had become a realist.

"Why dream on, old man? We have three choices: we can submit, we can run away into the jungle with Manco Inca, or we can die here. Myself, I chose my own grave, and it is here. This is where my grandfather began, and this is where his line will end."

"If we pray to the Sun," the old Priest began. The teacher interrupted him angrily:

"It is too late for prayers, Priest. We have forgotten what they were for, have forgotten too much for prayers to be of help now. Prayers did not help Atahuallpa. The Silver Men strangled him, ransom or no ransom, prayers or no prayers. Give me one of their armored long-legged llamas to ride upon and one of their fire-weapons to fight with, and keep your prayers." He turned his attention to the panting chasqui.

"How many, post runner?"

The chasqui held out a quipu, and the teacher studied the number and location of the intricate knots tied in the rope. "Too many. You have done your job, runner. I will not hold you here. What would you do?"

"Return to my family." The chasqui was still breathing hard from the long run up the mountainside.

"Go then, if you can avoid the Silver Men, and live long."

"Thank you, noble." The runner turned and fairly flew down the steep trail, anxious to flee the sacred city. He had heard of the barbarity of the Silver Men, of the atrocities they had visited even upon great Cuzco, and he had no desire to be martyred along with those who might choose to try to defend the citadel. Better it be left to Priests and nobles.

The old Priest let out a sigh. "The Empire is coming to an end. It is too bad."

"Too bad has nothing to do with it, Priest." The teacher made no attempt to conceal his bitterness. "I blame Huascar and Atahuallpa. If those two brothers had not spent the energy and wealth of the realm fighting one another over the succession, we would already have driven the Silver Men back into the sea, despite all their strange weapons and ways. Now, it is too late." He turned and gazed past the lower terraces, toward the first wall of the city.

"So now I shall die here, not for the Empire but for my ancestors and my oaths, which is all that has been left to me. What will you do, Priest?"

"I am bid to serve Inti, the Sun. I will pray to him for guidance, and if it be his will, I will perish in the temple at the time he chooses for me."

"Bah. Better to die fighting. Still, I am no priest, and I should not tell a priest how to die. Each must do what each must do."

"That is the law, my son." The Priest put a withered hand on the younger man's shoulder. "I cannot fight with you, but I can pray that you fight well."

"I accept your prayers, old man. They worked in the past, though the past is done. I go to organize the stone slingers."

He turned and started up the steps, leaving the Priest to stare worriedly down the mountainside. The morning sun glinted sharply off the distant white worm that was the Urubamba River. How soon, he wondered? How soon before the sunlight shines off the armor of the Silver Men? If only he could remember the old ways, the old magic.

But so much had been forgotten since the first Inca had started the Empire.

"We will confront them at the steepest part of the trail," the teacher told the assembled band of farmer-warriors. "If we cannot hold them back there, then we have no chance. Their long-necked llamas will have trouble climbing that place."

"A steep climb will not slow their fire arrows," said a voice from the back.

"Are you afraid of fire, Tamo?" asked the teacher. The man who'd spoken lapsed into silence.

"We are ready, then, save for the Priests and the children." The teacher prepared to step down from the speaking stone when another voice broke in:

"What of Yahuar?"

The teacher had to smile. "Crazy Yahuar? Let him play his pipes in peace. Perhaps the Silver Men will let him live. I have heard that they too have tolerance for the mad. Let Yahuar remain with the Priests and the Chosen Women, where he belongs."

Laughter rose from the warriors, and the teacher was glad. Now when the time came the men of the city would raise their legs at the Silver Men in defiance. If the gods willed it, the teacher would make a drinking cup of his enemy's skull. If not, at least they could die like the true children of Viracocha.

At the farthest end of the city, Crazy Yahuar sat on the lower steps of the temple, which were coated with the tears of the moon, and played his panpipes. Children attended him, still unaware of the importance of the coming battle. Women mocked him or smiled sadly at his innocence as they hurried to stock food and water for the men. The priests ignored him, busy making preparations for death.

Yahuar sat on the silver and played and smiled. And watched the sky across the gorge of the Urubamba. It was clouding quickly. Rain pelted his cheeks, ran in drops down his hooked nose. The haunting five-tone notes of his panpipes drifted out over the edge of the cliffs and down into the mists that rose from the roaring river.

"Filthy country, Capitan." The soldier tugged insistently at the reins of his reluctant mount while keeping a wary eye on the heights above.

"Filthy but rich, eh, Rinaldo?" Capitan Borregos scrambled to the crest of a protruding boulder and turned to survey the war party strung out down the mountainside.

He had fifty fighting men, twenty arquebusiers, and three hundred Indian auxiliaries. They had left the cannon at the bottom of the gorge since the men had rebelled at the prospect of hauling the six-pounder up the precipitous slope. Well, with any luck they'd have no need of it, and if worse came to worst, it could shield any retreat.

But Borregos had no intention of retreating. He'd worked too long to pry these men away from the comforts of conquered Cuzco. It had been less difficult than he'd expected, though.

Most of the wealth of that plundered city was well on its way to Spain by the time these men had arrived in Peru. Cortes and the Pizarro brothers had stripped the Inca capital of its gold and silver and jewels. The city had been full of desperate, anxious men eager for a chance at the loot that had aroused the interest of all Iberia. Such men made good fighters, willing to obey any order that promised a golden reward.

No Priest traveled with Borregos's party. The fathers made him nervous, with their moaning and whining over the deaths of infidel Indians. Their presence would make the necessary butchery awkward. So Borregos and his men had slipped out of Cuzco quietly, in clusters and couples, to avoid the attention of the authorities as well as the Church.

He turned and shouted to the Indian standing nearby. Omo started at the mention of his name, hurried over to the Capitan's rock. He was a Cotol, from a tribe of Puma worshipers who lived far up the coast. The Cotol had no love for the Inca. Many of Borregos's Indian allies were Cotol. A degraded race, Borregos mused, with none of the primitive dignity of their Inca masters.

"Are you certain of this trail, Omo?"

The Indian replied in broken Spanish. "Yes, lord. This is the right way. This is the *only* way. Soon we be there, at the greatest place in all the Four Corners of the World. It is small because it is secret, and more important even than Cuzco."

"And this is where the gold is?"

"Yes, lord. The temple atop the mountain city is consecrated to the memory of Viracocha, the first Inca, the Creator. The walls of the temple are plated with the sweat of the sun, its roof and floor with the tears of the moon. It is here that Huanya Capac, the last great emperor, brought much treasure for safekeeping. It was here that Viracocha first touched the earth amidst fire and thunder and sent down his children to be Incas and lords over the world.''

"You're afraid of this place, aren't you, Omo?"

"Yes, lord."

"Then why do you go onward? Why not return to your home in the far north?"

"Because my lord would have me killed." The Indian's gaze did not meet Borregos's. Which was as it should be, the Capitan thought.

"That's right, Omo. Until we've finished our business here. Then you can go home, with all the llamas you and your men can drive." Borregos could be generous. He had little use for llamas. It was gold he was after. Sweat of the sun, the Incas called it. His eyes gleamed.

"Come on, men!" he shouted at the struggling troop. "For good King Charles and for glory!" Drawing his sword, he brandished it at the cliffs overhead.

"He can keep his glory," muttered one of the bearded, dirty soldiers in the column as he urged his horse upward, "so long as there's plenty of gold."

"Don't forget the Chosen Women," grinned his companion. "This is a big temple place. There ought to be plenty of them, too, and no priests to trouble our pleasure."

"Aye, I'd forgotten them," the other soldier confessed. He shoved at his mount with renewed strength. "This will be a memorable day."

The farmer-warriors fought bravely, and the Priests prayed hard, but sling-stones and cotton armor were no match for bullets and Toledo steel. The Spaniards' close-order fire eventually drove the defenders back from the trailhead. Once the invaders crested the first wall and achieved relatively level ground where they could use their horses, the end seemed near.

The teacher retreated with his surviving fighters to the great temple of the sun that rose from the far end of the city. There the Spaniards paused, impressed but not awed by the massive stone structures. Sacsayhuaman in Cuzco had been larger and better defended, but it too had fallen.

For now the invaders contented themselves with looting and burning the thatched buildings of the city and enjoying a late afternoon meal. On three sides of the temple the cliffs fell away to sheer precipices thousands of feet high. Their prey had nowhere to go. Though the men were anxious to press in to the real treasure, Capitan Borregos counseled them to rest and regain their strength.

There was gold aplenty even in the common houses, and while the unchosen women were not as comely as those who served the temple, the conquistadores were momentarily sated. Within the barricaded temple the teacher and his warriors listened to the screams and shouts and bit their gums until they bled.

"What are we to do now?" asked one badly lacerated warrior.

"We should not stay here. We must go out and meet them and die like men," said the teacher.

"Perhaps we can bargain with them?" suggested another hopefully. "They do not kill everyone."

"They do when the mood strikes them," the teacher snapped. "Nor are these men of nobility, such as the few who led the army which took the capital. These do not even bring a Priest with them to remind them of their god. We can die in here, or outside, in the sun."

"Not even that," said another fighter mournfully. "The rain covers the sky."

"What is that infernal noise?" The teacher whirled, stared toward the back rooms of the temple, from which odd, piping music could be heard.

"Have you forgotten Crazy Yahuar?" said a warrior apologetically. "He sits by the hitching post of the sun and plays his pipes."

"Go and get him," ordered the frustrated teacher. "At least he can die like a man."

Two of the warriors hurried back through the passageways until they reached the little plaza open to the sky where the stone and metal obelisk of the Inti Huatana stood probing the storm. It was very dark there from the clouds. A strange rumbling was coming from the mountain beneath them, and the crown of the Inti Huatana was glowing like the sun as Crazy Yahuar played to it. The two warriors drew back from the holy place, for it seemed to them that as Crazy Yahuar played, the hitching post of the sun answered him.

"Better get the horses to shelter," one of Borregos's lieutenants suggested. "We can wait out this damn storm."

"I suppose that's best." Borregos was unhappy. He'd told his men to wait. Now they faced the prospect of spending a wet night waiting in the native enclosures or making an attack in the rain. "Curse the luck. Though our gold will wait for a pleasant morning, I suppose."

"Capitan!" Borregos whirled to stare at the soldier standing guard on the nearby rampart.

Something was rising toward the citadel from the gorge below, soaring into the clouds. Faces gathered at the windows of the temple of the sun. Even the priests were drawn from their final devotions. Above the rising wind and the deep-throated thrumming that rose from inside the mountain was the erratic whisper of Crazy Yahuar's pipes.

The sled was bright silver and gold, and it floated through the air like the condor. Riding the sled and clad all in tears of the moon was the form of a woman. Her silvery hair was long and stiff and formed a glowing halo about her. Of her face, some thought it beautiful and others the face of a coated skull. Her eyes glittered with inhuman fire.

She held in one hand the staff of the sky, a pale rod filled with a light too bright to look at. When it snapped downward, it sent a thunderbolt flying toward the mountaintop city.

It touched first Capitan Borregos, then his lieutenant, then the men next to them, turning them to ash and memory. Subsequent bolts sent stones as well as men flying from their positions. A few of the soldiers forgot their fear long enough to fire at the apparition, but bullets were as useless as lances against it.

And when the last invader had been cut down and destroyed, Mother Thunder whirled once over the citadel and touched downward with her staff before vanishing into the fading storm.

Trembling and fearful but alive, the survivors followed Yahuar out onto the steps of the temple and gazed at their city.

"Behold the work of Illapa Mama, daughter of Viracocha!" No one thought the words of the pipe-player mad now.

Where the crackling staff had last pointed, a hole had appeared in the roof of the mountain. A series of steps led downward, down out of sight, down into the unknown.

"Here is the way to the place of return," announced Yahuar. "Take down the sacred objects, the remnants of the Tahuantinsuyu."

The people hurried to obey, stripping the temple and its adjacent buildings of the tears of the moon and sweat of the sun and the sacred relics. Then they gathered food for the coming journey, a journey all knew would take a long time.

"The works of Viracocha came to naught because his people forgot his teachings. They fell to pleasuring themselves and did not work to maintain his memory, and busied themselves instead with petty squabbles and arguments," Yahuar explained. Among those nodding agreement was the now-silent, solemn teacher.

"But Viracocha was wise. One wise man of each generation was taught the special song, the song of remembrance, to be played only in dire need. The song that would bring forth Illapa Mama to rescue his children and show them the way to return to learning and peace.

"We must go back now to the home of Viracocha until it is time again for his descendants to return and extend their rule over this land. Know that I am the wise man, the song-player, of this generation, great-grandson of the first song-player, who was taught by Viracocha himself. Follow my song now." He put the panpipes to his lips and began to play.

Humming wordlessly to the familiar tune, the people of the city followed Yahuar down into the gut of the mountain, and they did not even tremble when it closed up behind them.

* * *

A great thunderclap was heard even in Cuzco. Some thought they saw a pillar of fire and a mountain ascending heavenward. Others said it was only a cloud lit by lightning. Still others heard and saw nothing and decried the words of those who did. Later travelers wondered what became of the people of the sacred city of Machu Picchu, even as they wondered at the western side of the great mountain that seemed to have split off and vanished.

Most of the city remains. So does the Inti Huatana, the hitching post of the sun, though no metal crowns it anymore. There are nights when the panpipes of a somnolent shepherd strike an odd resonance in the ancient pillar. No one thinks it remarkable, for many earthquakes plague the land once conquered by Viracocha, just as no one thinks to dig to see what may lie inside the great mountain . . .

THE CHAIR
(with Jane Cozart)

Story ideas come from everywhere. Even objects.

*In west Texas dwells a remarkable lady. Jane Cozart
was born into a theatrical family. Her father, for those
older readers, was none other than Smilin' Ed Mc-
Connell of radio and TV fame. Some might remember his
rubbery sidekick, Froggy. Jane elected to forgo a possible career in films when she broke her leg prior to the
filming of a minor epic in which she'd been cast. The film
was National Velvet, and Jane's part eventually went to
another teenage actress, name of Taylor.*

*Jane married and settled in west Texas to raise a few
kids, a lot of animals, and a little hell. Any mail that
arrives in that region addressed simply to the Wicked
Witch of the West goes directly to her. I was immediately
impressed the first time I met her because her personal
library was larger than that of the local school.*

*My wife JoAnn had scrimped and saved to buy me a
fascinating carved chair prior to our marriage. When I
described it to Jane one time, she allowed as how it might
form the basis for an interesting story. I was less sure
but told her that if she wrote it, I'd collaborate with her
on it. The chair itself still sits in my study, the face in its
back glaring at me even as I write this, its actual origin
still lost in the mists of time.*

*And if June Foray, she of the many cartoon voices,
happens to read this, Jane McConnell says hello.*

"NOT ANOTHER ANTIQUE STORE."
Dylan McCarey Grouchoed his eyes and did his best to

look as exasperated as he was tired. The Ford sedan idled nervously around him, anxious to please.

Across the front seat of the gold gas guzzler—currently road-dusted to a limp bronze—his wife folded her arms, pursed her lips, and threw herself into a first-class pout. It was a well-practiced posture, one that gave her the look of a martyred spaniel. The resemblance was compounded by her moss-green eyes and the black hair that fell straight behind her to tangle in the belt of her skirt.

Dylan had been the recipient of that pout numerous times in their frenetic, brief marriage. That didn't do anything to stiffen his resistance to it. Goering, he reflected, had known when the RAF and American bombers were coming across the Channel. That foreknowledge hadn't given him the power to stop their raids any more than Dylan's was able to prevent him from melting under Marjorie's pitiful little-girl expressions.

"All right, all right. But it better not be too far." He checked his watch. "I'd like to get home before midnight."

"Thanks, honey." The pout vanished faster than a starving hummingbird. "We're not far." She studied a slip of paper thick with hieroglyphics. "It's just south of Colorado, near Lake."

"Pasadena." They were already passing Covina off ramps, he noticed. They *were* close, and it was on the way out of LA. Time for him to take credit for some involuntary magnanimity. "Sure, sugar. No reason we can't stop and look for a few minutes."

But it took him longer to locate the store than he'd thought. The car made several passes in front of the right street numbers before Marjorie spotted the little sign set in among the brickwork, an identifying afterthought.

They parked nearby. Impatient to be on its way, the car grumbled when he turned it off. They didn't have far to walk. A Goodwill store, one dealing liquor, another pornographic books and magazines and FILMS, CHANGED EACH WEEK, 25¢.

A dim stairway to the right of the sign led up into the building, a narrow throat lined with flaking plaster. "Either it's a very old, exclusive store or else another secondhand store masquerading as an antique shop.'' He studied the stairwell warily.

''Why do you say that?''

He started up the stairs. ''He's on a second-floor walk-up in a run-down neighborhood. They have an old-line, class clientele that knows the location or else he's upstairs because he can't afford a street-level location.''

''Think you're pretty smart, don't you?'' She squeezed his arm affectionately, and he grinned back at her.

The door was the first one they saw at the top of the stairs. To the right and left, dark hallways ran off into silent oblivion. They could have run into other doors, other shops, or into the fourth dimension for all Dylan could see.

A name on the door: Harry Saltzmann. There was no bell. Several knocks produced no response.

''Nobody home.'' He hoped his relief didn't show. Three days of traipsing around the megalopolis had tired him out, and he didn't share Marjorie's fanatic fondness for antiques. He was disgusted with breathing the effluvia of industrial civilization. It was time to go home.

''It's Tuesday. How can they be closed on Tuesday?'' Marjorie sounded puzzled. ''There're no posted hours, though. Damn.''

''You'll find another antique store someday, Marj,'' he assured her. ''You can smell 'em.''

The door clicked, moved inward slightly. Eyes peered out and up at them. They were green as a young kitten's, the youngest feature of an old face. They formed an informal boundary between the narrow, lower face and jaw and the bulging oversized skull. The latter was fringed with white hair, the whole fleshy basilica seemingly too large to balance on the sunken cheekbones and thin jaw below.

''Oh, you're open.''

The man's voice was reassuringly firm, the accent southern: somewhere between Dallas and Nibelheim. ''Mebbe, young lady. Who're you?''

''I'm Marjorie,' she replied with her usual charming directness. ''This is my husband, Dylan. He's a writer. Are you Mr. Saltzmann, the owner?''

''Not much use denyin' it,'' he mumbled. He looked

resigned. "You want to look around? I haven't got much time."

"Not if you're closed. We don't want to cause you any trouble." Marjorie never wanted to make trouble, Dylan reflected wryly. She was the type to apologize to the tax collector for not being able to give the government more money.

"No, no trouble." The top-heavy face seemed to soften slightly. "You folks from out of town?"

"Yes. How can you tell?"

"You look happy. Whereabouts?"

Dylan was growing annoyed at the inquisition, but Marjorie threw him a sharp look, and he hung on to his retreating sense of courtesy. "Up the coast. Little town called Cambria. It's near San Simeon. You know, where the Hearst castle is?"

"Sure I know. They got a few nice pieces."

A few nice . . . either the old man was putting them on, or else the first of Dylan's suppositions was correct and the inventory within would not be cheap.

The door rode back on its hinges. "Come on in, then."

The shop was as organized as a Pacific tide pool. Furniture, clothing, and bric-a-brac were scattered about the high-ceilinged old room with an awkward yet eye-pleasing efficiency. One had the impression that whenever a new assortment was added to the melange it would spread itself like a wave across the existing stock, disturbing nothing, adding another layer of ancient creativity to the store's sedimentary deposits.

Light came in off the street through an old, high window. In the darker recesses of the nowhere-bright chamber, isolated small bulbs shone with feeble flavescence, like fat fireflies in an Ohio forest.

Masterworks and gutterworks crowded together, competing for scant display space. An old city garbage can held dresses that must have been over a hundred years old. In a scratched glass case junk jewelry lay heaped in piles of gleaming paste. There was also an old-style tiara sparkling with suspiciously genuine-looking emeralds and diamonds. One faceted green pool was as big as Dylan's watch face.

Curious, he called the proprietor over. Saltzmann

peered down over his belly to where Dylan's finger was pointing.

"The necklace? That's seven dollars."

"No, no. The tiara, next to it."

"Oh, that one. That's three hundred thousand."

Dylan missed a breath, stared at the slim, delicate filigree of gold and gems. "You're kidding, of course."

"Too much? Oh, well, if you really want it, I suppose I can let it go for two hundred and fifty. Belonged to Josephine . . . Bonaparte's gal."

Dylan tried not to smirk. "We'll keep it in mind."

There was a call for help from the far side of the shop. Marjorie was buried back among the old clothes there, running centuries through her fingers, trying on one era after another. Saltzmann waddled over to assist.

That left a bored Dylan to wend his own way deeper into the depths of the store. The long room seemed to run clear through the building. A ship's figurehead smiled down at him, and he admired it, tried to imagine it breasting the waves of the seven seas. He passed barrels stinking of long-drunk whiskey, kegs of railroad spikes, old cast-iron toys. There were baked and cracked horse collars and rusty farm tools dangling overhead that whispered of droughts and bad crops.

A corner led him to a back room, slightly better lit than the main store. Several pieces of furniture lay taken apart on floor and benches. He was just realizing that he'd stumbled onto the old man's workshop when he saw the chair.

It squatted off in a dim corner of its own, unadorned with antique Coke bottles or limp fur capes or power tools. To a writer of travel and adventure stories it was as irresistible as a guided tour of eighteenth-century Arabia.

Still, he paused long enough to peek back into the shop proper. Marjorie was holding a long black Victorian gown in front of her, dickering with the owner. The gown seemed to fit the nips and tucks of her Junoesque figure well. Somewhere an equally lovely form, the original wearer of that dress, was now dust. Quickly he drew back into the workroom and walked over to stare greedily at the chair.

It was straight-backed, with four legs, two straight arms, and a curved seat all hewn from some heavy, dark wood. Probably oak or walnut, he mused. In addition to the fairly standard clawed legs and swirling decorations there were more flagrant examples of the wood-carver's art.

Each arm ended in the head of a peculiarly anthropomorphic fish. At each upper corner of the straight back a deeply sculpted lion's skull, fangs agape, glared back at him. But it was the back of the seat that drew most of his enraptured attention.

Roughly half the smooth slab was filled with tiny carved faces. None was larger than his thumbprint, yet the amount of detail in them was astonishing. Peering closely at one, a middle-aged woman, Dylan could make out perfect carved teeth, eyebrows, hair. The expression was twisted and distorted, as were all the others.

Above this miniature gallery was a much larger face, so big that his spread palm could barely obscure it. It was extraordinarily animated and lifelike. The long nose appeared broken. Both cheeks swelled out into whorls of wind, gusting to either side of the chair to break against the smooth manes of the lions. Dylan studied the almost flexible carving, unable to decide whether the master wood-carver had shown a face laughing or screaming.

"This room's off limits, son."

Startled, Dylan nearly stumbled as he spun around. "Sorry. I . . . didn't see a sign or anything."

Glancing at the floor, Saltzmann located and picked up a dirty, battered rectangle of cardboard on which EMPLOYEES ONLY had been crudely painted. He muttered something to himself, set about rehanging it just outside the entrance.

While he was busy with that, Dylan beckoned his wife in.

"Sugar, come take a look at this."

Marjorie walked over, glanced at the chair, and grimaced. "That's your taste, all right. Gruesome."

"Oh, come on, Marjorie. Look at that workmanship; look at those faces, the detail."

"That's your way of saying you want it?" she asked evenly.

He was abruptly embarrassed. "Uh, did you find any-thing?"

She smiled tolerantly. "A couple of dresses."

"That's great. Buy whatever you want, hon."

"You always say that . . . after *you* find something you want."

"Welllllll . . ." He knew she was teasing him now.

"Never mind. I'm glad you found something, too. Just don't expect me to sit in it." Turning, she confronted the watching Saltzmann. "How much is it?"

"The chair? Well, you know, it really tain't fer sale." Dylan's hopes fell apart. "I've had it goin' on forty-five years." He looked at his watch. "But since I'm goin' to die 'round seven-twenty tonight, I s'pose you might as well have it as any other. That is, if its history don't bother you none. I'm bound to tell it to you."

"History intrigues me, never bothers me." Dylan turned a proprietary look on the chair, barely reflecting on the old man's macabre sense of humor.

"How old you think that chair is, folks?"

Dylan knew next to nothing about antiques. He let Marjorie guess. "A hundred years? No, two hundred."

Saltzmann was grinning, showing gold teeth alternating with dark gaps. His mouth displayed more masonry work than a Saxon fortress. "Little less than four hun-dred."

Uh oh, trouble, Dylan thought. A chair that old, in this kind of condition, would be expensive.

"It belonged to John Dee. Dr. John Dee?" Both Dylan and Marjorie waited expectantly. The owner looked dis-appointed. "He was court astrologer to Queen Elizabeth the First herself, after she got him off the hook for prac-ticing black magic. He invented the crystal ball; least-wise, he told fortune-tellers what it was good for." He paused for emphasis, added, "Made the only English translation of the *Al Azif.*"

"Never heard of it," Dylan confessed honestly.

Saltzmann grunted, mumbled something about the ig-norance of today's youth, and pointed at the back of the chair. "That's his face, Dr. Dee's, on the top there."

"That's interesting." Dylan had his wallet out. "How much?" He tried to sound casual.

"Oh, it don't matter now. Fifty dollars?"

Dylan made up for the earlier missed breath. "Okay. Sure."

Marjorie held the door for him while he wrestled the chair out into the hallway. "Hurry it up, son," the owner urged him. "I've got a lot to do before I'm taken."

As they finally finished securing the chair in the backseat of the car, Marjorie mentioned the oldster's earlier comment about dying at seven-twenty.

"He fancies himself a wit," Dylan told her, making sure the chair wouldn't slip on the long drive home. "Besides, didn't you hear him say as we were leaving that he was getting ready to be taken somewhere? Somebody's picking him up. Now, he can't very well go and die at the same time, can he?"

"I guess not." Marjorie slipped into the front seat, admiring her old new dresses.

They beat the fog in, for which Dylan was grateful. It curled in around him like a damp pair of pajamas as he climbed out of the car, stretched, and closed the garage door behind them. Then he was carefully extricating the chair from the sedan's backseat as Marjorie unlocked the service porch door.

"Can't wait to see what it looks like in the study."

Some minutes later Marjorie had fed the cats, hung her dresses, and joined him there. Forty feet below the wide window, surf slapped sharply on the seawall supporting the house. His desk backed that window. Books lined the other three walls, interspersed with hanging house plants, paintings, sculpture, an old rifle, a Polynesian cane, crossed battle-ax and saber, and other paraphernalia collected on their many travels. Somewhere offshore a ship's horn brayed at the fog like a hippo with sinusitis.

The chair rested behind the desk. "Got to polish it tomorrow." Loud barking exploded nearby. The study sided on another beach house. "Damn those dogs! A poodle I could maybe stand. But no, we move up here to be a hundred miles from noise and neighbors, and a month later he moves in with a pair of Great Danes not quite as big as ponies." The stentorian yapping sounded again.

"You'd better learn to live with it, hon. It's not against the law for a neighbor to own dogs." She indicated the chair. "And incidentally, you're going to polish that, not me. I'm not touching it. Gives me the quivers."

Making a face, teeth protruding over his lower lip, he advanced on her with clawed hands outstretched. "Ah, beware zee terror uf zee Transylvanian chair, my lufly!"

"Stop that. Cut it out, Dylan!" She backed away, swatting nervously at his hands. "You know how easily I scare."

He dropped his hands, looked disgusted, "Oh, for heaven's sake, Marjorie. It's only a dead hunk of wood."

"Fine." She retreated toward the bedroom to unpack. "But you polish it."

Shaking his head, he turned to admire his acquisition. Now he had time to examine the tiny faces cut into the wood below the large one, time to admire the rich grain of the wood as well as the craftsmanship.

"They don't build furniture like this anymore," he murmured to himself, sitting down in it. He gripped the fish heads, sat straight. "Fifty bucks!" The straight wooden back was a bit stiff, but that was to be expected. In sixteenth-century England they built for endurance as much as comfort. The tiny faces pressed into the small of his back, the larger portrait's gaping mouth between his shoulder blades.

"Hope you don't bite, Doc." It was very dark and quiet outside, the ocean a hidden, heaving mass idling and breathing beneath the fog.

Halfway to the kitchen, Marjorie stopped at a sudden sound, turned, and headed for the study. When she peered in, Dylan was hunched over the typewriter. The chair almost hid him, though the familiar hysterical chatter of the machine was enough to tell her what he was doing.

"Working now? I thought you were exhausted from the drive."

He stopped, looked back at her. "I just had a thought I had to get down. You know me, Marj. If I don't do it now, I'll forget it." A staccato cackle interrupted him.

"Those dogs! I've got to try and reason with Andrus again."

"Andrus is a lawyer, hon. You know you can't reason with him." She turned and headed back toward the kitchen.

The coffee was purring to itself, a dark liquid feline sound. She hefted the old-fashioned percolator, poured two cups. Dylan walked in, closing the door on disappointed morning mist. The paper was clutched in his right hand. "Foggy out still this morning, hon. What's the matter?"

His expression was solemn, thoughtful. "I wish I hadn't been so hard on Mark Andrus last night. I just ran into his housekeeper, Mrs. Samuels." Marjorie nodded, waiting. "Andrus died last night."

"Oh, Dylan, no." He nodded. "How'd it happen?"

He tossed the paper on the kitchen table, didn't bother to open it. She put his coffee in front of him, and he sipped delicately. Steam crawled upward out of the cup, slim shadow matches to the curls in his hair.

"Heart attack, the doctor said. That's what Mrs. Samuels told me she was told. It doesn't seem fair. He wasn't much older than I am."

"Isn't that kind of unusual, for him to have a heart attack? Not being forty yet and all." She stirred sugar into her own cup.

Shrugging, he opened the paper, laid it flat on the table. "Depends, I guess. If the men in his family had a history of heart trouble, then I suppose it's perfectly natural. Big fire up the coast near Eureka." He tapped the page. "If we don't get some honest rain soon here . . ."

He stopped, looked up at nothing. Marjorie knew that faraway gaze. Until he decided to return, she might as well talk to the coffee.

"You know," he finally told her, as though he hadn't been silent for several minutes, "it may seem a little sick, but this has given me a great idea for a story."

From behind the stove, she grimaced at him as she started the eggs. They made a sound like a desert sandstorm when they landed in the hot skillet. "You're right, that is sick."

"But it's a terrific idea." He pushed back from the table, stood. " 'Scuse me, hon, be right back." Marjorie sighed, watched him almost run toward the study. She'd have to call him to breakfast half a dozen times now, and his eggs would still get cold. Not that he would mind. In the fever grip of a new idea, he couldn't taste anything, anyway.

That breakfast was the beginning. From then on it seemed creation was only a matter of typing fast enough to keep up with the flood of inspiration. Everything Dylan wrote in the succeeding months sold, and the two books he managed to complete sold *big*. Not quite best-sellerdom, but considering the lack of advertising the publishers put behind them, the books did very well, indeed. That was enough to wake up the editors. If and when Dylan finished the third book, there'd be some spirited bidding waiting for it.

All of which, while gratifying, took a heavy toll on Dylan. It got so he rose explosively and raced for the typewriter. A hysterical day of writing left him barely enough strength to munch in slow motion through supper and stagger exhaustedly into bed.

Dylan used to be creative elsewhere besides behind the typewriter. Which is one way of saying his incredible surge of creativity was also taking a heavy toll on Marjorie.

"Hey."

"Hmmm?" Dylan didn't look up from the typewriter. She'd never cared much for the sound the electric made. Lately she'd felt as though each tap, each character printed, was a tiny bullet aimed squarely at her heart.

"I said, the housekeeper would like a word with the master." She stood leaning against the frame of the study door. Her insides had wound tighter and tighter the past week until her stomach felt as tiny and hard as a golf ball. Grayness obscured the view outside the study window, the inescapable coast fog of the north California coast.

"Damn it, sugar, I'm working."

"You're working, and I'm dying." She tried to sound furious. It came out in a sob.

"Don't be ri—" Something went click in his head, and he turned, stared at her curiously. "Hon, is something the matter?"

She didn't have to volunteer it now. He'd asked the question. "The matter? What could possibly be the matter?" She straightened, walked into the study.

"C'mon now, hon what is it?"

"Don't 'c'mon now, hon' me!" Her control vanished. "I haven't seen you, talked to you, done anything with you in months!"

"I've been working." His voice was soft but not gentle. "Working my ass off, for us. You know how well we've done lately. Our bank account . . ."

Usually his mock little-boy manner of arguing was ingratiating. Now it was simply irritating. "To hell with our bank account. I'd like my husband back. You've been so obsessed with your work here lately, ever since we got back from LA, that . . ." She stopped, stared at him open-mouthed.

"Obsessed, yes. Ever since you bought that god-awful chair."

"It's not god-awful. It's beautiful. You said so yourself."

"I never said it was beautiful, never! Well made, maybe, but I'd never've said it was beautiful. I'd remember."

"You're being silly, Marj. If anything, I'd have to say this chair's been good for me, considering how much and how well I've been selling recently."

"Maybe it's been good for you, but not for me. I—I want you to get rid of it."

"Get rid of it?" He looked at her as though she'd suggested some night swimming, now, in November. "This chair's one of my favorite things." He smiled patronizingly. "Don't tell me, Marj, that you're jealous of a chair."

"Will you get rid of it?" Her voice was low, edgy.

He sat quietly for a moment, then spoke calmly and with a chill in his voice that made her tremble. "You're a little hysterical, Marjorie. I can't talk sensibly to you when you're hysterical. We'll talk some more about it later. I've got ten more pages to do yet tonight." He turned back to the typewriter.

She stared at his back. *Tatta-ta-tat-tatta-tatta* . . . the letters fired at her, each one a little pinprick deep inside her guts. She opened her mouth, started to say something, then whirled and ran from the room.

He did not look up.

The doorbell rang, demanding. Sweating despite the coolness of the room, Dylan looked up from the machine on the third ring. Dazedly, he surveyed the evening's work. Nearly nine thousand words.

As the bell rang and he rose to answer the door, he vaguely recalled something disquieting about the evening. Oh, yes, he and Marjorie had had an argument of some kind.

That was probably she at the door. When she got mad or frustrated, she liked to take the car out and drive. Silly fool had probably forgotten her house keys and locked herself out. Try as he could, the cause of their argument escaped him. Well, he'd apologize for whatever it was, take the blame, promise never to do it again, and they'd kiss and make up.

He was composing excuses as he opened the door. Marjorie wasn't there.

Instead, he found himself staring blankly up at a tall stranger in a blue uniform. The man wore a white plastic helmet and sported insignia and buckles like a cubist's cactus. He favored Dylan with a solemn stare entirely out of keeping with his quasi-military appearance.

Dylan felt himself drowning in a sudden thick surge of conflicting thoughts and emotions. He heard a voice, distant and suspiciously like his own, saying, "Yes, Officer?"

"Mr. McCarey? Dylan McCarey? This is 1649 Oakhurst Place?"

"Marjorie . . ." Dylan leaned out into the steely dampness, tried to see into the garage. The door was up, open. "Has she been in an accident?"

"I'm sorry, Mr. McCarey. She died at the scene."

"Died?" He shook his head. That didn't clear it. He smiled crookedly. "Marjorie?"

"Apparently, in the fog, she missed a turn. About halfway between here and Goleta."

"Goleta? What was she doing way up near . . ." He stopped, remembered. They'd argued, and he'd turned away. Marjorie.

"Marjorie." He started out the door. A firm hand caught him, an arm barred his way.

"I'm very sorry, Mr. McCarey, very sorry. It was quick. Her car went over a three-hundred-foot cliff. I'm told she died instantly."

Dylan stared past the man, into the smothered night. Nothing was visible through the fog save a faint squarish outline in the driveway topped by a leering red light winking. Blood, fog, night . . . Marjorie.

"I'm Sergeant Brooks. I'm with the San Simeon station. If you'd like to come down there for a while . . ."

"Later, maybe. Not now," he replied numbly. "Later."

"You sure you'll be okay?"

"I'll be okay." He looked up. "Thank you, Sergeant. I have to make some phone calls, get in touch with people."

"Of course. We'd like you to come into Obispo tomorrow . . . or as soon as you can. Official identification. I'm sorry."

"Of course you would. I'll come in the morning. After I make the phone calls. Good night, Officer."

"Good night, Mr. McCarey." Brooks studied him professionally, reached a decision. "I'll be going now. If we can do anything, please call us."

"Yes. Thank you."

Dylan remained framed in the doorway, a weaving silhouette in the hallway light. He watched as the tall patrolman was swallowed by the fog. There was the sound of a car door slamming. Rumbling throatily, the blinking red light turned and receded into the distance. He stared until it had disappeared completely.

Reflex guided him back to the study, back to his desk. A detached part of him was coolly aware of the mournful dialogue of wind and wave below the window. Marjorie, Marjorie. What had they fought about, to send her blindly running from the house, from him? That silly fight over nothing, over a chair. A damned piece of furniture.

Turning, he looked at it. One little argument and his Marjorie was taken from him forever. One absurd little . . .

He froze, his spine rippling like an underground cable in an earthquake. Some unmentionable fear swamped his muscular control of self, and he shivered uncontrollably.

The back of the chair was altered, different. He could've sworn, would've sworn, he'd originally counted nine faces carved into the seat back. There were eleven now. On bulgy-eyed, close inspection, one resembled very much, quite impossibly, that of a recently deceased young lawyer and former neighbor, Mark Andrus. The other . . . oh, God, the other . . .

Long hair formed a cirruslike nimbus around the delicately rendered face. The tiny mouth was open, forming a deep little gash in the dark wood, while the miniature glaring eyes focused on some unseen but immediate terror. The complete expression was one a person would adopt on viewing some soul-twisting horror or a train abruptly bearing down on her, the earth cracking beneath her feet, or . . .

Rocks at the bottom of a cliff rushing up at her.

Shaking, cold, cold in the heated room, he bent around in the chair. A forefinger reached out unsteadily toward the tiny portrait. His voice was an echo.

"Marjorie?" He touched the carving.

It was warmer than the wood around it.

Dylan jumped out of the chair, hit the desk, backed away from it. His eyes never left the chair. He struck something—the wastebasket—and stumbled over it. Strange noises were coming from deep in his throat, a low grunting sound like someone might make while experiencing a nightmare in the midst of deep sleep.

Backing into a wall, he knocked precious books from their shelves and ignored them. A vase full of coleus fell, shattered, and stained the green carpet. Something else heavy was bumped, hit the floor with an imperative cushioned thud.

He looked down. The battle-ax lay smooth and clean among the dirt and humus and broken waxy stems from the cracked vase. Slowly he reached down, picked up the replica. Its weight blotted out everything else in the study. Cherry glaze blurred his vision.

Howling like a crippled wolf, he raised the ax over his head with both hands and rushed on the chair.

At the last instant it rose nimbly on four clawed legs and skittered aside.

The ax came down blindly, missing, gashing Dylan's right calf. Overbalanced, he spun, swung, and raised the ax again. It went through the picture window with a crystalline scream, and Dylan followed it.

Immediately thereafter a dull, distance-damped *thump* sounded from the rocks below. Then it was quiet in the study. Through the break, the fog began to enter, marching on the sound of winter waves forty feet below.

"I don't understand." The young girl looked happily at her fiancé. "It was so cheap."

He grinned at her with the superior knowledge of the older (he was two years older than she and had already graduated college). "Small-town estate sale, that's all. No dealers to bid against. It was sure a buy, though. What a way to start furnishing our apartment! Wait till Sally and Dave see it.

"Let's go. You've got classes tomorrow morning."

"Mondays, yecch!" She wrinkled her pretty face. "You'll have all day off to admire it while I'm slogging through Haskell's seminar."

"It'll be there when you get home." He slid behind the wheel of the van.

"Isn't it gorgeous, though?" She turned in her seat to stare back at the chair. It leaned up against the convertible couch, dogged down securely by rope. She admired the carved arms and lion's heads, the open-mouthed gargoyle crowning the back of the seat, and most especially the twelve miniature faces carved into the back.

Her fiancé frowned, looked in his rearview mirror. "Did you hear someone scream?"

She smiled at him, took his free hand. "Probably just some kid separated from his momma. I didn't hear anything but laughing, dummy."

"Laughing, screaming, who cares? We got ourselves

a helluva buy!'' He started the engine, guided the van out of the lot. They laughed as they rocked their way across several chuckholes and depressions in the road.

Behind them, the chair squatted expectantly as four wooden feet dug a little more deeply into the blue-red carpet . . .

THE INHERITANCE

I love cats. Always have, always will. I'm not allergic to them, and their hair doesn't make me sneeze. I've slept with cats the past fourteen years. They move around, they get your legs hot, and sometimes they snore. But they're great company. I like real cats, fictional cats like Gummitch, wholly imaginary cats, felines large and small. I liked Garfield better when he was a cat.

However, I have noticed through the years that not every member of the human race feels the same. There are people who like cats even though they're allergic to them: a pitiable situation. There are some folks who are indifferent to their presence. And then there are, astonishingly enough, individuals who outright hate felines.

There are even those who live in fear of the common house cat, whose phobia is a throwback to the Middle Ages and the terrors of the plague. No argument can alter their opinions, no logic dissuade their antifeline vitriol. In the very presence of a cat they will draw away in fear. It is an attitude I find incomprehensible, indefensible, absurd, and unreasoning.

Wouldn't it be hilarious if they turned out to be right?

". . . MY HOME, TRENTON, ITS CONTENTS, AND the sum of five hundred and fifty thousand dollars, after other and all taxes have been paid."

Every eye in the pecan-paneled room turned to Mayell. She remained composed in green sleeveless dress and pumps, managing not to grin.

"There are two conditions," the lawyer continued, his tone indicating disapproval of the manner in which the deceased's secretary's skirt had crawled an indecent distance up her thighs. "You must remain in residence at Trenton House for six months to enable the staff there to make a gradual transition to other employment."

"And the other condition?" Mayell spoke with the chiming notes of a gamelan, displaying a voice sweet enough to match her appearance.

The lawyer harrumphed. "There remains the matter of Saugen, the deceased's cat. You will henceforth be responsible for the animal's care. Full transferral of the aforementioned sum occurs six months from today, provided that Trenton remains home to its present staff for that length of time and provided that Saugen appears happy, healthy, well fed, and content at that date."

"That's all?"

"That is all." The lawyer evened the mass of paper by tapping the double handful on the desk. "This reading, ladies and gentlemen, is concluded."

Mutters rose like flies on a hot day from the small group, from disappointed distant relatives and modestly rewarded servants, from hopeful acquaintances, and from somber-faced business associates. Some had received more than they'd hoped for, others considerably less. None had fared nearly so well as the late Hiram Hanford's "secretary," the delectable Mayell.

Of the servants, none seemed as satisfied as the gardener, Willis. None had his reason to. For while Hanford had left him only a slight sum, Willis was heir to much more than was indicated in the formal will. He had inherited Mayell.

As she rose and turned to exit the lawyer's chambers, their eyes met in silent mutual congratulation. They had each other. In six months they would have the money and Trenton House. Soon they could live the life they'd endured in secret these past miserable five years.

"Nice kitty, kitty. Sweet Saugen-mine." Mayell knelt in the foyer of Trenton and cooed to the yellow tomcat. It slid supply around her ankles, meowing affectionately.

Willis's gaze was appreciative, but it was not wasted on the cat. Instead, he was luxuriating in the landscape provided by Mayell's provocative posture: kneeling, inclined slightly forward. It highlighted her burnished blond hair, the regular curve of delicate shoulders and hips, the cleavage better described in terms geologic than physiological, resembling as it did other remarkable natural clefts such as the East African Rift.

She stood, cradling the sleek feline in her arms. It purred like a tiny stove set on simmer. "See, he likes me. Saugen-sweet always did like me."

Willis noticed the cat staring at him. It possessed the penetrating, hypnotic gaze of all cats, magnified in this particular instance by overlarge yellow eyes. The black slits in their centers glinted like cuts. He shook himself. All cats stared like that.

"Good thing he does, too. That parasite of a lawyer will be around in May some time to check on the house and his furry nibs there. Keepin' the house and roses lookin' good is going to be my job. Keepin' the cat the same'll be up to you."

Mayell hugged the tom close to the warm shelf of her bosom. "That won't be any trouble, Willis. He doesn't seem to miss Hiram much." She gently let the cat drop to the floor. It made a moving, fuzzy bracelet of itself around her left ankle.

"That's something we have in common." Her perfect face twisted into an unflattering grimace. For an instant Willis had a glimpse of something less attractive hiding behind the beauty-queen mask. "Five years of my life, gone." She nestled into the gardener's arms. "Five years!" She clung tightly to his rangy, sunburned form. "Only you made it bearable, darling."

"We're gettin' fair pay back. One hundred and ten thousand for each year of hell." He glanced around the massive old house, at the garish neo-Victorian decor and the wealth of antiques. "Plus what this mausoleum will fetch. And no one suspects."

"No." She showed cream-white teeth in an oddly predatory smile. "I didn't think anyone would, not as slowly as I altered his medicine. Ten months, a fraction at a time. Otherwise the old relic might've gone on for another twenty years.'' She shuddered from a distant cold memory. ''I couldn't have stood it, Willis.'' Her voice and expression were hard. ''I earned that half million.''

''Six months and we'll leave this place forever. We'll go somewhere sunny and warm, as far from Vermont as we can get.''

''Rio,'' she murmured languorously, savoring the single soft syllable, ''or Cannes, or the Aegean.''

''Anywhere you want, Mayell.''

They embraced tightly enough to keep a burglar's pick from slipping between them while Saugen slid sensuously around the perfect ankle of his new mistress.

''Willis?''

''Yes, Mayell?''

They were sipping coffee on the heated, enclosed veranda of Trenton, watching bees busy themselves among the spring flowers of the garden. It was Saturday, and the remaining servants were off. They could indulge in each other without gossipy eyes prying.

''Do you think I look any different?''

''Different? Different from what, darling?''

She looked uncomfortable. ''I don't know . . . different from usual, I guess.''

''More beautiful than ever.'' Seeing she was serious, he studied her critically for a moment. ''You might've lost a little weight.''

She half smiled. ''Seven pounds, to be exact.''

''And it troubles you?'' He shook his head in disbelief. ''Most women would find that a bit weird, Mayell.''

She ran slim fingers through the tawny yellow-brown coat of Saugen, a puffball of fur asleep in her lap. ''I haven't changed my eating habits.''

He smirked, leaned back in the lounge. ''Could be you've been taking more exercise lately.''

She laughed with him, seemed relieved. ''Of course. I hadn't thought of that.''

He looked at her in mock outrage. ''Hadn't *thought* of it?'' They both laughed now. ''I guess we'll have to work at making it stick in your memory.''

* * *

A concerned Willis led the scarecrow called Oakley up the curved stairway.

"If she's as ill as you think, man, why didn't you call me sooner?" Grit and Yankee stone, the elderly doctor mounted the steps without panting.

"She didn't call me. I told you, Doc, I've been in New York all week, making arrangements for the sale of the house and land. I didn't know she was this bad until I got back yesterday, and I called you right away."

"Kind of unusual for a gardener to negotiate the sale of an estate, isn't it?" Oakley had a naturally dry tone. "Down this hall?"

Sharp old birds, these country professionals, Willis thought. "Yeah, She trusts me, and she's suspicious of lawyers."

That struck a sympathetic nerve. "Got good reason to be. Sound thinking."

"This is her room." He knocked. A faint voice responded.

"Willis?"

They entered. The expression that formed on Oakley's features when he caught sight of the figure in the old plateau of a bed was instructive. It took something to shake an experienced general practitioner like Oakley, and from his looks now he was badly shaken.

"Good God," he muttered, moving rapidly to the bedside and opening his archaic black bag. "How long has she been like this?"

"It's been going on for several weeks now, at least." Willis looked away from the doctor's accusing stare. How could they explain that they wanted no strangers prowling the house, generating unwelcome publicity and maybe some dangerous second-guessing questions? "It's gotten a lot worse since I've been away."

He took the chair on the other side of the bed. The hand that moved to grip his was wrinkled and shaky. Mayell's once satin-taut skin was dull and parchmentlike, her eyes bulging in sunken sockets. Even her lips were pale and crepe-crinkled though neither dry nor chapped. She looked ghastly.

Oakley was doing things with the tools of the physician. He was working quickly, like a man without enough time, and his expression was grim, a dangerous difference from its normal dourness.

A fluffy fat shape landed in Willis's lap. "Hello, cat," he said, absently stroking Saugen's ruddy coat. "What's wrong with your mistress, eh?" The tom gazed up at him, bottomless cat eyes piercing him deeply. With a querulous meow, he hopped onto the bed.

"Is he in your way, Doc?" Willis made ready to move the animal if the doctor said yes. Mayell put a hand down to stroke the tom's rump. It meowed delightedly, semaphoring with its striped maroon tail.

"No." Oakley hadn't paid any attention to the cat, was intent on taking the sphygmomanometer reading.

"Good Saugen, sweet Saugen," Mayell whispered. Willis was shocked, frightened to see how broomstick-thin her arm had become. She looked over at him, and he forced himself to meet her hideously protruding eyes. "He's been such a comfort to me while you were away, Willis. He kept me warm every night."

"You should've called the doctor yourself, Mayell. You look terrible, much worse than when I left."

"I do?" She sounded puzzled and oddly unconcerned, as though unable to grasp the seriousness of her condition. "Then I must get better, mustn't I?"

Oakley rose, looked meaningfully at Willis. They moved to a far corner. "I want that woman in the hospital at Montpelier. Immediately. Tonight. It's criminal she's still in this house."

"I told you, I was in New York. I didn't *know*. The last of the regular servants left three weeks ago, and we were going to do the same at the end of the month. She wasn't nearly this bad when I left." Despite the reasonable excuse, Willis still felt guilty. "What's wrong with her?"

Oakley studied the floor and chewed his upper lip before looking back at the bed and its sleeping skeleton.

"I don't know that I can give a name to any specific disease, or diseases, since I think she's suffering from at least three different ones. She's terribly sick. Can't tell for certain what's wrong until I get her into the hospital and run some tests. Acute anemia, muscular degeneration of the most severe kind, calcium deficiency probably caused by reabsorption . . . that's what's wrong with her. What's causing it I can't say. She can't have been eating much lately.''

"But she has been,'' Willis protested. "I know. I checked the refrigerator and pantry this morning when I made my own breakfast.''

"That so? Then I just don't know where those calories are going. She's burning them up at an incredible rate. Daywalking, mebbe. People don't consume themselves by lying in bed.'' He checked his watch.

"I'll want to travel with you to the hospital. It's after five. You have her ready by eight. I'll want to prep the ambulance team. We're going to put her on massive intravenous immediately, squirt all the glucose and dextrose into her that her system will take. Try to get her to eat something solid tonight. A steak would be good if she can keep it down. And a malted with it.''

"I'll take care of it, Doc. Eight o'clock. We'll be ready.''

It was hard to keep himself busy while he waited for the ambulance to arrive. He checked the window locks and the alarms. If they were going to be away for a while, best to make certain no one broke in and carried off their valuable furniture. He was still worried about Mayell, took some comfort from the fact that Oakley told him on departing that she would probably recover with proper medication and attention. She *had* to recover. If she died, his own hopes for an easy life would die with her.

Not unnaturally, his overwrought mind turned to thoughts of some sinister plot against them. Could someone, some disgruntled relative left out of the will, be poisoning Mayell in a fashion similar to the way in which they'd polished off Hanford? That was crazy, though. The house had hosted no visitors who might qualify as potential murderers while he'd been there, and Mayell had begun to deteriorate well before he'd departed for New York.

Besides, if he recalled the will correctly, in the event of any recipient's death, that portion of the inheritance was to go not to others but to several of Hanford's favorite charities. He remembered the faces present at the reading of the will, could not consider one capable of killing solely out of spite.

Saugen tried to keep him company, meowing and hovering about his legs as he kept an eye on the steak. He glanced irritably down at those fathomless feline eyes. Gently but firmly, he kicked the sable shape away. It meowed once indignantly and left him to his thoughts.

Some plot of Hanford's, maybe? Had he suspected what was being done to him, there at the last, and hired a vengeful killer to exact a terrible revenge?

There was the dinner to fix. Potatoes were beyond him, but he did right by the meat, and heating the frozen peas was easy enough. Recalling that honey was supposed to give one strength, he dosed her tea liberally.

As he mounted the stairs toward her room, the clock chimed seven times in the hallway below. An hour would give her enough time to eat.

"Mayell? Darlin'?" She didn't respond to his knock, so he balanced the tray carefully in one hand and turned the knob with the other.

It was dim in the room, lit only by early moonlight and the single small bulb of the end-table night-light. She was still asleep. He moved toward the other side of the bed. There was a pole lamp there. As he fumbled for the switch, he noticed a familiar shape on her ribs. It meowed, an odd sort of meow, almost a territorial growl.

Saugen moved, lifting to a sitting position on his mistress's chest. Willis thought he saw something glisten and looked closer, one hand on the light switch.

The carpet muffled the clang of the tray when it hit, but it was still louder than expected. Peas rolled short distances to hide in the low shag, and the juice from the still steaming steak stained the delicate rose pattern as Willis stumbled backward. He fell into the lamp, and it broke into a thousand glass splinters when it struck the floor. Funny, half-verbalized noises were coming from his throat as he tried to give voice to what he was seeing, but he could do no more than gargle his fear.

Eyes bright and burning tracked him as he staggered toward the door. A penetrating meow started his vertebrae clattering like an old woman's teeth. He could still see the fur on Saugen's stomach wriggling of its own accord as dozens of the thin, wormlike tendrils reluctantly withdrew from the drained husk of what had once been Mayell. They reminded Willis of tiny snakes, all curling and writhing as though possessed of some horrible life of their own. The hypodermic-size holes they had left in the wasted skin closed up behind them. Willis thought of the spiders he'd seen so often in the gardens, liquefying the insides of their victims and sucking them empty like so many inflexible bottles. The glistening he'd seen had been caused by moonlight reflecting off the myriad drops of red liquid still clinging to the tip of each unhair. He retched as he finally found the door and rushed out, thinking of how many nights the cat-thing had spent seemingly asleep on the girl's chest when all the while it had been silently feeding.

"Keep him contented and well fed," the will had stated. Ah, damn the old man, he'd *known*!

Nothing in the house looked familiar as he half fell, half stumbled down the stairs. His thoughts were jumbled, confused. The full bowls of cat food left untouched in the kitchen these past weeks, the privacy whenever Hanford had fed his pet, the regular visits of poor women from the city who had come expecting to fill one normal desire and who had left, their eyes darting and fearful, never to return a second time.

Somewhere in the gardener's shed there was a gun, a pistol he kept to ward off thieves and trespassers. He sought the front door. Oakley would be there soon with the ambulance and its crew. They wouldn't believe, but that didn't matter, wouldn't matter, because he would get the gun first and . . .

He stopped in midbreath, frozen as he stared forward, paralyzed by a pair of deliberate, mesmerizing yellow orbs confronting him. He tried to move, fought to look elsewhere. He couldn't budge, could only scream silently

as those fiery flavescent eyes held his swaying body trans-
fixed.

Its belly fur flexing expectantly, the plump crimson cat
left its place by the door and padded deliberately forward.

RUNNING

I always liked running. It's just that I was never any good at it, and I'm not any better now. Weak lungs have a lot to do with it, the product of severe bouts with infantile scarlet fever and adolescent tracheal bronchitis.

Nevertheless, I liked it. And I tried. There was something about the wind rushing past you, the world becoming a pastiche of impressionistic shapes and colors. Maybe I was trying to find the subways of my infancy.

Trouble was, my body wouldn't cooperate. The pain would arise shortly after I began to move, intensifying until my lungs felt like newspaper in a fireplace: little crumpled sheets of blackness twisting and darting as they ascended up the chimney. I'd have to slow down and gasp for air while others, seemingly without breathing at all, would rush past me, their arms and legs functioning in perfect harmony, their feet never touching the earth.

As time passed, running somehow became "jogging." I think I know what jogging is now. It's running, only in designer clothes. Its emblem is a set of shoes that cost only slightly less than a good color TV; shoes that can be bought at K Mart without a ridiculous name stitched on the side for one-tenth the cost of a pair with a name. Its flag is a set of compact headphones, attached to a portable tape player blaring music the runner is too exhausted to hear. Jogging is a world inhabited by strange, misshapen creatures who unsmilingly haunt the countryside and city while insisting that they're having a wonderful time. A strange basis for a society.

Running seems to me more honest.

THE WOMAN IN BED WITH JACHAL MORALES WAS not his wife. That honor belonged to the portly gentleman who had just unexpectedly entered the simply decorated bedroom.

The eyes of the hausfrau snuggled contentedly in Jachal's arms expanded from somnolent to terrified as she espied her husband. Reflexively, she wrenched the covers up tight about her neck. This had the effect of completely denuding Jachal. The sight of his lithe, naked body further inflamed the thoughts of the already apoplectic man standing in the doorway.

Calmly Jachal sat up, slid out of the bed, adopted his most ingenuous smile, and approached the older man with a comradely hand extended in greeting.

"I apologize for this, citizen Pensy. Quite honestly, things are not what they seem to be."

How odd to finally use that line without lying, he mused. Unfortunately and expectedly, citizen Pensy did not believe a word of it.

Even worse, the poor old fool had a gun.

"You rotten, dirty blaspet," he sputtered, shaking with fury. "I'm going to kill you. They'll have to scrape you off the walls of my house!"

"That'd be a foolish thing to do, sir. Bad for both of us."

"Worse for you." His finger tightened on the trigger.

Jachal had no more time for diplomacy. He feinted to his left and, as the gun swung shakily to cover him, kicked up and out with his right foot. The little pistol went flying out of the banker's hand. It struck the floor at his feet, where it had the extreme discourtesy to discharge.

Banker Pensy slowly looked down toward the little hole in his jacket, which was framed by a slowly expanding circle of red. Jachal gaped at the gun. Likewise banker Pensy's wife, who promptly stumbled out of bed to embrace her collapsing husband. She cradled his head in her lap and turned a shocked stare on her almost lover.

"You've killed him. Musweir man, I should never have listened to your sweet words. You've killed my poor Emil."

"Now just a minute, lissome, I . . ."

At that point it occurred to her that it might be useful, not to mention seemly, to scream. She did so with admirable energy, her anguished wail echoing around the room and doubtless out into the rest of the apartment complex.

Ignoring her as well as the unlucky banker slowly expiring in her arms, Jachal turned and dressed quickly. The second-floor window opened onto a broad dirt street. Too broad, but it was a cloudy morning, and most of the populace would be at work.

Closing the curtain of her screams behind him, he gauged the drop and jumped. His legs stung with the shock of contact, and his hands touched the ground to give him balance. Dark eyes darted right, then left. He had to get out of sight and fast, before the banker's wife, now more siren than siren, alerted the entire community.

Caution never insured against bad luck. He'd been telling the truth to the poor, dead Pensy. The banker should have been at work this morning, preparing to fleece some farmer, not returning home at just the wrong moment.

Jachal had been in quest of information, not sex. Specifically the control codes that would have given him access to the central credit line of the fiscal computer controlling Pensy's small bank. The banker had caught him in the act of theft, all right, but not the kind the poor man had thought.

Jachal blended into the shadows of the small street he turned into, six feet of man, lean and dark as cured lumber, black of hair and eyes. He did not think of himself, even as he ran, as a bad man. He never worked to break the law as much as he did to circumvent it. Bad timing, the bane of a precarious existence, had finally caught up with him.

He forced himself to slow to a fast walk. He was out of range of the distraught widow's screams. The sight of a stranger racing through the streets would attract unwanted attention.

Embresca was a new town, growing slowly but steadily via an influx of bucolic types who sought to make a fortune from the incredibly productive soil of Dakokraine. Jachal wove his way through streets lined with prefabricated buildings imported from manufacturing worlds. They were not a luxury but a necessity, for Dak-okraine was nearly devoid of useful building materials. Stone and adobe were not fashionable.

In any new community of modest size word traveled quickly. Jachal was doing his best to keep ahead of it as he maintained a steady march toward the airport, where he had a chance of losing himself among the flow of goods and settlers from the northern dispersal points. No one had stopped him yet. Perhaps his luck was returning.

It had been an accident. If anything, he'd acted in self-defense. Cuckolding someone was not grounds for shooting. Self-defense, sure . . . and naturally the bereaved widow would testify on behalf of her would-be seducer. Sure she would.

Jachal walked a little faster.

Rounding a corner, he caught sight of the cluster of armed men blocking the single entrance to the airport facilities. They carried a variety of weapons and made agitated gestures with them.

He didn't hesitate but turned and headed back through town. The airport was sealed off, along with his future. If the locals were determined to get him, he'd never have a chance to plead anything. He'd go down "while fleeing from arrest." He'd seen that obituary on the graves of too many acquaintances to wish it for himself.

If they would leave it open to him, he had one chance left. A slow suicide instead of a quick lynching by gunfire. He opted for it instantly.

Two of Dakokraine's three moons were high in the evening sky when he approached the towering electrically charged fence that ringed the town of Embresca. Barely visible to the left and right were automatic gun emplacements. He ignored them. They were programmed to watch for something else, not for him. Their lethal, transparent barrels pointed outward.

Outward over the rolling, world-girdling plains that formed most of Dakokraine's surface, out over the green and brown ocean that the settlers fought to tame. Out over topsoil measured in depths of many yards, which supported an endless sea of grasses and grains that was mined by the settlers as tenaciously as any precious metal to feed the exploding and ever hungry population of man.

Here, near the town, the native grasses had been plowed under and imported hybrid grains grew to fantastic heights, nourished by an ideal climate and soil. Rising among them were the twenty-foot-high fences, charged versions of the heavier-duty barrier that shielded the town itself.

The fences and weapons ringing Embresca were designed to prevent entry, not egress. Jachal had no trouble making his way outward. He adjusted the small pack of supplies he'd barely had time to gather together, pulled it higher on his back, and hurried out into the first field. It was planting time, and the grain was barely up to his knees. In three months it would tower above his head. Then it would hide dangers of its own.

No point in worrying about that now, he told himself. A glance back over a shoulder showed the sparkling lights of Embresca dancing against the Dakokrainian night. There was still no sign of pursuit.

Turning to his chosen path, he set himself the task of covering ten miles before sunrise. His legs pumped steadily, rhythmically, carrying him over the firm loam and the flexible stalks of the seedlings. Two moons led him eastward, and a third beckoned from just below the horizon.

One man among the armed mob that halted inside the fence line wore a uniform. He represented half of Embresca's police force. His partner remained at the station, monitoring calls.

It had been an eventful night. The agricultural community was relatively crime-free. Its people were uncomplicated, hardworking types interested only in wresting a living from the bountiful soil, not from one another. Usually the cop's job was dull and uninteresting. He liked it that way.

Now this visitor had caused a genuine uproar, rooting the cop out of a sound sleep, bringing him on-shift early, and forcing him to adopt a tiring pose of authority. Not to mention all the official forms that he still had to file. A murder, no less. A killing, anyway.

Privately he reconstructed the scenario that had been played out in the banker's bedroom and wondered who was really guilty, if anyone.

But Embresca was a little world unto itself. The population was tightly knit. He was only one man, and there were combative farmers out for this stranger's blood. Banker Pensy had a lot of friends.

Fortunately, the subject of their ire had been polite enough to flee into the Veldt. The farmers wanted his blood, yes, but not enough to follow him out there. If he attempted to sneak back into Embresca, then the officer would be forced to cope with him. If he'd just stay outside the fence lines, Dakokraine would handle the administration of justice. That would be a lot simpler. He offered some silent thanks to the unknown maybe-murderer, wherever he was out there among the grasses. He even wished him luck.

"It's all right," he told his angry civilian posse, nodding toward the moon-swept fields of triticale-four rising beyond the fence. "He's gone Veldtside. There's no way he can get back into town without being noted, and I've alerted the airport monitors to watch for him.

"Now, everybody go home and get some sleep. Unless some of you would like to follow me out after him?"

Faces burned red from daily exposure to the sun turned sullen, then resigned as they studied the silvery landscape. No, not at night would they march out after the intruder, the stranger who'd upset the easy routine of their lives. Not even for poor Mr. Pensy's widow. Not out into the Veldt.

The officer was right. There was nowhere for the murderer to escape to. He could go anywhere he wished, and it would do him no good. Dakokraine would take care of him. They turned away from the barrier and started back toward their homes.

The twenty-foot-high electric fences had not been raised to keep children out of the corn.

It was still dark when Jachal let himself collapse in the last of the cultivated fields. He dragged himself a little farther . . . and found himself lying among native grasses. Civilization had spread west and south faster than eastward.

The grass was taller than a man, much taller. Blades fifteen feet and higher soared overhead. They swayed in the night breeze, occasionally obscuring the stars.

He'd fled without any long-term plan in mind. His only desire was to get out of the town and beyond the clutches of improvised justice. If he could just survive out here for a few weeks, memories of his exploit would be replaced by more prosaic concerns in the minds of the citizenry. Then he might have a chance to slip back into town beneath the relaxed electronic guard they had doubtless alerted to watch for him.

From there he would somehow get aboard an aircraft. Thence to a large city, a shuttleport, and off this world. Let me but accomplish this one escape, he assured the cosmos, and I will henceforth restrict my adventures to more urbane societies.

He'd seen no evidence of pursuit and doubted that he would. There was no reason for it. He'd been on Dakokraine long enough to know why even heavily armed parties never traveled outside the charged fences except in aircraft.

Climbing to his feet, he pushed outward. His legs protested at being employed so soon after his marathon flight. A short walk brought him to an outcropping of volcanic rock. It rose slightly above the crowns of the grass sea.

Ages ago a lava bubble had burst, creating the small circular cave into which he now settled himself gratefully. He would be reasonably safe there from the smaller predators that roamed the Veldt. They didn't like to come out of the cover of the grass.

And he could see the stars. There were a great many of them, for the skies of Dakokraine were bigger than those of most worlds. Their permanence lulled him into a troubled sleep.

In the morning he mounted the highest point of the little outcropping and examined his surroundings. There was nothing to hint that the town of Embresca lay not far to the west. It lay hidden behind hills cloaked in green and brown. But he still worried that some fool friend of the unlucky Pensy might decide to do some daytime hunting on his own rather than leaving local nature to take its course. Though the chances of spotting a fugitive in the high grass were slim, Jachal decided not to take any chances. He had to get farther from town.

He breakfasted on some of the concentrated rations he'd managed to gather before taking flight, then strode down from the rocks into the grass, heading east. There were many small streams meandering lazily through the vegetation, and he didn't lack for water.

Occasionally he would dip down into a little valley, and the grasses would grudgingly give way to shelf and stool fungi of equal size. A ten-foot mushroom would nicely supplement his diet if he could decide which ones were edible and which toxic.

It would be a cold, raw diet he'd have to survive on, he knew. Only in the rare safety of such spots as his cave of the night before could he risk a fire. It wasn't the possible sighting of any smoke that he feared. A grass fire on Dakokraine was something any sensible person hoped never to come within reach of.

He heard many animals but saw few. Insects in profusion swarmed through the Veldt, feeding on the endless supply of tree-tall grass, nibbling at the bases, munching on roots as thick as his arm while aerating the soil. None of them bothered the solitary human. His concern was for the carnivores that skulked through the grassy forest in search of those who fed upon it.

Ironically, it was a herd of herbivores that nearly got him. He heard them approaching long before they reached him, a deep swishing sound like soft thunder, too inconstant to be the result of a rising wind. Wildly he searched for something to climb. There were no trees. He scanned the ground, found no cover. The grass began to bend toward him, and the soft rustling had become a rumbling in the earth.

A hole, there, a glint of light off rock—something's den. Without hesitation he plunged into it, squirming to fit himself feet first into the gap.

The mufleens stampeded over him, their long hair brushing the entrance to his refuge as they ate their way northward. His eyes stung from the dust the herd stirred up, and he saw nothing but shaggy bellies and cloven hooves the size of a man's head. He feared he might suffocate. The slab of granite that formed the roof of the burrow he'd appropriated quivered whenever a mufleen strode across but did not descend to smash him into the dirt.

When the herd had finally passed, he emerged from the hole, filthy and shaken. Already the trampled grass was beginning to display its inherent resiliency, the flattened stalks arching skyward again. Something had nibbled away part of his left shoe heel. If it was the owner of the burrow, still ensconced in darkness behind him, Jachal hoped he found it nourishing. He would have gratefully given up the rest of the shoe, except that he needed it for something more important than food.

A steady afternoon rain began to fall, cooling and cleansing him. He continued eastward, too tired to wonder at his narrow escape.

He'd expected the Lopers to have found him sooner. There were no fences out here to hide behind. He did not expect to find them and certainly did not expect to have the upper hand when the dreaded confrontation took place.

The single Loper lay alongside the pool in the rocks and stared back at Jachal out of hugely pupiled eyes. It was impossibly thin and would stand about twelve feet tall when on its feet. That made him about average, Jachal knew. Though he was not interested in Dakokrainian ecology, it had been impossible for him to miss hearing about the Lopers. They were a principal topic of conversation among the settlers.

The humanoid head was oval-shaped except where the chin drew up in a dramatic point. Two wide, membranous ears projected out from the sides of the head. Air gills pulsed on the long, elegant neck. The lean, muscular body was covered with a stubby, yellow-gold fuzz.

The Loper wore a beige loincloth and a small, elongated sack slung over one shoulder. Its spear lay out of easy reach, carefully stowed to one side next to the lethal bone boomerang men had dubbed a flying flense. Jachal knew it could snip his head off as easily as he could prune a rose.

One long leg lay in the pool, bent back at an unnatural angle. Man and Loper regarded each other across the shallow water. Jachal carried only a small knife, but it hung from his belt. Unlike spear and flense, it was not out of reach.

The Loper's gaze traveled from the human to its own weapons. It tried to shift toward them, but the attempt was aborted by the pain that promptly shot through the thin body. Jachal studied the injured leg. Possibly a bad sprain, more likely a break, he decided.

He hesitated, his thoughts churning. His odds for surviving the necessary weeks alone in the Veldt were very poor. He knew that as surely as did the locals who'd permitted him to flee into it. Here might be a chance, just a chance, to improve those odds markedly. If he was gambling wrong, well, at least he wouldn't have to worry anymore.

It took time for him to gain the Loper's trust. He began by feeding it, pushing food within reach of those gangly arms and then backing off to watch. It took more time before the native would let him touch the damaged leg. The angle of the break had prevented the Loper from trying to make repairs of its own.

Eventually Jachal managed to get it splinted, using parasitic vines to tie the dead grass stalks to the leg. With his aid, the Loper succeeded in standing up. Despite its height, its weight was not great. Throughout the entire process it had not uttered a sound.

As the leg healed, man and Loper had time to examine each other. Lopers healed fast. They had to, living nomadic lives on the ever-dangerous Veldt.

Fighting between settlers and Lopers had been nearly continuous since the first farm had been established on Dakokraine some fifty years before. Despite the fact that they were armed only with the most primitive weapons, the Lopers fought hard and had become a real menace. Built like hyperactive giraffes, they could run at speeds close to seventy miles per hour in short bursts and could maintain a steady pace of thirty to forty for an unknown length of time. Their natural coloring permitted them to become part of the landscape, and they were damned clever. A man caught out in a field, no matter how heavily armed, was as good as dead if the Lopers found him.

Only the expensive electric fences could keep them out of populated areas. Even so, they occasionally penetrated a field or two. Harvesting had to be carried out under guard, in armored reapers with air cars riding overhead. The expansion of the great farms was slowed but not stopped.

Attempts to forge a truce were few and ineffective. The fighting continued. The Lopers absolutely refused to allow a new farm to be established without contesting it strongly. Such battles inevitably resulted in a number of dead Lopers and a dead settler or two. But once a fence had been set in place and charged up, the Lopers were forced to retreat.

The deaths of the Lopers did not trouble the settlers. Not one whit. Only a few bleeding-heart xenologists grieved over the casualties.

What the farmers couldn't understand was the Lopers' persistence. Dakokraine was still ninety-nine percent theirs. There was plenty of room for settler and Loper alike. Then why did they oppose the occasional new farm so strenuously?

Just ornery, the settlers thought. They just like to fight. Well, we know how to fight, too.

And, of course, the fighting continued.

Eventually the injured Loper's tribe found him. Jachal was not upset by the appearance of the three dozen or so warriors and their families. He'd been counting on it. Pulling his knife, he made a show of laying it down and moving back from it. Then he calmly waited for whatever might follow.

The Loper whose leg he'd set ignored him, delighted to be among his own people again. When the greetings had concluded, a few warriors came over to stare down at Jachal. No one made a sign of thanks; no one offered him back his knife.

But they did not kill him. Not yet.

They settled down on the rocks, the children playing solemn games of hide-and-seek among the surrounding grasses, the females preparing food, the males engaging in an energetic discussion that seemed to have Jachal as its focal point. For his part, Jachal contributed an occasional imploring look whenever he could catch a vast, golden eye looking over at him. It had no effect on the argument.

Finally the group broke up. One large male, who in addition to loincloth and pouch had several necklaces of bone dangling from his long neck, approached. Jachal tensed. The warrior was fifteen feet tall and unusually muscular for a Loper.

It showed him an empty backpack and made gestures indicating that Jachal was to climb inside.

He frowned but saw no good in arguing. There wasn't a thing he could do about it if they chose to stuff him into the sack by force. So he climbed in, settled himself gingerly, and waited.

Then he was flying through the air in a short arc. He readied himself for the expected smashing against the rocks. It didn't come. Instead, he found himself settled against the Loper's furry back. Straps appeared, were used to bind him into the sack to keep him from falling out. Or from escaping.

The Lopers muttered among themselves, and Jachal listened intently in hopes of picking up a word or two. He was bobbing about against his captor's back, twelve feet above the ground. The Loper language was smooth and sharp, like an angry Polynesian's.

Then he was flying, or so it seemed. The tribe, having broken its brief camp, was moving out into the Veldt.

Stiltlike legs ate up the ground with long, effortless strides, dodging taller grasses with ease, dashing over shorter ones. The wind rushed past the passenger's face as he considered his position.

They had not slain him immediately. It was known that the Lopers were resourceful. Perhaps they were keeping him alive for tomorrow's lunch. The Lopers were omnivores, like most humanoids. At this point nothing would surprise him, including the possibility that the male whose leg he'd repaired had been designated to do the carving.

What did surprise him was when the tribe halted for the night next to a free-flowing stream hidden by twenty-five-foot-tall blue-green stalks and his towering captor looked down at him and asked, "Why midget come alone to the Veldt?"

In all his encounters and conversations with settlers, not once had Jachal heard them mention the possibility that the Lopers could understand human speech, much less use it. But then, Lopers and men did not sit down in conference to detail to each other their respective abilities. The few attempts at peacemaking had been performed by human xenologists utilizing the Loper tongue. Verily were the Lopers a clever folk.

The fact that they had revealed this knowledge to him was a sure sign they had no intention of letting him go.

"Why come midget alone to Veldt?" the giant repeated.

"I was compelled to," he found himself answering. "It was important to me." He forbore from giving details. Most primitive tribal societies understood and did not sympathize with murder.

"Lone midget, by self, far out from skylegs or multicaves. Not understand compelled to. Why?"

Jachal was very tired. He was confused, and the strain of wondering when someone's flense was going to remove his head had begun to addle him slightly.

"I was running," he explained. "I've run all my life, and this was just one more time I had to run. I don't suppose you can understand that."

Of exhaustion and confusion are fortuitous remarks sometimes born. Misinterpretation, become thy savior . . . or was it misinterpretation?

Jachal did not have the strength to consider this at the time. All he knew was that his reply set off an extremely violent discussion among the members of the tribe. A few seemed close to coming to blows. Seven-foot-tall infants cowered in the grass.

Finally the giant in charge of Jachal came back to stare down at him.

"Midget live for a time. Elders find it interesting. Later more talk."

"Sure, I love to talk. Listen, while we're talking, could you take me to Reshkow?" He tried to describe the location of the nearest town other than Embresca that possessed an airport. If he could actually manage to reach Reshkow, he could easily get aboard a local transport, make it to a city, get off this . . .

"No go near multicaves of midgets for ourselves. Surely not for midget. Stay you with us. Elders find it interesting."

And that was that. But Jachal did not give up hope. "It," meaning he, was found interesting. Later more talk. That was far more promising than later become meal.

"How did you learn human . . . midget . . . speech?" he asked his captor.

The giant stared down at him, firelight flickering off great, dark eyes. "One daytime skylegs drop down among us. Midget get out, seek peace signs. Elders consider what usefulness can come of this. So midget stay with us for a time and teach us. Want to make peace. Finally Elders ask if midget can have killweeds-of-coldstuff taken down. Midget says no. We must first come in and give up weapons. Midget informative but crazy. Wasting not, we ate it."

"I see," murmured Jachal, endeavoring to become more interesting than ever.

A week passed and then another. Jachal did not become a meal. One morning he was preparing to enter his carry sack when the giant waved him away. It slung the sack loosely over its shoulder.

"What's wrong, Apol?" He studied the plain of seedlings that lay west of the campsite.

"No more carry midget. Elders decide. You always running, say you. No more carry. Now you run with us."

Jachal at last saw how misinterpretation had kept him alive. He dared not explain that what he'd meant that night weeks ago about always running had had nothing to do with physical movement. Or did it? He was becoming confused himself. And hadn't he always been in excellent shape? He'd had to be to stay ahead of the law.

They'd kept him alive because he was an anomaly, a midget who talked of always running instead of skylegs . . . air cars. Perhaps they saw something familiar, something of themselves, in him.

His calves throbbed in expectation of the ordeal to come. But he had no choice but to try, to do the best he could. Apol was adamant. "Now you run with us." He would have to try.

He ran until his lungs threatened to burst, until his legs felt like iron weights, until his chest heaved and his throat roared with pain. He ran until he could run no more, and no one complimented him on his gallant attempt. No human, not the finest marathoner, could hope to keep pace with a Loper.

He gave out and collapsed in a cluster of grasses with horizontal leaves that grew at right angles to the central stalk. The sky was a sweat-smeared blot of blue-white. A wide-eyed oval face peered down into his own. It was not Apol.

It belonged to Breang, the Loper whose leg he'd mended.

"Ja'al run well, for a midget."

He didn't have the energy to reply, simply nodded weakly and hoped the Loper would understand the gesture.

Long, thin arms of surprising strength were under his own then, helping him up, forcing him to his feet. He tottered there, feeling faint, his body having given up its reserves, his heart hammering against his ribs as if trying to break free.

"Can—can't run—anymore, Breang. Can't." He smiled faintly. "Midget—not Loper. Can't run with—"

Breang showed him something. It was the carry sack Apol had employed. "Rest now. Run later. Run well for midget, Ja'al. Well much."

Jachal eyed the sack hungrily. He'd never been so tired in his life. But he hesitated, knowing other eyes were on him. "The Elders say I'm not to be carried."

"Owe I a leg to you. Can by law lend mine to yours."

Eye for an eye, legs for a leg, thought Jachal. By accepting his offer, maybe I'm doing Breang a favor. Maybe he's never said anything to me before this because he owed me and had no way to work off the debt.

He climbed gratefully into the sack. As he did so, he saw a couple of the Elders staring at him. Were they watching approvingly, or was their attention simply a fig-

ment invented by his oxygen-starved brain? He didn't
know and didn't care. It was dark in the carry sack. He
closed his eyes gratefully.

In an hour he was running again.

As the weeks became months he learned why he'd been
spared. As he supposed, his declaration that he'd always
been a runner had struck an important and responsive
chord within the tribe. Running was not merely a means
of locomotion to the Lopers. It was their reason for being, their religion, and their gestalt. They did not run to
live; they lived to run. It was as important to them as
eating and breathing. The feel of air rushing past the
moving body, the land disappearing beneath moving feet,
oxygen coursing over neck gills—these were the crucial
sensations of life, the rationale for existence.

A body at rest was an incomplete form, any other
method of transport alien and degrading. One might as
well be as inanimate as a rock or dead stalk of grass.
Real people defined themselves through movement,
through the action of running, by showing their independence from the fixed earth. This separated them from the
inanimate spirits that were fixed to the ground. To be
demaru, to be truly alive, one had to run.

Midgets, humans, did not run. They used machines to
transport them about on the ground and skylegs to carry
them through the air. Therefore, they were not properly
alive.

No wonder all efforts to make peace between settlers
and Lopers had failed. The Lopers would find the very
idea of sitting down at the peace table repugnant.

The tribe hunted and slept and gave birth to an occasional infant who would be up and running in a few
months. They killed an elemorph, a monstrous bear-thing
that charged and swung great claws at its tormentors but
could never quite catch them. They ran it to death.

They ran whenever they weren't hunting or sleeping or
giving birth. To run was to be free.

Freedom . . . Jachal had a thought, sidled close to
Breang one night beneath a roof of grass thirty feet high.
The broad, spatulate leaves curved together overhead,
forming the nave of a green cathedral.

"Why do the Lopers hate the midgets so?" he asked.

"Beyond the fighting, beyond the fact the midgets do not run. Why so?"

Breang considered. "Midgets new grasses make grow. No trouble. Midgets make Veldt even all over. No trouble. Midgets killweeds-of-cold-stuff put up." His dark eyes studied the green sky. "Big trouble this."

That was understandable, Jachal thought. He tried to explain. "Killweeds-of-cold-stuff is there to protect the farmers not only from you but from the mufleens and other Veldt animals who would trample down or eat the farmer's new grasses, which are very important to them."

Faces were suddenly intent on him, speculating, judging. Elders and children had stopped chatting and turned to listen.

"No trouble that," said Breang surprisingly. "No trouble midgets' new grasses. Understand want to keep out mufleens and morpats and polupreas." Now it was Breang who was looking at Jachal imploringly.

"Many runs have you lived with us, Ja'al. Much have you learned. Is not the sky clear-blue to you yet?"

Jachal thought back on what he'd just said and on what he'd learned, and suddenly it was sky clear-blue.

"Really stupid," he was telling the xenologist who'd come by aircraft all the way down from the provincial planetary capital of Yulenst to participate in the conference.

She sat opposite him inside the tent that had been set up outside Embresca. The formalities had been concluded out on the Veldt. Government functionaries were working out the details of the treaty with the various Elders of the different tribes. The discussion was taking place on the run, or course, the inadequate legs of the humans being aided by mechanical supports that gave them the temporary ability to run alongside the Lopers.

"The farmers put up the fences to keep out the grazers of the Veldt as well as the Lopers. All the time they thought the Lopers were against the farms, when in reality all they objected to were the fences." He paced back and forth. For some reason he was unable to sit still these days.

"The fences cut across many of the old runs, blocked

traditional paths across the Veldt. The farmers couldn't understand why the Lopers didn't just go around the fences. They didn't understand that they were preventing the Lopers from their proper way of running. As everyone now ought to know, running is everything to them. It's not just something they do to move from place to place."

"The Tuaregs of track," the xenologist replied, brushing at her gray hair. She smiled. "The gates in the fences will be sufficient, do you think?"

Jachal nodded as he paced. "That and the agreement which states that any new farm will permit the Lopers free passage through its boundaries."

"You've opened more than one kind of gate for the Lopers, Jachal Morales."

He shrugged. "Sometimes you have to live with people to understand their needs and wants."

She studied this peculiar man curiously. "What about you, speaking of gates? What will you do now? I've heard about the incident you were involved in here. You'll have to come to trial, of course, but it will be before a legitimate magistrate, not a mob. If you need help or a reference, after what you've done, I'm sure that I can arrange . . ."

He grinned at her and moved to the tent exit. Outside, atop the nearby hill whose volcanic convolutions protruded above the Veldt grasses, he knew Breang and the others would be waiting.

"Thanks for the offer, but I don't think I'm ready to stand trial. Not just yet, anyway. See, I've been running all my life. That's what I told them." He gestured toward the distant, beckoning hill. "They misinterpreted what I said. Misinterpretation in this case led to mutual understanding. What I didn't realize at the time was that it worked both ways.

"See, when nobody's chasing me—" He left his last words behind him as he fled through the portal, advancing in long, steady, free strides toward the far hilltop. "—I've discovered that I *like* running."

UNAMUSING

After ideas, readers usually ask how a writer comes up with his characters. Sometimes they can be based on real people, but more often they're wholly imagined. Frequently they're a composite of many people or many individual traits drawn from real life, spiced up by the author's imagination.

Most of my characters are entirely imagined for a very good reason. Just as I write science fiction and fantasy in order to see places I'd never otherwise be able to visit, so I populate these far reaches of the mind with individuals I'd like to meet. Or in the case of the bad guys, with people I wouldn't like to meet. Just for variety, I once wrote a book where I flip-flopped completely and based every character in the story on someone I'd actually met (the book was Cachalot).

Never did I have the audacity to base a character on a colleague. But as I mentioned previously, there are times when a story forces itself on the writer. There's nothing tougher to banish from your mind than a story that insists on being written, even if it doesn't take long to tell it.

The character trait I saw in this colleague that so intrigued me I also saw in other creative individuals to a greater or lesser degree. I could not, would not make the character in the resultant story a straightforward portrait of my colleague. My work is fiction. That does not prohibit a real person from serving as the springboard for a tale.

Readers are always asking what this or that writer or artist or composer is really like, how he or she functions, how, as Vaughn Bode said, they "do the trick." Creative *inspiration takes many forms, and motivation arises not always in the head.*

I FIRST ENCOUNTERED NEVIS GRAMPION AT THE one-man show of his work the Met put on last winter. Or maybe I should say the show he put on for the Met. Never was an artist greater than the sum of his aesthetic parts than Grampion. He was his own best canvas, utilizing words with the same skill as he did his palette. His paintings were bold, shocking, sometimes outrageous, never dull. He'd perfected his technique through twenty years of arduous practice in his barn-loft studio. Arizona is full of old barns and new artists. The longevity of the barns usually exceeds that of the artists.

His work ranged from the competent to the brilliant. Not that the critics cared. Grampion was good copy, and they delighted in provoking him to comment on the state of art today, the position of critics, the power of the large museums and galleries. Grampion's response rarely disappointed them.

What attracted me to him, however, was neither his skill with the brush nor his calculatedly abrasive personality but rather the demon squatting on his right shoulder.

He was not an easy man to isolate. People clustered about him like cat hair on an angora sweater. He both attracted and repelled. Nevis Grampion, the Elephant Man of art. I watched the people watching him and was reminded of witnesses to an auto accident.

Eventually I managed to get him alone by dint of following him through the gallery hall until the novelty that was himself had begun to wear off. He was polite to me, indeed, cordial. I think he sensed something of a kindred artistic spirit. Besides, I didn't want something from him. Only to chat. I think that made me unique among those attending the show.

We discussed respective influences, I alluding to Wyeth and Bierstadt and Lindsay, he to Goya and Klee and Dali. We debated the relative merits of acrylic and airbrush, which I prefer, to his choice of oil. He bawled me out for employing the easier media, and I suffered his well-meant criticisms patiently.

Eventually I could stand it no longer. I gestured toward his right shoulder, said, "Nevis, maybe I'm crazy—"

"Ain't we all?" he put in. He was unable to resist a chance to be clever. A congenital condition, I believe, that did not endear him to his public. The moreso because he usually was.

"—but is there or is there not what appears to be a small gargoyle perched on your shoulder?"

For the first time that day some of the slick veneer he wore for his fans slid away, and I had a rare glimpse of the real Nevis Grampion.

"I'll be damned. You can see him?"

"Quite clearly." I moved close to study the apparition, which was ignoring me completely. I believe it was asleep at the time. It was quite solid, with nothing of the aspect of a dream about it.

"It is bright red, with splotches of orange, about a foot high in its squatting position, and has four horns projecting from its bald skull."

Grampion nodded slowly, watching me closely. "You see him, all right. You're the first . . . no, the second one, ever. Maxwell was the other."

I thought of Jarod Maxwell, Grampion's close friend and an exquisite portraitist in his own right.

"What," I asked, "is it doing there?"

Grampion made that funny half-pleased, half-angry grin that was featured so prominently in the papers. "His name's Clamad. He's my artistic muse."

Having already accepted the presence of this strange creature, it was easy to accept this new revelation. "Your artistic muse? You mean he inspires you?" In truth, upon close inspection I thought I could see certain qualities in the creature's face that had been reproduced numerous times in Grampion's paintings.

"You could say that. Clamad's been with me a long time. If it wasn't for him, I wouldn't be a painter."

"Really? What would you be?"

He shrugged. "Something more relaxing, less demanding of the mind. A long-haul trucker, maybe, or a librarian. But not a painter. Too painful. But I determined to be one long ago. I worked and worked at it, and one day, whammo, there he was. He's been with me ever since.''

Of all of us, I'd always thought of Grampion as a born painter. To learn otherwise was something of a letdown, though it in no way detracted from the brilliance of his work.

"Can't you get rid of him?"

He smiled sadly. "Don't you think I've tried? He helped me master my technique, bring to the fore everything I always wanted to say in my work. But once I'd accomplished that, he refused to leave. He drives me to keep topping myself, to hunt for perfection. Won't even let me sleep unless I at least begin a new study every day." His eyes were growing slightly wild as his voice dropped to a whisper.

"Look, you can see him. That means you must understand, at least a little, even if your own work is still too facile, too untested. What if I could persuade him to switch places? Would you have him?"

The offer took me aback. Around our little corner the party continued to seethe. Conversation, cookies, dried-out little sandwiches, liquor, and carbonated waters, and in the middle of it Grampion, the demon, myself.

Clamad the muse shifted slightly on his clawed crimson feet, grunting in his sleep. I shivered and even so was tempted.

"If I agree, what will happen to me?"

"Not much," said Grampion a little too eagerly. "He'll sharpen your style immediately, fasten on what natural uniqueness you possess, refine your technique, clarify your visions, bring out the hidden inside you and show you how to put it to canvas. Or Masonite, or art board, whatever you choose. You'll be world-famous within a year."

"And what does he demand in return?" The demon yawned.

Grampion eyed his shoulder. "Only responsiveness and artistic dedication. His pleasures are simple. He fastens himself to artists with potential because he likes to see the results. Paradoxically, he can't paint a lick himself."

"Let me think about it." Suddenly the hall seemed

dark, the overhead lights dim. The conversation around us had begun to fade as if something had deliberately muted all other talk, and I felt my throat constrict.

"Sure. Sure, you think about it. Think about what you're missing with your silly pretty pictures. Acclaim, fortune, the admiration of your colleagues. Think about it." He was as disappointed as he was sarcastic.

"If he's such a prize to have around, why are you so anxious to get rid of him?"

"Who said I was anxious? I'm just trying to help out a younger artist, that's all. I—I need to rest. I've done it all, accomplished everything I'd hoped to do as a painter. It's time to share the wealth. Maybe I'll take up tatting. You think about it. When you're ready, come see me." He fumbled in his pocket, produced a business card. "You know Paradise Valley?"

"A little."

He nodded once, then turned and vanished into the crowd. I watched him borne away by several obsequious collectors, Clamad the demon visible like a red searchlight above the clutter of humanity. A searchlight only I could see.

I don't know why I went up to the house that night. Temptation, temptation. A subject I'd often tried to render in paint and now was acting out.

I went home thinking of Grampion's words, of the wealth and independence his work had brought him, the independence to thumb his nose at even the most influential critics, those same critics who casually dismissed my own work as purely "commercial," a stigma I had striven for years to escape.

Nowadays I am wiser, but then I was young and impatient.

There was no answer to the bell, but the door was unlocked. I considered. Had I not established a rapport of sorts with Grampion? Surely he would not object to my surprising him, even at so late an hour. He was said to be fond of surprises. I fancied he would be happy to see me, for though he had many casual friends, he knew few who understood him.

I called out past the opened door. There was no reply. Now that was odd, I thought. Surely he would not go out and leave the place unlocked. I entered, made my way through the central atrium, the kitchen area, down a hallway toward bedrooms unslept in. By my watch it was eleven o'clock. The moon lit my path.

Gone out for a minute, I thought. Artists are notoriously unpunctual eaters. Cake and chocolate at midnight in place of a balanced meal. I resolved to wait until he returned.

A grandfather clock boomed portentously from the salon, announcing the time. I perused the well-stocked library, the objets d'art.

Then there was a sound. A stifled cry, almost a whining. I frowned and debated within myself. Grampion had many enemies. The door, unlocked. Could I have stumbled onto a burglary or worse? Was Grampion lying somewhere nearby, bleeding and in need of immediate help?

I armed myself with the nearest heavy object—a trophy of carved marble, presented by some society of European avant-garde artists—and moved cautiously in the direction of the sound. As I drew near a part of the house I had not yet visited, the rhythmic roll of anxious breathing reached me. I was reminded of a marathon runner well along his course.

A door was open, and light stole from beyond. Cautiously I pushed it open all the way.

Grampion stood in his vaulted studio, in front of an easel. A half-completed canvas rested there, full of mad, violent colors and strokes. The subject matter was still indistinct, but the breathtaking talent behind the work was already in evidence.

Crouching behind Grampion was a giant, glowing, red thing. Its eyes were open now, the pupils black slits that probed the canvas. No longer decorative and modest, it was immense and muscular. Each of its huge, clawed hands held one of Grampion's wrists prisoner. There was a brush in each hand.

Grampion turned and saw me. I was shocked at his appearance. His face was flushed, his eyes bulging and red, his expression one of desperation born of complete exhaustion.

"Help me, Malcolm!" he pleaded, his voice hoarse,

the words painful. "For the love of God, make him stop!"

My gaze moved from the thin, drawn specter of the painter to the demon who would not let him rest, who drove him to brilliance and madness and near death. At that moment he, Clamad, noticed *me*. He let out a threatening growl that turned unexpectedly into something else. Something at once less and more inimical.

A flicker of interest.

I turned and fled screaming from the studio, from that accursed house, down the road outside, my path lit only by the moon. I fled past my parked car and did not stop running until I was aboard a city bus and on my way home. The other passengers stared at me. I did not see them.

I saw Grampion several times after that. He was always unnaturally subdued in my presence but unapologetic. Only I knew the real reason for those circles around his eyes and the nervous, jittery movements of his body. Clamad rode his shoulders as always, asleep as always, each time seemingly a little plumper. I wondered just how he fed off Grampion, for it was evident that he did, but by mutual consent we restricted our subsequent conversations to art and related topics.

I've given up art for art's sake. Now I make my living in advertising, where there is little need for the dirty inspiration a muse like Clamad can provide. But every so often I will see a thoughtful shadow flitting about the room, probing the work of Mark or Jillian or Carrie, searching for promise, for talent, for a victim.

I avoid mirrors.

THE THUNDERER

The wonderful thing about English (the rotten thing is spelling, but that has nothing to do with this story) is that it's like a big vacuum cleaner. It sucks up everything, useful or not, and compacts it in one place where you can pick through stuff at your leisure, sorting out the useful from the lint and dead things. Not only individual words and phrases but patterns of speech as well.

Not long ago The Economist *magazine did an extended survey of international English, remarking on its versatility and ready adaptability to the needs of today. The gist was that a supplier of raw materials in Bombay could talk to his dealer in Singapore to ship via Kenya to London and New York even if he couldn't talk to his neighbor down the block. Putting Urdu and Hindi aside, neighbors would end up conversing in English.*

Because the English language lives while others wither and die. In English words are never thrown out with the garbage. More often than not they're resurrected and given new life and meaning. Witness "gay," "cool," and "gas" as examples of old words given new meanings. Sometimes a word can acquire and lose several meanings in a mere lifetime, such as "bitchin'." Words are discarded as rapidly as new ones are invented to take their place, so we have "rad" replacing "reet."

Speech patterns can be as fascinating as the words they employ. When stirred together, they form a linguistic gumbo that can create a mythology all its own. Plain everyday talk can suggest any number of phantasmagoric possibilities.

"His feet big and flat-bottomed like heavy pirogue. His legs, dey thick as oaks and tall as slash pine. His body one great slab o' rock that flake off side o' tired old mountain an' de arms hang from dat like twisty cypress.

"He got a cane field full o' hair and skin de color o' de best bottom soil, cloud-big cheeks all sunk in and eyes like swamp pool wid no bottom. When de trees bend, when de ol' river talk loud, when de bull gator roar his lovey song, when de crook-flash walk de dark sky, den we say dat de Thunderer walkin', de Thunder stalkin', de Thunderer . . . he *talkin*! . . ."

—Old Louisiana folk tale

OUT SOUTHWEST OF NEW ORLEANS THERE ARE places in counties with names like Iberia and Cameron, Vermilion and Terrebonne, where sometimes even the rain has no ambition. Instead of falling hard and quicksilver, it just sort of dribbles down out of a winter sky the color of soiled mattresses. By the time it's worked its lazy way through the obstructing leaves and bushes and Spanish moss, you can almost hear it sigh in relief as it finally touches ground.

The Texon geologist tugged the slick bill of her rain cap lower over her forehead, and still the rain crawled for her eyes.

"You sure that place is around here, Crossett?"

"Yes, ma'am." The guide grinned. His narrow face erupted with alternating squares of ivory and gold, a thin parody of a Vasarely print. His hand, which always shook slightly, was an extension of the outboard motor. Voice of man and voice of motor were also much alike: steady, unexcited purrs.

"Jean Pearl been living here since before I was born," he added conversationally, peering to one side to see ahead. "Nobody around here knows who come first, Jean Pearl or Jean Pearl's cabin."

Mae Watkins looked back at him. "Since before you were born?" The geologist giggled, an infectious cotton-candy sound that shoved aside the somberness of the rain-sogged swamp. "He must be *old*, then."

"Nobody know, ma'am." Crossett leaned affectionately on the motor's arm, and the boat swung slightly to starboard. The trees closed wooden arms above. Watkins felt as though they were sliding weightlessly down a gray-green tunnel. The world here was composed of gray permutations, swamp colors homogenized by the storm. Trees were gray-green and gray-brown, the occasional heron white-gray, and gators and anhingas so gray as to be rendered invisible. Gray moss drifted on gray water.

There was a click forward, and she turned her attention to her assistant. "Lay off, Carey. You know how the company feels about shooting for sport."

The other geologist was barely into his thirties and less out of childhood. Reluctantly, he slipped the safety back on and set the rifle across his knees. "Mae, he was a twenty-footer if he was an inch!"

"Africa's ten thousand miles away, Carey." She jerked her head to her right. "You're a geologist, not Frank Buck."

"Frank who?"

"Before your time."

He still looked disgusted. "Nobody had to know. I had a clean shot."

"I'd know." She let that percolate, then added, "If this trip pans out and we can confirm the hopes of the aerial survey, the company will buy you your own pool of gators, and you can indulge yourself in an orgy of slaughter." Seeing his glum look, she said less accusingly, "And when you do, I want at least three pair of shoes, different styles, and bags to match."

He tried hard not to smile and failed. Flustered, he turned away, scanned the nebulous line dividing island from water. It was hard to stay mad around Mae Watkins. No matter that she was fifteen years his senior and his superior on this trip. Anyone who could switch from boss to mother to coquette in the same sentence kept you eternally off balance.

Anyhow, he consoled himself, there was always a chance a gator might charge them. Held tight in his palms, the wood of the rifle was hard and warm, slick, comfortable.

Crossett saw the geologist's fingers tighten around the gun and smiled. He could sense what the younger man was thinking. On the bizarre happenstance that some crazy gator did burst out of the water nearby, that fool white boy was more likely to blow off his own foot than anything else.

Though in weather like this, one couldn't discount surprises. His own rifle lay near his feet. It was nicked and worn, and the barrel was wrapped with steel tape to hold it together. No matter. What counted was where the bullet ended up, not what it emerged from.

Rain tickled his eyebrows. Fog and drizzle teased his vision. "There she be, ma'am. Just like I said."

"Yes, Crossett. Just like you said." She arranged equipment, poking into the lockers set below the seats. The photos and charts she ignored. The rain wouldn't hurt them. They'd been laminated before they had set out from Styrene three days ago.

Carey Briscoe set his rifle down, sniffed resignedly as they neared the island. The shack drawing closer resembled the exoskeleton of a long-dead bug whose innards had long since decayed and putrified, leaving only a shell behind. Dozens of sheet metal and tin roofing scraps covered the roof, a quilt held together with nails instead of thread.

Two faded windows flanked the center door, rectangular eyes bordering a sagging nose. A front porch sagged alarmingly in odd places. There were no signs, not on the building, not on the collapsing jetty that thrust out into the bayou.

They slid neatly up to the tiny pier, bumping against the frayed eye sockets of old tires. "Watch your step, folks." Crossett was looping a line around a splintery piling. "Jetty's kind of worn."

"Worn, hell." Like a kid testing a hot bath, Briscoe gingerly put one foot and then the other onto the first planks. He gave Watkins a hand up, studied the cabin. "How does he make a living here? Who can he sell to?"

"Trappers, mostly." Crossett was lugging two large gas cans out of the back of the boat. They clanged noisily against each other, fruity echoes of distant thunder. "No tourists out this way." He laughed, a single sharp "ha!" "No roads out this way. But the swamp folk, they know he's here."

They slogged toward the cabin. "Interesting old structure." Watkins somehow found beauty even in the dump
they were approaching. To her it was picturesque. To
anyone else, it was a slum. Semantics, mused Briscoe.

"As to why it, and its owner, are here, that's obvious," she said cheerily. "The man likes his privacy.
Suppose he ran a store in a big town like Lafayette? What
would he do with the extra money? Buy a private place
out here in the woods and have to commute."

"Very funny." Briscoe gave her a sour look as they
stepped up onto the porch, out of the rain. There was a
dog there, lying against the house. Probably supporting
it, he thought. The shaggy lump was an amalgam of all
dogs, a true *weltburgher* of pooches, a canine compen-
dium of all the breeds of all the lands and ages. A mutt.
There was little difference between his coat and the moss
dangling from nearby live oak branches.

At their arrival it raised its head and surveyed them
with a practiced eye, then dropped to the porch again. It
did not let its head down. It literally dropped, landing
with a distinctive *thump*.

Crossett moved to knock. The door opened before he
could. Standing in the portal was either the most Gallic
black man or the blackest Frenchman Watkins had ever
seen. Also the oldest. It was fitting that he was all of a
tricolor. Hair, mustache, teeth, and eyes were white; skin
was black-blue like ink; and in keeping with the day's
coloring, his clothes were gray. He was slightly bent at
the waist but seemed alert and lively. Not at all like the
ancient wreck she'd expected from Crossett's description.

" 'Lo, Charlie Crossett." His voice was husky but not
cracked.

"Jean Pearl." Their guide nodded minutely, held up
the two cans. "Gas?"

"Yep."

Conversation hereabouts, Watkins mused, was as
muted as the scenery.

"I'll get it for you." The old man took up the two
cans and retreated inside, closing the door behind him.

"Friendly sort," said Briscoe, meaning the opposite.
"He stores his gasoline inside his house?"

"In back." Crossett picked his teeth with a piece of porch. "Oh, Jean Pearl, he friendly enough." A rodent of indeterminable pedigree scampered into view, and Crossett spit at it. "Like the lady say, he just like his privacy."

He also liked to take his time. While they waited, Watkins and Briscoe passed the minutes discussing anticlines and salt domes. Around them the rain intensified. A really worthwhile storm unfolded, droplets hammering the rich earth with liquid persistence.

Eventually the door was pulled inward, and Pearl re-emerged. He handed the filled cans to Crossett.

"Goin' back now, I 'spect?" The query was unexpected.

"No, Jean Pearl. These folks down from Styrene. Oil people."

"Huh! Know-it-alls."

Watkins smiled at him. "I suppose you don't think much of us, do you? Tearing up your beautiful swamps with our rigs?"

Pearl surprised her by responding with a wheezing chuckle. "You crazy fool people! What I care about swamp? You go tear up all you want."

"Don't you like it here?" Briscoe was unable to resolve the statement with Crossett's insistence that Pearl loved his privacy.

"Like it? Like the swamp? Like copperheads and water moc'sins, gators and rats and skeeters big as you little finger? You crazy for sure, boy." He shrugged. "But what Jean Pearl to do? I born here, I live here too much my life. For sure I gon' die here. I got no place else I know, no place else to go. Like it? Boy, you want tear up the swamp, you got Jean Pearl, his blessings." Abruptly his attitude changed drastically.

"But not 'round here, not tonight, yes?" His voice had turned solemn, anxious instead of challenging. "You good fella, Charlie," he told their guide. "I know you family from when 'fore you born. I know you momma and papa." He gestured callously at the two geologists, speaking as though they weren't there.

"These folk, I don' know, I don' care. But you pretty good guy. You go back nort'east, Charlie. You don' go west, you don' go south. I tell you, the Thunderer, he out on night like t'is for sure."

"You a good man youself, Jean Pearl." Crossett regarded the oldster affectionately. "We thank you for you warning, but we have our business."

"Warning?" Briscoe looked interested.

So did Watkins. "What's this Thunderer he's talking about, Crossett?"

Their guide looked embarrassed. "Pay him no mind, ma'am. It an old local folk superstition. Country tale. The Cajuns, they claim they get it from the Indians who here first, and everyone else get it from the Cajuns." His smile returned. "The Cajuns, they great storytellers. It make a nice tale to scare the children with during a fry or when everyone out frog-giggin'."

"I'm always interested in folk legends." Watkins looked kindly at the recluse. "What's a Thunderer, Mr. Pearl?"

"You oil people. You should know." Pearl snorted. "The Thunderer, he make you oil for you."

Briscoe struggled not to laugh. "With all due respect, sir, petroleum is formed when decomposing organic matter is subjected to tremendous heat and pressure. Nobody 'makes' it."

"You smart boy, you. Ol' Jean Pearl, he can' fool you." Pearl waggled a wrinkled finger at him. "You find Thunderer, maybe then you find some oil, yes."

"In that case he's just the chap we'd like to meet," said Briscoe gently.

"What is he supposed to be like?" Unobtrusively, Watkins had pulled out a pen and was fishing in her diary for a blank page.

"Not 'supposed' . . . is."

"Excuse me. What is he like?"

"Not for me to say. The Thunderer, he shy fella. Stay asleep under swamp all time 'cept few nights every year like this one. He big 'round as cypress, have biggest gator in swamp for toothpick. Like to drink oil, and when he can' find it, he make it."

Having lost interest, a bored Briscoe had turned away and was studying a chart.

"I see." Watkins's pen squiggled on the page she'd

opened to. She finished jotting, looked up. "He's sort of a local bigfoot, a southern Sasquatch. Like a big hairy man, is he?"

"You smart oil people, I can' hide nothin' from you." He stared imploringly at Crossett. "I can' stop you goin', Charlie. I see that. You been in city too long much. You forget you momma's talk."

"No, Jean Pearl." Crossett spoke softly, humoringly. "I haven't forgotten her, or Papa, either. I haven't forgotten they had nothin' and that I got a boat and will soon have a new one, and a new gun, for helpin' these folks in their work. I don' forget easy, man. Thanks for you concern."

Pearl turned away, looking so distraught that Watkins was moved to reassure him. "Don't worry about us, Mr. Pearl. We're armed, and Carey here's a pretty good shot, just as I'm certain Mr. Crossett is. We'll be okay."

"You have trouble," Pearl replied firmly, "you fire t'ree time. If I hear, Lightning and me—" He indicated the dog, which might have twitched at the mention of its name and might have not. "—we send for help."

"That's very gracious of you," she said. "How much do I owe you for the gas?" She had her wallet out.

"Four gallon and tenth, only five dollar."

"Jean Pearl . . ."

The old man glanced angrily at Crossett. "I take back what I say about you bein' good fella, Charlie. *Mirableu* . . . four dollar, then."

The geologist pulled a damp five from her billfold. "Here, keep it, for your concern." She noticed Crossett's disapproving look, did not react.

Back in the boat, slipping the line from the piling, Crossett said admonishingly, "You shouldn't do that."

"Why not?" She settled herself back on the outboard's center seat. "He looked like he could use the money, and Texon can afford it. Even if we don't find any oil."

"It not that." Crossett got the engine started, headed them out into the bayou. "Now he always think he put one over on you."

"I don't mind," she said easily. "His concern for us was touching, even if misplaced."

"Bigfoots," snorted Briscoe. He spit out warm rain-water. "Let's check out these coordinates, plant our charges, take our readings, and get the hell back to Sty-rene. I feel like I'll never be dry again."

They did not reach the place marked on their charts that night. As they turned to land on a high island, the wind picked up, moaning through the trees and moss, making the swamp sound like the recreation room of an asylum. Rain blew sideways, sneaking around inside their hoods to crawl wetly down ears and necks.

"What do you think, Crossett?" Watkins peered out of the pop tent at the sky as the guide jogged back up from their beached boat, a locker under each arm.

"I think it plenty damn wet, ma'am." He handed her the lockers one at a time, then slipped inside the tent, a roll of thunder on his heels. "I think we should make supper and listen to the radio."

As she spooned in her meal, Watkins reflected that advances in science still hadn't found a way to make freeze-dried food taste like food. It was tasty, even spicy, but it was the taste of spiced cardboard. She put aside the tin of macaroni and tuna, fiddled with the dial on the radio until she'd located the marine weather band.

"Tropical storm," she announced eventually, echoing the now silent broadcaster. She nudged the radio into a corner. "Not a hurricane, not yet. And it's moving west. Ought to miss us by plenty even if it should develop into something." She eyed Crossett. "What's your opinion?"

He considered briefly. "I think we only in danger of getting mighty soaked. You want to stay and work, I stay, too."

"I didn't ask for acquiescence, Crossett. I asked what you thought. You know this country better than we do. I've been through two hurricanes for Texon, one at Sty-rene and one at Maracaibo. That's enough."

"I gave you my honest opinion, ma'am. I think we be okay."

"Good." Briscoe was sopping up the remainder of his cheese sauce with a biscuit. Watkins winced as she watched him. He actually seemed to like the stuff. "I'd hate to motor back to town and have to tell them we wasted over a week of company time."

"That's settled, then. We stay. Carey, see if you can find something interesting on the radio."

He nodded, set down his scoured plate and pulled over the unit. "Anything in particular you'd like to hear?"

She leaned back onto her bedroll. "Beethoven or Bee Gees, it doesn't matter to me."

The wind continued to howl incoherently around them, battering fitfully at the nylon walls of the tent. It shrugged off all attempts to force entry, the tubular aluminum frame forming a snug, secure dome overhead. Their weight kept it tight against the ground.

Watkins found herself awake, turned her head sluggishly. A figure was moving about inside the tent. "Carey?"

"No ma'am, it me," came the deeper whisper.

"Oh, Crossett." She let her head flop down on the pillow, irritatedly adjusted her hair net. "What's up?"

"I afraid the water rising, ma'am. Oh, we okay way up here in the trees. But I want to make sure of our boat."

"Good. Be sure and snap the flap on your way out, will you?"

"You stay nice and dry, ma'am. I'll be careful."

She had a brief glimpse of gray in motion. The thrumming of rain and wind was momentarily louder as the guide slipped out through the flap. She heard the flap snap catch behind him, lay back down.

"What's going on?" It was Briscoe's blanket-muffled voice.

"Crossett. Gone to check out the boat. Shut up and go back to sleep."

She found herself able to return only halfway to the relaxing oblivion of sleep. The uneven ground seemed to bother her more now than when she'd first lain down, and she tossed and turned restlessly.

Suddenly she discovered herself sitting straight up, wide awake in that occasionally unreal fashion that will strike without warning. She looked around. The tent was unchanged. Outside, rain continued to pummel the earth. It sounded as though the wind had dropped slightly.

"Carey. Carey," she whispered insistently, "wake up, man."

"Huh . . . wuzzat . . . somethin' wrong?"

"What time did Crossett go out?"

Briscoe was rubbing his eyes, yawned. "How the hell should I know? He went out?"

"To check on the boat. Remember?"

"Oh, yeah. Yeah." He glanced idly toward the third bedroll. It was empty. "Not back yet, huh?" He looked vaguely puzzled.

"No." She had a thought, fumbled through her bag and extricated her billfold. In the near blackness she had to feel for the bills and credit cards. Everything seemed to be there. She wasn't embarrassed either by the thought or by her action in following it up. After all, she was a child of the city, not the country.

"Maybe he's having trouble with the boat," Briscoe suggested.

She shook her head impatiently. "I'll bet it's been at least an hour." Rolling over, she unlatched the tent flap, looking out into driving rain. Nothing. A flash of lightning revealed the outboard, securely beached and tied to a cypress stump. But no Crossett. The lightning faded, leaving blue patches on her retinas. Thunder skipped like a stone across her ears. She let the flap fall, didn't bother to secure it.

"Well?" Now awake, Briscoe was sitting up on his foam pad and staring at her.

She shook her head negatively, chewed her lower lip.

"Don't look so damn solemn," he advised her. "Probably he wandered off somewhere, maybe looking for a better place to tie the boat up. Want some coffee long as we're awake?" He leaned on one side, began hunting in the darkness for the lantern.

"Huh uh, thanks. Crossett would've come back and told us if he was going to be gone this long."

A glow filled the tent as Briscoe got the Coleman going. "Not necessarily. Polite as he is, he might not want to wake us. It could be, though, that he hurt himself. Easy to slip out in that muck." He sounded sympathetic and disgusted all at once.

"I don't relish going out looking for him. I agree that if he's not back in, say, fifteen minutes, we probably ought to get dressed and go hunt him up." He stopped moving, one hand holding the tiny grasshopper stove, and the other a packet of coffee.

"What is it?"

"Shut up. There's something outside," he whispered.

She froze. Several minutes went by during which they could hear only the steady percussion of the rain and the puffing wind.

"Nothing, I guess," he said finally. He grinned. "You know, I just had a thought. Maybe our good guide's using this opportunity to show us city slickers that out here in the swamp anybody can be deluded by a little bad weather and a rambling tall story." He got the grasshopper going, set a pot of water on it.

"Okay, Crossett!" he abruptly shouted. "Come on in and get yourself warm. The coffee's boiling, and we're not."

There was no response. Below, agitated water lapped at the meager shore. Briscoe shrugged. "Let him get soaked, then. I swear, if he comes tumbling in here and drenches us—"

"NURRRRRR . . . !"

It was thunder, but dull thunder, not sharp and clean like the kind that walked the treetops but a rich, rasping ululation that had nothing to do with electrical charges. It sounded again, on a rising inflection this time, and while it did not originate in the heavens, it came from a source almost as primal. A feral thunder.

Watkins found herself turning upside down as she rose into the air. The flaming grasshopper stove tumbled past her and shot out the open tent flap. Lockers, radio, food, charts, bedrolls, all fell in a surreal stream past her. Her head was bent to her chest, and her hands went out instinctively. Then she did a complete somersault, her hips falling past her head. Somewhere above her Briscoe was yelling about his legs, up at the other end of the tent. Aluminum tubing snapped like fresh popcorn around her.

So this is how a cat in a sack feels, she thought wildly. Then there was air and rain in her face. Seconds later there was pain, splitting her backside and racing up her spine, as she hit the ground.

Rolling over, she mumbled weakly. "Carey?" A voice was alternately screaming and cursing in the hazy dis-

tance, legs and pain and guns all whipped up together in
a verbal froth of anger and terror. Her mouth was full of
mud. She started to lift up on her hands, collapsed as an
unseen tormentor jabbed a long needle into her coccyx.

"Oh, God." She lay on her side, her right arm under
her. The screaming and demanding went on behind her.

Her gaze turned toward the noise. At the same time
she became aware of a thick, rich stench like creosote.
Lightning danced in a night sky of gray crepe.

Outlined in the light was the Thunderer. Occasionally
it would let out a querulous bellow, a rumble like a sim-
mering volcano. It shook her, mostly inside. She thought,
a mite hysterically, of the reported sightings of such legends as the yeti and bigfoot, describing a hairy man or
manlike ape eight or nine feet tall. How silly and foolish
people are! she thought chidingly. Even the greatest of
imaginary horrors fail when measured against the real
thing.

What stood in the faded discharge of energy and light
was at least seventeen feet high at the shoulder, and it
stood in a hunched-over position. Long arms dragged the
ground, ending in great burl knuckles that backed steam-
shovel-sized paws. Long white claws curved back into
the palms. It was only remotely manlike, a grotesque
hybrid of simian and gargoyle. It had ears like a bat's,
vast black eyes, and a prognathous jaw from which protruded a pair of upcurving tusks like a warthog's.

She'd glimpsed a short, twitching tail, bald as a rat's.
The entire slowly heaving mass was covered with short,
bristly hairs, sparse but evenly distributed. Between the
hairs the skin was composed of large scales like those of
a tarpon.

It was holding the collapsed tent in one paw. She
started to crawl away, not yet thinking of retreating to
the boat but only of putting distance between herself and
that transcendentally hideous form. She also worked to
ignore the steady sobbing that was coming from within
the smashed shape of the tent.

"UNNN . . . NURRRRR . . . ." it bellowed. Another
hand the size of their boat came off the ground, closed
over its companion, and squeezed. There was a last, mer-
cifully short shriek from within the tent. Then silence,

save for rain and wind. The creature appeared to be exerting great strength. Watkins imagined she could detect a faint glow emanating from between those tightly pressed paws.

Thoughts of the size of those paws had reminded her of the boat. Thought of the boat reminded her of the guns lying within. As she painfully dragged herself through the muck, she considered poor Carey's modest .30-30, Crossett's ancient over-and-under. She struggled to her feet. One hand pressed tight over the fire in her lower back as though that would somehow ward off the agony. As she stood, another needle pierced her left ankle, and she nearly fell. Broken? She couldn't tell.

She might as well throw mud at the gigantus as use either of the guns. But there was something else: a tightly wrapped pack of gelignite charges for making soundings. If she could set a detonator in just one charge, place it where the monster might step nearby, it ought to discourage it. Perhaps even kill it.

She had no time to consider where the monster was, refused to consider what it might be doing with what remained of Carey. All her energies, all her thoughts, were concentrated on reaching the boat. It appeared undisturbed, bobbing nervously in the fractured water. In the middle, beneath her seat, should be the small reinforced locker holding the charges. She reached the bow . . . and slipped.

No doubt about it, she thought with an odd disinterest, her ankle was definitely broken. She lay breathing heavily, rain pelting her mud-streaked face. Her arms moved weakly on the wet ground.

Have to . . . get . . . charges . . .

Despite the pain, she inched forward. The earth grew wetter, more slippery beneath her. Must ignore the pain, she told herself. Pretend it doesn't exist. Refusing to accede to positive thinking, the pain grew worse. Her femur was a log in a fireplace, burning evenly.

She paused for breath. Moisture covered her mouth. She licked her lips. Not water: thicker, pungent . . . familiar.

She glanced downward. She was lying not in thin mud or a puddle of rain but in thick oil. It must, she thought wildly, be a natural pool, oozing to the surface. That meant a potentially huge field requiring little drilling. Just drop in the pumps and suck it out. The company would be pleased.

The boat, the boat . . . she forced herself ahead. Hand, knee, hand, knee . . . Maybe it wouldn't notice her, a dim, slow-moving little lump in the darkness. Her head bumped something: the side of the boat.

Up now, she ordered herself. Hand grip gunwale, other hand grip, pull . . . pull, dammit!

Her head was over the side. Ahead, still secure beneath the center seat, was the small metal locker holding the charges. It was neatly latched and untouched. She started to pull herself into the boat.

Something made her nose wrinkle.

Creosote.

They found the boat and the remnants of the tent a week later. The hurricane had spent its strength and petered out over Alabama.

"Damn shame," Hardin muttered, kneeling to pick up a battered, broken shape. "This might've been the radio."

"Might," agreed his disconsolate companion. Weinberger had worked in Styrene with both missing geologists. His eyes surveyed the storm-battered swamp, the bayou behind them where an iron ring was still tied to a stump of cypress. It was all they'd found of the survey party's missing outboard.

Nearby was a small pool of oil, a smudge on the earth. Stains showed it had recently been modestly larger. Shreds of clothing lay scattered around and within the stained soil.

"Looks like the storm tore the clothes right off their backs."

Hardin, his hands on his hips, nudged the blackened fragments of polyester and nylon. "Hundred-twenty-mile-per-hour winds could do that, sure. Looks like they found some oil, too."

"Afraid not, Sheriff." Weinberger eyed the stained earth and the bit of fluid remaining with an experienced gaze, indicated the traces of two similar pools nearby.

"They must have had it with them, though I'm damned if I can figure why. That old geezer back upstream said they only bought gas from him."

A glint of metal caught his eye, and he bent, recovering an oil-stained lump of dull gold-colored slag. It was about the size of a belt buckle.

"Wonder what this was." He chucked it aside, sighed. "Oh, the oil? It's fresh, new. Hasn't come out of the ground. No, I'm afraid they didn't find anything at all."

PLEISTOSPORT

Sitting atop the TV in my study is the skull of a saber-toothed tiger (Smilodon californicus), cast in resin from the original and painted to look exactly like it. The lower jaw raises and lowers to show how the great slashing saber teeth passed neatly outside the bone. A stuffed Garfield sits beneath those impressive teeth, grinning imperturbably. Relatives, it would seem. I talk again of cats.

When I was growing up, paleontologists were so busy trying to sort out which head belonged to which skeleton and whether Iguanodon walked upright or on all fours that they had little time to devote to visuals. Color does not fossilize. Within the past decade or so artists such as William Stout, Richard Bell, Linda Broad, and John Sibbick have done for prehistoric life what Chris Foss did for spaceships. Patterning replaced monotones, and color took its rightful place in our picture of the ancient world.

Great gray eminences such as the sauropods and therapods were colorized not by Ted Turner but by reason and logic. Suddenly they were transformed from towering symbols of a bygone eon into living, breathing creatures. They acquired Color. Color for attracting mates, color to warn, color to camouflage. Nature did not invent man and the paintbrush simultaneously. Previously the Mesozoic was thought to be a dull place. Dinosaurs were large like elephants, so naturally they were portrayed in elephantine gray.

The later mammals fared no better. Herbivores were as brown as bison. The big cats and catlike carnivores were sandy yellow, like lions. It was obvious and most likely inaccurate. The ancient environments were as var-

ied as those of today. As animal life expanded to fill spe-cific niches in those environments, what more natural than that they should change color and size to fit them? No less could be expected of possible subspecies of Smi-lodon.

As far as I'm concerned, someone who hunts for food occupies higher moral ground than do those of us who go to the supermarket to buy our meat preslaughtered. But one who hunts for a "trophy" dwells below the moral and intellectual level of a diseased Neanderthal. To the former, respect and even admiration. To the latter, this story.

There is a beautiful painting done in colored scratch-board and airbrush by the noted California wildlife artist Lewis Jones that illustrates this tale.

THACKERAY ENJOYED THE PLEISTOCENE.

Oh, he also liked the rest of the Quaternary period, but the Pleistocene was his favorite. It contained a greater variety of large animals than any other part of the Quaternary. And if you were lucky, you might catch a glimpse of one of the protohominids that might or might not be your great-grandpa several million times removed.

It was a shame, though, that the time puncture didn't encompass any more than the Quaternary. Still, one to five million years gave a man plenty of room to explore. If you tried for anything more recent than one million, the Chronovert just sat in its station stall and whined petulantly. Try for beyond five million and the Chron-overt (and likely as not its passenger, too) ended up a pile of expensive slag.

If only the technicians could add another hundred mil-lion years to the puncture! What he wouldn't pay to be able to come back with the head of a tyrannosaur or a Deinonychus to mount in the aerie he'd built above Santa Fe. The boys at the club would vote him a life member-ship, at least.

Of course, those limp-wristed wimps who belonged to the Time Preservationist Society would launch into their usual tirades, just as they did now whenever he or a friend brought back a trophy. Ranting and raving they'd be about preserving the ecology and inviolability of the past. Well, he knew why they were so vitriolic in their condemnation of the Quaternate hunters. It was because none of the faggots had the guts to travel in the past themselves.

He scrunched lower in his seat. Snow was falling steadily outside the blind. The camouflaged tent kept him concealed and cozy warm. Ice goggles let him penetrate the drifting whiteness with relative ease.

The Wincolt .50-caliber lay close at hand, its forty-round high-power drum locked tight into the barrel, telescopic heat-sensitive sight ready to warn him if anything came within killable range, laser pickup itching to pick out a fatal spot. Thackeray was proud of his equipment. After all, he was a sportsman.

He reached behind the cushioned, electrically warmed chair and picked up the thermos of coffee. Part of his muffler blew into his mouth, and he irritably shoved it aside while he sipped the hot Kona. Beyond the triangular entrance to the blind and downslope tumbled a foaming river. To his right lay the edge of the primordial ice sheet. Somewhere beneath those miles of solid ice lay land that in his own time would be the province of Canada, subterritory of British Columbia.

Behind him were the almost modern crags of the Canadian Rockies. Beautiful country still, but not as wild and dangerous as this. Only a few cougars and bears roamed the modern Rockies. The Quaternate Rockies, on the other hand, were alive with all manner of impressive beasts. And no game wardens. The National Rifle Association had seen to that.

Thackeray relished a challenge. Most of his fellow hunters preferred the warmer regions to the south. The area around the La Brea tar pits was particularly popular. You could always count on bringing back a decent mastodon head from there or, if you were lucky, a cave bear. Dire wolves were thick as fleas. An animal trapped in tar wasn't too hard to stalk.

Well, Thackeray had had enough of that. After all, he was a sportsman.

There was no thrill if there was no challenge, no work, no discomfort involved. Anyway, he'd already grabbed off the best the tar pits had to offer. His trophy room was crammed full of record and near-record heads: *Smilo-*

dons, dire wolves, American lions, giant ground sloths, mammoth and mastodon, and a new, as yet unclassified smaller relative.

Now he was after the only major trophy that had eluded him: the woolly rhinoceros. The paleontologists had decided that the woolly rhino had never been very common. The mammoths were more efficient subglacial browsers, the musk-oxen more intelligent. Competition was tough.

Hell with that, Thackeray had decided. He wanted a woolly rhino head, and by God, he meant to have one. He was convinced the paleontologists were in league with the preservationists, anyway. Surely the history of the Earth wouldn't suffer from the loss of one lousy rhino.

The wind howled mournfully around the blind. If there was a real storm coming, he'd have to close up and wait it out. Or worse. He glanced over a shoulder.

Behind him squatted a tubular metal chair surrounded by a molded plastic body impregnated with special circuitry. He could always climb back into the Chronovert, pack up his equipment, and be whisked back to the time station in twenty-second-century Albuquerque.

To do so would be to admit failure. Thackeray didn't like to fail. He didn't like it in himself, and he didn't like it in his employees, who unfortunately could only be fired and not shot. Besides, Chronoverting was expensive, even for one of his considerable wealth.

Not many could afford to Chronovert. Not many had the financial wherewithal or the health (he was only forty-three).

He was determined to have that woolly rhino head for his trophy room. He'd reserved room for it on the west wall, a blank space he was sick of listening to comments about. That smarmy oilman from Qatar, Musseb Tuq, had noticed it right off during the New Year's party.

Well, Tuq didn't have a rhino, either. Thackeray knew because he'd visited the oilman's home. This was one time he intended to be first.

Unless the paleontologists beat him to it. They were hunting woolies, too, but for breeding and study. Thackeray decried the waste of good travel money.

The heat sensor on the Wincolt's sight beeped once.

Quickly he put down the thermos, wiped coffee from his lips. He raised the weapon and cradled it on his lap as he stared out through the drifting snow.

The river was a good location for a blind. It flowed from the base of the distant ice sheet out of the mountains and down into a burgeoning lake surrounded by relatively flat land. Herds of camels and small horses grazed contentedly around the lake. They were huddled together against the snow now. This was a transition zone, where inhabitants of the glacial front mixed with migrants from the warmer subalpine regions. There was free-flowing water and plenty of forage. Perfect rhino country.

He'd chosen a location on the flank of a hill, just below the more inaccessible bulge of the Rockies. He could shoot downhill from there. A bulky creature like a rhino wouldn't be able to muster much of a charge uphill. Thackeray was a sportsman but a prudent one.

He raised the Wincolt and squinted through the telescopic sight. Plenty of mammoth in view, a large herd of zebrelles, but no rhinos. Probably the gun had beeped for a zebrelle.

He was about to put the weapon back in its resting place when he heard the scream. It was sharp and high, and the wind carried it straight to him. Not an ungulate, of that he was certain. He'd heard too many of them scream when they'd been shot. This was something different.

Braving the snow, he stuck his head out of the blind. A rustling sound, a soft thrashing, came from somewhere behind his shelter. He frowned. It was snowing hard, but there seemed no danger of it turning into a whiteout. Could it be a trapped rhino, maybe, stuck in the snow? The wind could've distorted the scream. If so, his kill would be easy. He debated whether to go and have a look.

Unlikely to be a mammoth. The trail up the slope was too narrow, and there was no reason for a mammoth to come this way, anyhow. But a hungry rhino, maybe, just maybe.

Hell, it was worth a minute to check it out. Cradling the Wincolt tightly, he stepped out of the blind. The wind struck him full force and chilled him instantly. He worked his way cautiously around the shelter. The snow wasn't deep enough to hinder his progress. It whipped his exposed cheeks and made him think of his warm den back in Santa Fe.

There was nothing in view, and he was about to return to the blind, when the thrashing sound reached him again. It was fainter now and close by, beyond a slight rocky rise. Carefully he checked the location of the blind, which was white to match the snow. No harm in going another few feet. The possibility of a trapped rhino goaded him on.

The climb up the slight slope made him breathe hard. Near the crest he fell to crawling until he could peer over the edge of the snowbank.

He caught his breath. It wasn't a woolly rhino. It was Something Else.

The Phororhacos was dead, the three-meter-tall form of the giant carnivorous running bird stretched out in the snow. Its vestigial, tiny wings lay tight against its body. The enormous head with its razor-sharp bill lay limp, the eyes closed in recent death.

Not many creatures would dare to tangle with that feathered monster, whose appetite and ability to snap off the head of its prey in one bite made it a match for the legendary roc. Thackeray had a similar if smaller skull mounted in his trophy room. He'd shot the beast from a tree blind, not dar—not wanting to meet it on the ground.

Something had slain this one. He thought of the thrashing sound that had brought him out of the blind. Blood still seeped from its mouth and the place where a single bite had nearly severed its neck. Probably it had come upslope in search of the large agoutilike rodents that made their homes in caves along the mountainside. Now it had become prey itself.

There was only one Pleistocene carnivore with enough power and cunning to make a meal of the huge bird. But never, never had Thackeray dreamed of anything like this.

It was a *Smilodon* standing over the corpse, a saber-toothed cat. But it was unlike any *Smilodon* he'd ever seen described. Instead of the familiar tawny brown coloration, this killer was cloaked in a magnificent coat of white with black spots. In addition, a full black ruff ran around the neck. It blended perfectly with its environment.

The uncat glanced up from its recent kill. Thackeray burrowed lower into the snow. In his excitement at envisioning that exquisite skull mounted in his trophy room he'd forgotten that he was outside the armored walls of the blind. Olivine eyes flashed through the frozen breath that emanated from between nine-inch-long sabers. The tips of those extraordinary weapons were still stained with the blood of the Phororhacos.

The flattened forehead and the positioning of the ears on the side instead of the top of the head marked this creature as a real saber-tooth and not one of the true, modern cats. He was of a line destined to drown in the river of time. A line suited to a wilder, more feral age.

Must be a new species, Thackeray thought anxiously. He could even name it. *Smilodon californicus alpinus*. No, no. *Smilodon californicus thackeray*. Much better. What would Musseb Tuq say to *that*?

Regulations said that in such cases his first duty was to call in a paleontologist. Damned if he'd do that. He'd discovered the beast. It was *his*. A paleontologist would just want to try and take it alive, anyway. That was hardly what Thackeray had in mind.

Besides, he was outside his blind, unprotected. He had to defend himself, didn't he?

Slowly he lifted the Wincolt and slid the muzzle through the snow. The shells it fired were specially designed to kill by penetration only. They would not shatter or explode. That could ruin a good trophy. He lowered his gaze to the telescopic sight, activated the laser, and squinted.

The Phororhacos remained in the cross hairs, the red dot of the laser playing across wind-ruffled feathers. Of the *Smilodon* there was no sign.

He jerked his eyes away from the sight. Damn. He'd taken his eyes off it for a second, and it had vanished into the storm. Probably heard the gun moving and got spooked.

For a wild moment he thought of going after it. Only for a moment. The storm could intensify any minute.

Anyhow, he was no tracker. He was a sportsman. Sportsmen hired trackers. They didn't try to imitate them.

Maybe it'll return for its kill, he thought. If so, the Wincolt's heat sensor would alert him. Meanwhile he could turn the blind so it was pointing this way. To hell with the rhino. He'd stumbled across something far more worth killing.

Better get about it. Turning the blind would be a job, and Thackeray wasn't used to physical labor. He started back down the slope.

As he neared the entrance, the gun started beeping softly. He turned a wild circle, keeping the muzzle pointed outward. Snow whistled in his ears, mocked him from behind naked rock. Nothing else moved in the Quaternary evening.

Then he saw the sides of the blind moving. The sabertooth hadn't run off. It was inside.

He did not panic. Some men do not panic because they are brave. Some do not panic because they are too frightened to move. A few, like Thackeray, do not panic because of an overriding arrogance.

This should be easy, he thought. Even easier than up on the hill. Holding the rifle at the ready, he slipped around the blind until he was standing facing the entrance. When the *Smilodon* finished its exploration of the interior, it would come out. There was only the one exit. Thackeray would have his trophy.

Not on the wall, this one. Not with that pelt, he mused. Make a rug of it.

Time passed, cold time. Thackeray's face was beginning to get numb. His hands were starting to chill even through the thick, insulated gloves. He couldn't shoot into the blind for fear of hitting the Chronovert.

Come out, damn you. Why don't you come out? Come out where I can kill you.

It occurred to him that having discovered a nice, warm shelter, the saber-tooth might be settling down to wait out the storm. Surely the blind was more comfortable than whatever cave it had been living in.

It had to come out. Thackeray was a little concerned now. It must be hungry. Soon it would emerge to drag the body of the dead Phororhacos back to its new lair.

Soon, soon . . . Thackeray discovered he was shaking from the cold. If he waited outside much longer, he'd be shaking too hard to aim the rifle. Also, it was almost dark. He couldn't wait for full night. In the dark anything could happen. He never had liked the dark.

For the first time he began to think of the saber-tooth as a possible danger instead of an unmounted trophy.

The Wincolt's stock boasted a number of specialized controls. Thackeray made a decision, used numbed fingers to push one control several notches forward. Now the weapon was on full automatic. He could spray forty shells in as many seconds. Not very sporting, but then, neither was freezing to death. He'd played the sportsman long enough. It wasn't his fault if the dumb animal was refusing to cooperate. He wanted a defrost supper and some hot coffee.

If he was careful, he could catch it easily. Maybe it would be sleeping. He'd just have to be careful of the Chronovert. He was freezing.

Slowly he approached the entrance. Dim light showed inside, activated by a photocell as night descended. With the tip of the rifle he nudged the material aside, played the laser pinpoint over the blind's interior. Nothing moved inside. And the heat sensor wasn't beeping anymore.

As he moved inside he saw the hole in the back of the blind. It was impossible, of course. The material should have been impervious to anything like a simple tooth or claw. Not that there was anything simple about a nine-inch-long saber. The ragged edges of the gap flapped in the wind.

That decided it for him. He couldn't guard two entrances. Forget the coffee, skip the supper. Still holding the rifle, he made his way to the Chronovert and settled himself into the padded seat. He'd return home and come back to these same coordinates with a bigger, stronger blind, a professional tracker, and proper snow travel gear. Maybe an air car. Then he'd go out and hunt down that damn uncat.

He could see it clearly as he activated the Chronovert's instrumentation: the spotted skin spread out on his trophy room floor, those terrible serrated saber teeth propping up the flattened skull, green eyes replaced by equally bright spheres of glass.

Oh, he'd bring it back, all right. You just had to have the right tools. He'd come after rhino, not mountain saber-tooth.

He activated the controls. The Chronovert started to hum, the puncture field forming around it. The outlines of the blind's interior began to waver.

Something grunted in the machinery. He frowned. This was no time for a mechanical problem. The Chronoverts were supposed to be foolproof. They had to be. You couldn't find a time physicist shop in the Quaternary. The field, however, continued to brighten properly. He turned to check the projectors.

Staring out of the cargo compartment were a pair of bright green eyes. They were barely a foot from his face. A snarl rose from beneath them. It was a hungry snarl, as Thackeray had correctly surmised.

He screamed across ten million years.

Thackeray had always enjoyed the Pleistocene. It was only fair that the Pleistocene enjoy him.

NORG GLEEBLE GOP

When I began reading science fiction, women's issues generally referred to what brand of washer-dryer to buy for the house or whether one's habitation suffered from the dread waxy yellow buildup. The latter always suggested to me some insidious, infectious alien disease (is there a story there?).

My, de times how dey do change.

I never had any problem with equality, as it were, perhaps because from the start so many of my editors, not to mention my agent, Virginia Kidd, were women. Just to prove it (largely to myself, I suppose), I made the protagonist of my second novel female. A character I would have enjoyed meeting.

Much more difficult than writing a character who happens to be of the opposite sex is trying to do a story in which that character has to deal with a problem particular to his or her gender. It's as if C. L. Moore had tried to do a story dealing with Northwest Smith's fear of impotence.

The only way, I believe, that a writer can handle such a difficult situation is to discuss it with members of the opposite sex. Even then, there is always the fear that you're treading psychological water instead of getting at something real.

"IT'S JUST THAT THEY'RE SO CUTE," DEERING SAID. Her friend and fellow xenologist Al Toney disagreed. "The Inrem are a primitive, utterly alien race that we still know next to nothing about, which is why SA has gone to the trouble of sponsoring this expedition. Although the attitude of the natives toward us thus far has been friendly, we don't know nearly enough about their culture to start making generalizations. 'Cute' qualifies as a generalization, Cerice, and not a very scientific one at that. These people are hunter-gatherers who have developed a complex social structure we are just beginning to understand. Their language remains incomprehensible, with its floating internal phrases and switchable vowel sounds, and their rituals no less confusing.''

Cerice Deering leaned back in her chair and stared out the glass port at the surface of Rem V. The sun was slightly hotter than that of her home, the atmosphere thick and moist. And it boasted that rarest of all discoveries, a native intelligent race. How intelligent remained to be determined. She considered herself fortunate to be counted among those designated to do the determining.

Not only was being a member of the expedition exciting and enlightening, it could be a career maker. *If* she could come up with something spectacular. The competition to be first with a breakthrough was keen among the expedition's scientists. As one of the youngest, it would be hard for her to make a mark for herself. Or so her colleagues thought. She smiled a secret smile at her private plan. Fortune favors the bold, or so the old Latin claimed. She intended to find out.

She could not confide in Toney. While he was a friend, he was also a competitor, and he certainly would have disapproved of her intentions.

''Where's your sense of adventure, Al?'' she asked teasingly.

''In the scientific method. In the careful filing of observations for collation at a later date, at which time the real discoveries are made. In learning patiently and assuredly. This isn't a play, Cerice. The Inrem are not special effects. You don't plunge blindly into an alien culture. That can be dangerous.''

She couldn't keep from laughing aloud. ''The Inrem? Dangerous? Are we talking about the same aliens, Al?''

''Never trust appearances. That's a truism from human anthropology that applies just as well to aliens.''

''So we squat here and pick up a useful datum or two a day. Science at a snail's pace.'' She put her long legs up on the table, knowing it would distract him. "Take this *Gop* ceremony they're having tonight. How the hell are we supposed to study it if we're forbidden to attend?"

Toney looked uncomfortable, partly because of the question, partly because Deering was wearing only shorts and a halter. Rem V was a hot world and getting hotter, he reflected.

"We can't study it. We'll have to wait until we're invited in or until Dhurabaya and his people crack this ridiculous language and we learn how to ask permission properly."

"It's not ridiculous. The Inrem don't realize that to us their language sounds like baby talk."

"I know. But it's still hard to keep a straight face when the local chief waddles up to you and says with all seriousness something like *'Neemay goo ga weeble fisk,'* or whatever it was he told us yesterday."

"That's one reason why I think they're so cute."

"He might've been cursing me out."

"Bull. You're paranoid, Al. The Inrem have been downright hospitable ever since we set up camp here. They've been curious and helpful every time we've asked them for something—except for excluding us from the occasional ceremony."

"You've got something on your mind." Toney looked up at her sharply.

"Who, me? I'm just a junior researcher. Half the senior scientists on this barge don't think I have a mind." She pulled one knee back to her chest and locked her hands around her ankle.

Toney swallowed, staring, and forgot about the warning lecture he intended to inflict on his associate.

Night and the creaks of an alien world. Whistles and hoots, squeals and buzzes assaulted the encampment. Deering wasn't worried as she slipped out of camp and made her way through the forest toward the big Inrem village where they'd been conducting their field studies. The expedition had been on Rem for six months, and nothing bigger than a biting bug had challenged them. Violet leaves caressed her thighs. Webbers scurried out of her path, their big fluorescent eyes glowing in the light of her glowtube.

It was about a mile and a half over level, relatively dry ground to the village. She could hear the steady susurration of the chant long before she located a good place to make her observations. The Inrem were very big on ceremonies, performing at least one a week. They politely permitted the visiting humans to study most of them. Only a few had been declared off limits, such as this *Gop* ceremony tonight.

Deering knew it was an especially important ceremony, but she and her colleagues had not been able to determine why. Much of the interspecies communication between human and Inrem still took the form of signs and gestures as the expedition's linguists struggled to crack the complex if silly-sounding native tongue.

She was breaking a taboo as she set up her recording equipment on the little rise overlooking the village, but she wasn't frightened. An expedition botanist had accidentally killed an Inrem adolescent two weeks ago, but even that hadn't been sufficient to provoke their anger. They seemed to respond with understanding and even compassion for the distraught visitor.

The village consisted of stone and wood longhouses arranged in a circle around a central square. There were small openings in the ground in front of each longhouse. As near as they had been able to discover, the openings led to an intricate complex of tunnels of unknown extent. They were too small to admit humans (the Inrem averaged about three feet in height), and so what studies they had been able to carry out had been done only with instruments. The consensus so far held that the caves served to store food and provide private links between longhouses. They were not for defense. There was no war among the Inrem.

The ceremony was already under way. There was no carved image, no deity to be worshiped. The Inrem rituals remained an open book, attendant upon multiple interpretations. She hoped tonight's work would allow her to make several. If nothing else, merely recording the forbidden ceremony would be a real feather in her cap.

She was just inserting a new cube in her recorder when half a dozen armed Inrem materialized from the trees behind her. Eyeing them warily, she moved to put the recorder between the natives and herself. She had a small pistol with her, but using it on a native, even in self-defense, would result in her being censured and sent home in disgrace.

Nothing in the Inrem's expressions or movements betrayed a hint of hostility, however. The senior warrior stepped forward. Like all of his kind, he walked on a pair of thick, stumpy legs. His squat body seemed to have been fashioned from gray putty. There was no neck, only a tapering of the torso that was called a head. His short tail twitched as he sniffed at her with his flexible trunk and its rosette, fringed tip. The teeth in his mouth were blunt, and something akin to a squashed derby decorated his bald pate.

"Si mokle reerip ba boovle," he declaimed. *"Norg gleeble gop."*

As always, Deering had to repress a smile. Not that the expression would have meant anything to the Inrem. "Look, I don't mean to intrude." The words were for her own benefit, since no native could understand a word of English. She turned both hands palm up in a universal gesture of conciliation. "I just want to watch." Now she did smile. "I'll leave if you insist."

The Inrem had built-in smiles, like porpoises. *"Norg gleeble gop,"* the senior repeated.

"Oh, okay, whatever. *'Norg gleeble gop.'* "

This appeared to please the warriors no end. Apparently she'd said exactly the right thing. Poor Toney and his paranoia. A pity he and the other old fogies weren't here to witness this minor triumph of improvised interspecies communication. You just have to go at it boldly and with the right spirit, she reflected.

The senior uttered another delighted *"Norg gleeble gop"* and gently took her hand to lead her down to the village. No one objected as she picked up her still functioning recorder. She felt gratified and exhilarated. This was what science was all about, the rush that came from making a breakthrough discovery, the thrill of observing what none had seen before her.

A few of the villagers paused in the middle of their clumsy but high-spirited dances as she was led into the square. For the first time she sensed something akin to hostility, until the senior warrior escorting her raised a hand and declared loudly, *"Norg gleeble gop! Sookle wa da fookie!"* Then the performers were all smiles again.

No one bothered her as she set up her instruments, angling them on a group of elder Inrem females. The species had three sexes: male, female, and neuter. Behind her the alien music rose to a deafening din as a cluster of musicians pounded, tootled, and plucked furiously at their instruments. It was by far the most impressive performance so far witnessed, and Deering concentrated on her recorder. There was a driving, atonal beat to the music that was distracting and fascinating.

With a cry, the performers and dancers scattered. Normally this signified that the ceremony was at an end, but the *Gop* was different. Instead of the chief matriarch retiring to her longhouse, she gathered her favorite male and neuter around her and joined the rest of the population in forming small groups in front of the numerous cave openings. Deering adjusted her angle from narrow to wide, trying to include as many groups as possible.

Then she gasped and looked up from the eyepiece of the recorder.

Something was coming out of each of the holes in front of the longhouses. Slowly at first, tentatively searching, each pale pink worm was as thick as a man's arm. They tapered to points and were innocent of features: no eyes or ears, no mouths, no nostrils. The worms swayed back and forth as if in time to the now silent music that had called them forth.

Occasionally a worm would touch one of the chanters, whereupon the individual so blessed would tumble onto its back and begin writhing in ecstasy. Deering worked her recorder frantically. Here was some kind of solemn symbiotic relationship no one on the expedition had so much as suspected. What the Inrem derived from the worms was a matter for future speculation. Their mere existence, not to mention their special relationship to the natives, would cause pandemonium among her colleagues. She had slipped secretly out of camp seeking something unique and had been rewarded beyond her wildest dreams.

The worms were now swaying low over the twisting, jerking bodies of the blessed, doing something—it was difficult to see because the standing members of each group blocked her line of sight. She shoved another cube into the recorder.

Something touched her lightly in the small of her back.

Whirling, she found one of the worms not a meter from her face. Despite its lack of eyes, it seemed to be studying her curiously. Probably had a highly developed tactile sense, she told herself, breathing hard. It leaned forward. As she stood frozen to the spot, it brushed her right forearm. She held her ground. There were no teeth to defend against, no poison. Only a thin, pleasantly fragrant secretion of some kind.

Moving slowly so as not to alarm it, she adjusted her recorder for close-up work. All around her the worms were lightly touching and swaying over fallen villagers. A truly wild thought came to her.

What if the worms were not individual creatures but merely the tentacles, the limbs of something much bigger that pulsed and lived beneath the village? She envisioned it rising in response to the *Gop* music, digging its way surfaceward from unimaginable subterranean depths to gently caress and commune with those who had summoned it forth.

The worm touched her again, startling her this time. She felt herself quiver all over, almost as if she'd received some kind of injection. That was impossible. The worm—(tentacle?)—had nothing to inject with. But it had left a glistening patch of that perfumed secretion on her arm. Suppose it could be absorbed through the skin? For the first time she felt uneasy. She was out there alone, surrounded by delirious aliens and giant pink worms. She'd learned enough to ensure herself a commendation. Better not push her luck.

A warm sense of tranquillity and well-being was spreading through her. She started to collapse the recorder. "I—I think I'd better be going now," she said to the Inrem nearest her. It smiled back up at her placidly.

"Norg gleeble gop?"

"Yeah. *Norg gleeble gop.*"

She hoisted the recorder and turned. She made it to the edge of the forest before she collapsed.

She awoke in a bed in the camp infirmary. Chief Physician Meachim was staring down at her. Disapprovingly, she thought.

Since nothing was holding her back, she sat up.

"They found you just outside the camp perimeter." Meachim was frowning to himself. "Your cubes have been played back. Everyone's arguing with everyone else. The biologists are going crazy."

She touched her forehead, her temple. She felt fine. Better than fine; she felt terrific. "I must've passed out. It was pretty exciting. I'm okay?"

Meachim shrugged. "You look great to me, but that's nothing new. Funny thing, though. I tried to bring you around with compol and damrin. Your system rejected both. But your vital signs stayed perfectly normal, so I didn't press it. You started to wake up about five minutes ago. The monitor notified me. Now you sit up by yourself with no apparent ill effects. Trying to put me out of a job?"

She slid off the bed, did a few experimental jumping jacks. "Sorry, but there's nothing wrong with me, Meachim. Know what? I'm going to be famous."

"That's what everyone's saying. The captain would like to have you drawn and quartered, figuratively speaking, but the scientists won't hear of it. They're slavering over your recordings and can't wait for you to lead a full-scale survey group back to the village. I imagine they figure you've got a special in with the Inrem."

"All it takes is guts, in science the same as everything else. I can go?"

"This infirmary's for sick people, Cerice. You aren't sick." He turned and gestured. "Someone waiting to see you."

Al Toney entered. "You ought to be shot. Instead, I think they'll canonize you. You've made a discovery that's more important than everything we've learned about the Inrem to date."

"I know."

He shook his head. "I wonder if you have any idea how lucky you were."

"Luck had nothing to do with it, Al. I just had the Inrem figured right. Cute, remember?"

"I guess so. Oh, Dhurabaya's made some progress. Maybe when we go back to your village—that's what everyone's calling it now, your village—we can ask the right questions."

"You don't have to know how to ask the right questions if you've got the right attitude. The Inrem know empathy when they feel it."

Toney nodded, looked thoughtful. "Silly-sounding speech they have, but logical once you work out the roots. That's what Dhurabaya's people say. Take *'Norg gleeble gop,'* for instance. The Inrem have been using that phrase over and over for months." He started toward the door. She went with him, anxious to bask in the admiring stares of her envious colleagues.

"I remember. They were using it quite a bit during the ceremony."

"Really? Maybe that explains what kind of ceremony it was. *'Norg gleeble gop'* means 'pregnant.' "

BATRACHIAN

Metamorphosis is a marvel of nature that's always intrigued me. Did when I was a kid, and still does today. It takes many forms, not always that of caterpillar into butterfly. The thought of beginning life in one body and ending it in something inconceivably different is hard for humans to imagine, starting and ending as we do with essentially the same shell. I tried to deal with certain aspects of metamorphosis in a book called Nor Crystal Tears, *which opens with the line "It's hard to be a larva."*

Arthur C. Clarke stretched the concept in the classic Childhood's End. *Eric Frank Russell took a different approach in his novella* Metamorphosite. *I wonder if the author of the book* Cocoon *ever read that story.*

You take a familiar concept and run it into something common and everyday, and sometimes you get a story.

"FORGET IT, MAN. YOU'LL NEVER GET NEAR HER." Shelby moved a pawn two squares forward, trying to protect his king. "Every guy in the building's tried, and a few of the chicks, too."

Troy advanced his knight, and one of his friend's bishops was removed from the board. Shelby frowned at the development.

"I can imagine they have. Immature jocks, most of 'em. I'll bet you and I are the only two grad students in the whole complex. She's just waiting for someone with a little maturity to come along, that's all."

Shelby reached toward his remaining bishop, thought

better of it, and returned to studying the board. "Sure she is. Bet you can't get inside her door."

"What'll you bet?"

"Dinner for two at Willy's."

"Done. The important thing is, is it worth getting inside her door?"

His friend nudged a castle sideways, looked satisfied. "I've seen her going out. It's worth it. Believe me, it's worth it."

"What does she look like?"

"Different. Exotic. Dresden china stained dark. She's a little bitty thing, but something about her intimidates the hell out of me, even at a distance. I'd go up to her and stammer till my teeth fell out. Wouldn't know the first thing to say."

"That's one of the things I've always liked about you, Shelby. You know your limitations."

"And you don't, Troy. Your successes are grander than mine, but so are your failures, and you have more of both."

"That's called living."

"Don't get philosophical with me, man. Save that for Gilead's class. Now, move something. I'm getting hungry."

Troy's queen crossed nearly the entire board. "Checkmate."

Shelby stared at the quilted pattern of squares and pieces. "Well, hell. Where'd you learn that one?"

Troy rose from the couch. "Improvised it."

His roommate sighed. "You'll have to do more than that to make it with Ms. Strange upstairs."

Troy's gaze lifted ceilingward. "We'll see."

The bell rang many times before the door was opened a crack.

"Who's there, please?"

Odd accent, for sure, he thought. "Excuse me. My name's Troy Brevard. I'm on the third floor. I understand you're a student at State."

"That's right." He tried but could not see into the room beyond. The voice was smooth, soft, assured despite the fact that it was obviously utilizing a second language.

"I'm a grad student. Poli Sci. I'm having a lot of trouble with a paper I'm doing on motivations in World War I, and I was wondering if maybe you could help me." Surely a foreign student would be interested in a world war, no matter what her actual major might be.

Silence from the other side. Then, "You're a graduate student. I'm an undergraduate. Why come to me for help?"

"Because there are stupid grads and brilliant undergrads."

"What makes you think I'm one of the brilliant ones?"

"Aren't you?"

Laughter then, or something akin to laughter. The door swung inward, announcing his minor triumph.

"All right, Mr. Brevard. Come on in and I'll see if I can help."

He stepped over the threshold. The apartment was nearly identical to the one he shared with Shelby except for the view. They lived on the third floor. This apartment was on the sixth and topmost. Off to the left of the small den would be a bathroom and bedroom, to the right the compact kitchen. Through the tall picture window he could see the sunbathed campus of Arizona State University.

The door hid her, and so he didn't see her right away. His attention was caught instead by something else. The den was swamped with frogs.

Stone frogs of Mexican onyx and soapstone lined the wall shelves, guarding endless rows of textbooks. A turquoise Zuni frog fetish sat in a position of honor atop the glass coffee table fronting the couch. Stuffed frogs stared bubble-eyed from the back of the couch, on which lay several hand-sewn frog pillows. There were ceramic frogs and jade frogs, stylized frogs of stainless steel and traditional frogs of wood and pewter, cardboard put-together frog cutouts and paper frogs dangling from the ceiling.

Portraits of frogs in oil and watercolor, pastel and pencil, and acrylic decorated the walls. Terraria bubbled and burped as spotted green things moved lazily about behind glass walls. He stepped inside and found himself standing on a thick frog rug.

"You like frogs," he said dryly.

"My collection," she replied.

Then he turned to face her and forgot all about frogs.

Placing her proved impossible. Her skin was coffee-colored. That implied a home located anywhere from the Congo to the tanning salons of southern California. Her features were slight to the point of rendering petite an indication of grossness. Except for her eyes. They dominated that delicate face, huge, damp orbs in which a man could drown with little effort. They were a bright, electric green, as pure as anything generated by a laser, as alive as the floor of a rain forest.

Aware he was staring, he forced himself to look elsewhere.

"Mind if I sit down?"

"Oh, excuse me. I forget my manners sometimes. I don't have many visitors."

He flopped down on the couch. Frogs eyed him from high shelves, inspected him from the top of the crowded coffee table. He readjusted a frog pillow behind him and arranged his notepad and books.

"It's real neighborly of you to help me out like this."

"Why didn't you use the library?"

"Libraries can't give you every viewpoint, especially contemporary ones. Besides, I'm lazy. I'd rather ask someone. Especially a pretty someone."

Good Lord, was she blushing? It was hard to tell with that skin. Could it be that no one had had any luck with her simply because no one had tried?

"I'm not pretty. Actually, I'm still kind of ugly."

Was she playing with him? The woman was gorgeous! Slight, almost boyish, but with features that would put many a professional model to shame. If it was a put-on, though, she was playing it well. If it wasn't, maybe it explained something else.

"Is that why you like frogs so much? Because you see yourself as unattractive and they're the same?"

"Oh, no," she said intently. "They're beautiful. I try to see myself as them." As if she'd already revealed too much of her private self, she became suddenly business-like. A tiny hand indicated the study materials he'd brought with him. "Now, what's your hang-up, and how can I help you?"

He made a show of shuffling through his notes. "How about going out with me Friday night? That would be a helluva help to me. Improve my mental state no end. I know a great place for Mexican. Willy's."

She smiled apologetically, shook her head. "Sorry. I don't go out."

"Someone as pretty as you? Come on!" He had a sudden inspiration. "*I* know what it is. You're from a foreign country, right? You're not sure how to act, how to react to our peculiar American customs. Don't let that make you a shut-in. Half the time us natives are just as confused about how to act. Just relax. You can't do anything to embarrass me. I don't embarrass. And I won't push you into anything that makes you nervous. I just think you'd enjoy my company. I know I'd enjoy yours. How about it?"

"You're right, Mr. Brevard. I am from a foreign country."

"Just Troy, please. What do I call you?"

"My real name's a bit longer than you'd find comfortable. I use Eula for short."

Eula. That was no help. "Ethiopia? Somewhere in the Caribbean, maybe? Jamaica?"

She shook her head, showing a shy, reluctant smile. "Too close."

"India, then?"

"I won't tell you, Troy. Let me hold on to some secrets."

"You seem to be all secrets, Eula, but okay. See, I said I wouldn't push."

"I don't think you will." Oh, those eyes, he thought. "I think I will go out with you Friday night. Yes, I think I will. It should be educational."

"Real dedicated student, aren't you? Intense observer of local culture."

"I have to be dedicated, Troy. I'm going to graduate this June."

"Me, too. Going to grad school?"

"Yes, but not here."

"Whereabouts?"

"Back home."

"Which is where?"

She wagged a warning finger at him, and it was his turn to grin.

"Okay." He raised both hands. "Guilty. I won't do it again." Maybe she was a refugee from one of the several minor wars that always seemed to be going in the Third World. He could see where that might embarrass her. Time enough to find out.

She wasn't the usual date, but he'd expected as much. Quiet, watching everything and everyone no matter where they went. As he slowly won her confidence she let him take her anywhere, except for parties. She absolutely refused to go partying.

"I don't like them," she told him frankly. "The people are noisy, they drink too much, and then they get silly and out of sorts. You can't learn anything from people in that state. They all act like preadolescents."

"Not like us mature folks, hmm?"

He was joking, but she wasn't.

"We're not mature, Troy. We're both still adolescents."

"Maybe you think of yourself that way, Eula, but I don't. I'm twenty-three."

He could not interpret the look she gave him. Finally she said, "Each of us has an image of ourselves, Troy. I know what I am. I won't be an adult until I graduate. Until I go home."

He shrugged it off. "Hey, I really don't much care for loud parties myself. I just thought it was something you might find educational."

Her smile returned. "I probably would, but not enough to overcome my distaste. Let's go somewhere else tonight." She softened her criticism by moving close to him. It was a first, of sorts. He put his arm around her, no easy task. At six feet, he was a foot taller than she was.

Two months, he thought, enjoying the warmth of her

lithe body. Two months to warm her up this much. Yet the old sense of thrust and parry, of chase and conquest, had left him weeks ago. This girl was not just another mark. She was special, unique, and he'd been more deeply affected by her than he'd realized at first. Her quiet sincerity, her honest shyness had reached something deep inside him, had struck something dormant and now slowly awakening.

To his great surprise, he understood that he was falling in love.

Shelby had noticed it, too.

"You're really hung up on this chick, aren't you, man?"

"Yeah, aren't I, lowlife? And don't refer to her as a chick, please."

Shelby put up both hands defensively. "Excuuuse me! Well, it's your life, Troy. Just don't let her run it."

Troy glanced up from the history text he was perusing. It hurt to know that Eula was only a short elevator ride away. But she insisted on separate study time as well as on her privacy. She refused to let him monopolize her.

"I won't. She doesn't want to."

"She still doesn't intimidate you?"

Troy shook his head.

"Well, she would me, man. When I saw that first blank stare on you, I thought I'd better do a little checking, since you were obviously too far gone to care. I mean, we've shared this dump for three years now. You're a good buddy, Troy. I wouldn't want you to get into something over your head."

"What the hell are you talking about?" He closed the book, shoved the snake-necked Tensor light aside.

Shelby studied the fingernails on his right hand. "Just that she's the hidden wonder of the senior class. You ever ask her what she's majoring in, how many units she's taking?"

Troy shook his head. "She likes her privacy, remember. I think she's some kind of general major."

His roommate laughed. "You're right there. I guess when you're taking everything, that qualifies you as some kind of general major. She's a regular Einstein, man!

She's carrying three majors: world history, anthropology, and botany. Seventy-six units. What's more, she's doing each curriculum under a different name, and none of 'em are Eula or anything like it.''

Troy struggled to digest his friend's information. He could not conceive of any human being carrying that many units. Of course, he didn't really know much about her school hours. He rarely saw her during the day.

"That's physically as well as mentally impossible."

"That's what I thought, man, but she's doing it. I wonder why the three aliases."

Troy thought furiously. "You said it yourself. She's shy, private. If what she's doing got out on campus, she'd have her picture plastered over every paper in town."

"Yeah. Yeah, I guess she would. And when the two of you are out together, she doesn't make you feel inferior?"

"No, never."

"Sparing your male ego, I bet."

"No. That's not like her, Shelby. She's not like that. For all her intelligence, she's still unsure of herself. She's got to be at least twenty, yet she always refers to herself as an adolescent."

He kept his friend's information to himself, afraid to reveal what he'd learned to Eula. He didn't want her to think he'd set Shelby to spying on her. He hadn't, but convincing her of that might be difficult.

"After graduation," he told her one night as they sat parked on Camelback Mountain overlooking the lights of Phoenix below, "maybe we can take a vacation together. Nothing intimate," he added quickly. "Just a trip to enjoy each other's company."

"I have to go home, Troy," she told him sadly. "I'm graduating. You know that."

"Yeah, I know. I'm graduating, too, remember? Surely you can take a week off. As hard as you've worked, you deserve a real vacation." He let his excitement spill out. "My folks have money, Eula. Old money. We can go anywhere, anywhere you want to. Africa. Europe. The Seychelles. Frog hunting up the Amazon."

She laughed at that, filling the night with beauty. "You

know me a little, Troy. More than anyone else I've met during my schooling. Yes, I'd like to go looking for frogs up the Amazon. But I can't. I have to go home. I have to graduate. It's not something I could avoid even if I wanted to. And Troy . . ." She hesitated, looked away from him. There was a vast sorrow in her. "You might not like me anymore after I graduate."

He frowned uncertainly. "That's a hell of a thing to say. What difference does graduation make? I'm going to get a master's. We're graduating together."

"No, Troy. We're not. Where I come from graduation means something more than it does for you. I'm graduating out of adolescence as well as school. It's a big change."

"Well, change, then, but don't worry about me still liking you afterward." He couldn't hold it back any longer. It seemed time was running out on him. On them. "Don't worry about me still loving you afterward."

"Troy, Troy, what am I going to do about you?"

"How about this for right now?" He leaned over and kissed her. She resisted only briefly.

He looked for her during the graduation ceremonies but couldn't find her in the crowd of caps and gowns. That wasn't surprising. If Shelby's information was right, she could have been with the graduating class of any one of three different departments. So he had to content himself with waiting out the speeches of the honored guests, the turning of the tassels, and the throwing of their mortarboards in the air by the new lawyers before he could break from the crowd and rush for his car.

She didn't answer her door. He waited all that day, dully accepting the stream of congratulatory calls from his parents and relatives back east, checking Eula's door and phone every ten minutes. Day became night, and still no sign of her. Had she gone already? Skipped the ceremonies and disappeared? Surely, knowing how he felt about her, she wouldn't just pack up and leave without even saying good-bye.

Or maybe she would, he thought desperately. Maybe she'd think it was better this way. A clean, quick break, no tears, no lingering emotional farewells. Maybe that was how they did it in her country.

He raced upstairs. Her door was still locked. He ignored the stares of the other residents as he kicked repeatedly at the barrier, kicked until his leg throbbed and his feet were sore. Eventually the door gave, collapsed inward.

Save for the rented furnishings, the apartment was empty. Every personal effect was gone, down to the last tiny porcelain amphibian. He searched nonetheless, yanking out drawers, scouring closets, finding nothing. Clothes, makeup, toiletry articles, everything gone.

He ran back out into the hall, checked his watch. Eleven o'clock. She might be anywhere by now. His first thought was to check the airport. Then he realized he still didn't know her last name. If Shelby was right about her multiple aliases, he might not even know her first name.

Shelby was standing there in the hall next to the elevators, watching his friend.

"Where is she, man?" He gripped his roommate by the shoulders. "Where'd she go?"

"She said she was going home. I was surprised to see her. Thought she'd be at the graduation ceremonies, like you. That's all I could get out of her, man. Honest. She was shipping her stuff out. I don't know what she took with her, but there was a big Salvation Army truck loading up downstairs while she was moving out. Maybe she gave all her stuff away."

"Not her frog collection," Troy muttered. "She wouldn't part with that. Not that. You sure she didn't say how she was leaving? Plane, train, bus?"

Shelby shook his head. "I saw her drive off in that little rented Datsun of hers. Didn't look like she had much luggage with her."

"Which way did she go?"

"Hell, what difference does that make, Troy?"

Shelby was right. Troy let him go, thinking frantically. If she was traveling that light and going farther than Ethiopia, she had to be taking a plane. That implied a connection through LA or Dallas. Could he check that, using her description alone? It seemed so hopeless. He never should have left the building this morning without her.

Then he remembered the place. Her favorite place. Out toward Cordes Junction, where the interstate climbed high out of the Valley of the Sun toward the Mogollon Rim country. A vast, empty place. They'd driven up there several times to luxuriate in the solitude and privacy. She hadn't said good-bye to him. Would she leave without saying good-bye to her favorite place? It was the only place she'd ever taken him. He was always the one who decided where they'd go. Except for this one favorite place.

It was a chance, probably a better one than the airport. If she'd gone to the latter, then she was probably already winging her way overseas. He rushed down to the garage and burned rubber as he sent the Porsche roaring out onto the street.

As soon as he cleared the city limits, he opened the car up, ignoring the speedometer as it climbed toward a hundred. He passed the traffic on the steep grade below Sunset Point as if they were standing still. Truck drivers yelled at him as he sped past.

Then he was off onto the side highway, and then fighting gravel and dirt as he spun off onto the country road leading up into the mountains. The creek they'd cooled their feet in so many times gurgled down the dark recess paralleling the road. There, there ahead, was the little slope that overlooked the valley below. Mesquite and scrub oak and juniper made clownish shadows against the moonless night.

The abandoned Datsun sat forlornly by the side of the road. He pulled off, fumbling for the flashlight he kept in the glove compartment. Exhausted and sweaty from the long drive, he stumbled out of the car and began playing the light around the grove.

He heard her voice before he saw her. "Troy? Oh, Troy! What are you *doing* here? Go back, Troy. Go home!"

He started for her, was amazed to see her slim form backing away from him. "What's wrong, Eula? Why'd you run out on me like that? I would've understood, but dammit, you at least owe me a good-bye."

"No, Troy, no! I tried to make you understand. I tried. Go home, Troy. Don't you understand? I've graduated.

I'm not going to be an adolescent anymore. I can't—''
She broke off, her gaze turning slowly, expectantly skyward.

There was something overhead, something above them in the night. It was immense, soundless, and falling rapidly toward them. Troy stood frozen, his head back, the flashlight dangling from his hand as the gargantuan shadow descended. A few tiny lights glowed from its underside. It blocked out the stars soundlessly.

A brighter, intensifying light drew his attention back to the trees, to where Eula had been, the Eula he'd known, the Eula he'd loved. The Eula who had graduated and left her adolescence. In her place was a vicious, twisting, explosively beautiful pillar of green fire. It towered over the grove of mesquite and juniper, writhing with incredible energy, so bright that it stung his eyes and made them tear. He tried to look at it and shield his face at the same time. Hints of yellow and white crawled across the fiery apparition; bright little explosions of intense color danced within it.

It moved toward him, and he stumbled fearfully backward, falling to the ground. The earth was cold under him, but he didn't notice it. The overpowered flashlight was forgotten. It was no longer necessary, anyway. Night was witness to a temporary emerald dawn.

It whispered to him, full of an awesome incomprehensible strength. *"I tried to tell you, Troy. I tried."*

Then it rose into the air and vanished into the massive dark presence overhead. The stars returned as the Visitor disappeared. Troy's hands went to his ears, and there was momentary pain as air was explosively displaced by the Visitor's departure. It was gone, and so was what was Eula.

For a long time he lay there, breathing hard but steadily, considering everything that had transpired. He was frightened, but as the night noises returned to normal, he slowly relaxed. Quail peeped hesitantly into the darkness, and an owl made a sound like a metronome. Down in the creek frogs resumed their staccato conversations. That even made him smile.

He understood a little now. About the frogs, anyway.

Eula had gone home, to a country farther off than he could have imagined. She wasn't an adolescent anymore.

He stood, dusting off his pants. His legs still worked, carried him toward the car. No need for remorse, he told himself. No need to blame himself for what had happened or for how he'd behaved.

After all, all little boys love to chase after tadpoles.

THE TESSELLATED
TETRAHEXAHEDRAL
YELLOW ROSE OF TEXAS

Clifford Simak's not with us anymore. Cliff was one of those writers, like Poul Anderson and Jack Williamson, whose stuff slides down so smooth and easy that we just take it for granted. Until it's gone. Only then do we take notice and realize that, hey, nobody else really does write quite like that, no matter how simple and straightforward and uncomplex it seemed upon repeated readings.

Cliff's ideas were subordinate to his characters and to the atmosphere he so effortlessly seemed to create. Like a Turner painting, it was the light that was important to Simak, the illumination he provided and not the subject matter, whether ship or skyline or train. A Simak story was like a Piranesi prison suddenly transformed into a galactic flower stall, or a sound picture by Delius, or one of D. W. Griffith's early cinematic efforts such as True Heart Suzie.

So much science fiction takes place in metropolitan settings or is at least overlaid with an urban sensibility that when stories do move out into the alien territory of the countryside, it's usually done by the author with a slight titter. We utilize the funny folks with the hay in their teeth and the dirty denim coveralls largely as comic relief, or mad murderers, or golly-gee-whiz victims of alien invaders. When was the last time the hero of a science-fiction or fantasy novel was a farmer?

Not that we have many real farmers left. Nowadays they're all into agribusiness and have degrees in economics or business. They raise their beef via artificial insemination, a problem with too much of today's science fiction.

Several editors thought the following story too long for what it had to tell. There was a time long ago when that would not have been a criticism. Now we live in a time when we're engulfed by information, when there's never enough time for reflection or contemplation. Movies become sitcoms, novels metamorphose into video games, and political and philosophical debates are reduced to sound bites. Reality is what you can put a good spin on.

That's not how most of the world lives. That's not even how most of this country lives.

"SIR, I'VE GOT SOMETHING VERY PECULIAR HERE." The lieutenant assumed an irascible expression and walked over. Mobler was not a particularly pleasant man, due in part to an unfortunate childhood disease that had given his skin the form and consistency of a golf ball's surface. This pebbled epidermis would turn color according to his emotions. At present both cheeks resembled obese anemic strawberries.

Despite this, he was respected, if not especially well liked, by the enlisted men and women who served under him. This was sad because Lieutenant Mobler was competent and intelligent. It wasn't his fault he looked like a sniffly adolescent instead of a soldier.

It was dark in the long, sealed room. Illumination came from bulbs, purposely, dim set in the ceiling overhead and from the numerous dials, switches, and screens that lined both walls. Smartly uniformed people sat intent before the instruments. When they conversed at all, it was in whispers. A natural somberness kept talk soft and furtive, not orders. The purpose behind this room was well known to all who worked in it, and this itself was enough to inspire reverence and quiet.

Now that businesslike attentiveness had been broken, and Mobler would know the reason why. Standing behind the young electronics spec. seven, he peered over his shoulder at the circular screen in front of them. It was lit from within by a rich fluorescence the color of pea soup. Right away he noted the cause of the specialist's comment without detecting the declared peculiarity of it.

"So you've got a track, Davis. What's so startling about that?"

Grimacing uncertainly, the specialist pointed to several small gauges set into the console at the screen's lower left. Mobler leaned close to read them, a movement shoving his prominent Adam's apple taut against neck skin. Then he frowned, turning the tiny craterlets on his face linear.

"It's not possible," he finally announced. His voice was surprisingly deep.

"That's just what I thought, sir." The specialist stared now not at the screen but at his superior. He was waiting for orders but hoping for an explanation.

Mobler turned, looked down the long row of seats. His tense words were unnaturally loud in that funereal atmosphere. "Colson, Matthews. Specialist Davis's instrumentation insists it's got a small object reentry coming in from the west on irregular descent at three thousand kilometers per."

One of the women started. "Pardon, sir," Matthews queried, "*three* thousand and irregular?"

"I know," Mobler concurred. "That's much too slow, and the approach path is cockeyed all to hell. Let's have some confirmation."

Abruptly the room looked like an anthill before an impending thunderstorm. Those not among the two designated to confirm the impossible sighting were hard pressed to attend to their own tasks. The level of noise in the room rose alarmingly, but Mobler couldn't blame them.

Eventually, disbelieving reassurance came from both additional stations that the track was legitimate, that both the speed of reentry and the zigzagging descent path were correct. Mobler turned back to Davis's screen and saw to his dismay that the tiny blip, the cause of all the commotion, was still there.

Almost absently he ordered, without turning, "Matthews, Garcia, Abramawicz. Taking into account all shifts in path, I want the best prediction of a touchdown site you can come up with. I've a hunch this baby isn't going to burn up."

"What do you think it is, sir?" Davis asked wonderingly. But the lieutenant was busy nearby, speaking into a rarely used phone. Davis strained to overhear, found he could make out the local half of the conversation.

"No, sir," Mobler was telling someone softly, "three thousand. No, no change in angle of descent, not yet, anyway." A pause, then, "They're certain? That's what I hoped, too, sir. Yes, I'll wait." He turned slightly, saw every eye in the room locked on him.

"It's not Soviet or Chinese," he announced in response to the many unspoken questions. An almost audible sigh rushed through the room. "Absolutely no launchings in the past ninety-six hours, and all orbital devices accounted for in number and mass." He turned his attention back to the phone, listening intently.

"Yes, sir . . . I agree, sir. The angle is much too sharp for that speed. It's coming straight down, comparatively. No, sir," he added after a glance at Davis. "It's still intact. Yes, sir, I know it doesn't make any sense." A longer pause, and Mobler leaned to his right to study a chart hanging on the wall.

"No, sir, it's not one of ours. Impossible. The last reentry we had was OGO eighteen, the geosurv satellite, and it burned up on schedule two and a half weeks ago. Nothing of ours, or theirs, for that matter, is set to come down for at least three more months.

"Yes, sir, we're working on a possible crash site now. It shows indications of shifting its path from time to time. There's a straight line in there somewhere, though . . . assuming it doesn't go ahead and burn up, after all. Just a second, sir."

Mobler looked back down the room toward the three technicians whose assignment he was plotting. He said nothing, but his cheeks turned slightly darker. Knowing the signs, the three specialists worked faster.

It was Garcia who spoke up excitedly. "No path yet, but I've got something else, Lieutenant. The object is no larger than three meters in diameter and not less than point eight. Its general shape is spherical." He hesitated, added, "That's all only a guess, but it's a good guess."

Mobler nodded once, reported the new information to whoever was on the other end of the line. Meanwhile Matthews completed a final check of her instruments.

"If it doesn't burn up and if it maintains its present general heading, sir, it's going to strike somewhere in the southwest or south central states," Matthews called out.

"Can you pin it down any better than that, Matthews?" Mobler asked. She chewed her lower lip, made some hurried calculations.

"I'd estimate somewhere between El Paso and Dallas longitudinally and Tulsa–Galveston latitudinally."

"Thank you, Matthews," Mobler said gratefully. This prediction was relayed dutifully across the phone. The lieutenant put a palm over the receiver, spoke to the technician hopefully. "Both Colorado Springs and Washington would like to know if you can narrow it down a little more. They'd like even a preliminary impact point prediction."

Maybe it was the excitement of the situation, but more likely it was the almost indifferent mention of those two names that spurred the specialist's abilities. After several minutes of frantic computer work, she turned and declared guardedly, "I'd say anywhere in an area up to three hundred kilometers east of Dallas. That's a general radius, sir."

Mobler reported this to the phone. "Yes, sir. Thank you, sir. Yes, we'll notify Point Mugu also and relay what we have. They'll send it on to White Sands and Houston. Very good, sir. Yes, sir. Good-bye."

Hanging up, the lieutenant spared a casual glance for the room. Everyone returned instantly to his or her assigned tasks, which were quite as important as what had just happened. He said nothing, simply stood thinking. Then he leaned back and stared upward, trying to see through the triple-reinforced ceilings of the tracking station.

Somewhere up there, above the palm trees and sands devoid of tourist hotels, far above thick Hawaiian clouds, something almost surely not of this Earth was speeding past.

As soon as Point Mugu picked up the rapidly dropping object, fighters near White Sands scrambled in hopes of intercepting it visually before impact. Unfortunately, that entire area of the United States was awash in winter thunderstorms. The few planes aloft had enough to do fighting buffeting winds and instrument distortions engendered by lightning. The object was never sighted.

Worse still, when it finally went tropospheric, all contact was lost. Important people in places far from one another raged impotently at the uncooperative weather and chain-smoked many substances whose sole point of commonality was that all were encased in paper tubes and then fired.

So it was that a tired Josiah Chester, Major, USAF, found himself standing in the office of General MacGregor, to which he had been summoned posthaste.

Chester's skin was numb from the steel lashing of the frigid Texas wind outside as he started to remove his heavy winter overcoat. The general only allowed him to finish his salute, however.

"Just stand there, Joe," MacGregor ordered him gently. "No point in removing your coat; you don't have time to warm up."

Chester moved his hands from the buttons. "I came as fast as I could, sir. The weather's brutal tonight. Something's up?"

"Something." MacGregor snorted teasingly as he reached for a bottle concealed out of sight. He poured and downed half a shot glass neat, offered the same to Chester. The major accepted and duplicated the general's efforts—to ward off the weather, he insisted to himself.

"I should have taken that job National Avionics offered me in Washington," the general told empty air. Just as easily, he cocked a querulous eye at the standing officer and asked, "Joe, do you believe in flying saucers, UFOs, that sort of thing?"

Chester had thought himself as well prepared as possible for one summoned unexpectedly to a meeting with his base commander at nearly two in the morning during a near blizzard. So the speed with which he lost his composure was unsettling.

A host of conflicting thoughts fought for attention. The Ruskies were trying something . . . no, if that were so, he'd have been called to his plane, not the general's office. We're being invaded . . . but if that were the case, he'd hardly be alone here.

He finally decided that something very important was going on that higher-ups wanted as few people as possible to know about. His last thought before replying was that he probably wouldn't have a chance to telephone Charlene to tell her he wouldn't be able to attend Mary-Ellen's ballet performance at the school today.

"No, sir, I don't, but then, I don't disbelieve, either."

"The little green men's agnostic, is that it?" essayed MacGregor. He added irritably, without giving the major a chance to comment, "Oh, for heaven's sake, at ease, Joe!" Chester relaxed as the general pushed the bottle forward on the desk.

"Like another? A cigar, maybe? Havana."

"No thank you, sir."

MacGregor sighed, folded his hands on the desk. "Why don't you believe in UFOs?"

Chester considered the answer as seriously as the question was being asked. It was a question that every pilot had been forced to contemplate at one time or another during his flying career.

"Not enough evidence, not enough facts to support their existence," he eventually stated.

"The saucer advocates say they *have* sufficient facts and evidence," countered MacGregor.

"They have yet to convince me, sir."

The general sat back, apparently satisfied. "Good. That's what I wanted to hear." He rolled his chair across the acrylic carpet protector and pulled down a wall map of Texas. Rising, he hunted around on the map for a bit, then tapped something near its middle.

"Come around here, Joe." Chester did so, fighting hard to keep a growing list of questions from overpowering him.

"Know this area?" the general inquired, tapping the map again. Chester studied the region in question.

"I've been clean across the state on Interstate 20, sir."

The finger froze. "This is a town called Cisco."

Chester shrugged apologetically. "Never been there, sir."

"Neither have I," confessed MacGregor. "They claim to have the world's largest man-made swimming pool there. We think they may have acquired a new attraction." He put his finger in the metal ring at the bottom of the map, pulled, and then let the plastic sheet slide shut without a snap.

Chester took it as a signal for him to return to his former position in front of the general's desk. "You've been over to the Manned Space Center?"

"Numerous times, sir," Chester admitted. "There's one thing, sir," he asked hesitantly. "May I be permitted to telephone my wife? She's expecting me home by five."

"Go ahead. No reason you can't, though of course you won't be allowed to say anything about your mission—where you're going or how long you'll be there." At Chester's distraught look of resignation the general added, "You may tell her that you're not going out of the country this time."

Chester looked happy. "That'll satisfy her, sir. Thanks. Where am I going?"

"To Cisco and the surrounding countryside. But first you're to proceed to Houston to pick up three people at the Space Center." Exploring his desk, he located a notepad filled with scribblings. "Couple of fellows named Calumet and Tut."

"Perham Tut?" wondered Chester. MacGregor appeared mildly surprised.

"You know him?"

"Only by reputation, sir, and through a couple of articles. It's not a name you read and quickly forget. I don't know this Calumet."

"Jean Calumet," MacGregor elaborated, studying the note. "And a Sarah Goldberg."

"That's another name I know." Sometimes Chester wished the general would begin his puzzles with the border instead of loose pieces. "She and Tut are both associated with all aspects of the search for extraterrestrial life. They both worked on the directional programming for Pioneers sixteen and seventeen. I guess Calumet's in a related field of study, if not the same."

"You'll have a driver," the general continued. "All five of you will proceed from Houston to Cisco." MacGregor's expression turned solemn. "We have evidence," he began slowly, "unconfirmed but pretty impressive, that a small object that may be of extrasolar construction survived entry into the Earth's atmosphere earlier this morning and came down in one piece somewhere in a circular region of 120 kilometers with Cisco at its center.

"You understand," he went on, both hands twirling a pencil back and forth, "the reason for total secrecy and for informing no one of this information."

"What about local sightings?" Chester asked.

"The same rotten weather that caused us to lose this thing over New Mexico has apparently helped us, too. We've been monitoring everything from fifty-thousand-watt radio stations down to personal CBs in the area. No one's reported seeing or hearing anything unusual.

"That might also mean that the damn thing's gone and burned up during final descent. In fact, the experts tell me that's probably what happened." He glanced up from the pencil, and his eyes were cold. "Naturally, we can't take that chance.

"Given the suspected small size of the object, the weather, and the fact that people live pretty far apart from each other up in that part of the country, it's just possible something could have set down intact without anyone noticing it, even if it made a good-sized bang on impact.

"You'll take an unmarked station wagon from the Space Center. It'll hold the five of you and the minimum amount of equipment the three scientists are being allowed."

"Not much room for instrumentation in the back of a wagon," Chester observed.

The general smiled. "From what I hear, this Goldberg and her friends would like about six two-and-a-halfs packed with all kinds of gadgetry. Obviously we can't have the kind of attention a convoy would attract in that area."

"Obviously," Chester echoed.

"We want to try and hide our interest without hiding it," MacGregor explained. "Nothing seems to attract attention like people trying not to attract attention. So you and the driver will wear uniforms, and the three scientists, of course, will be in whatever they want.

"*If* this isn't someone's idea of a bad joke, and if the object really exists, and if it's come down in recognizable chunks, then we'll move in with larger forces."

"Does that mean I can get whatever I need if I need it?"

"Use your own judgment," the general instructed him. "Keep in mind that we want this kept as quiet as possible but that in addition to the Air Force, you're serving as representative for all the armed forces. Special units at Fort Hood have been placed on emergency standby. On your word, they can reach the Cisco area by copter inside an hour.

"Also keep in mind that I, General Hartford at Fort Hood, and a few others here and at the Space Center are in constant touch with NORAD and Washington.

"Again, there's a walloping good chance you'll find nothing but cold beef on the hoof and a lot of mud. On second thought—" The general grinned thinly. "—you may be spared the mud. I understand the high up that way's been well below freezing lately. Better have your woolens."

"No problem, sir," said Chester, smiling back. "I'm wearing them."

"That's good, because your driver should be waiting for you outside by now."

Chester glanced involuntarily toward the closed door. When he turned back, he saw that MacGregor was standing. Coming to attention, he saluted, and the general saluted him back.

"One last thing, Joe," MacGregor declared. Chester paused with his hand on the doorknob.

"What's that, sir?"

"Probably worrying you needlessly. Kauai was the first of our stations to pick this thing up. Midway missed it, but we can't tell if that means the Russians did, too. We haven't had any queries from them, but that doesn't necessarily mean anything. Given the potential of this, if it's what we hope it is, well . . . I'm not saying they'd try anything crazy, but. . . ."

Chester didn't reply, merely patted his left underarm in a significant fashion. "I understand, sir. I'll brief the driver accordingly."

"He's already been briefed," explained a grim MacGregor. "With those three scientists jabbering among themselves, we couldn't very well keep him in the dark, anyway. It'll be up to you and him to take care of the three people from NASA. They won't look beyond the end of their gauges."

"Yes, sir. Good night, sir."

"Good night, Major Chester. Tell the driver to take it easy. The roads are bad."

"I will, sir."

Chester turned, walked wordlessly through an outer office, a waiting lobby, and down a corridor, then out into the subfreezing night.

"Dad?"

"Huh—what?"

"Dad!"

Jesse Shattuck blinked, rolled over in bed. In the moonlight filtering fitfully in through the broken clouds and the big window he saw the anxious face of his sixteen-year-old, David.

"What is it, boy?" Then he put up a hand for silence as his son started to reply.

The wind was a sad echo of its former might—the storm had obviously passed, he told himself—and the barking reached him clearly from somewhere back of the henhouse. A shadow stirred on the other side of the bed and sat up. It had a small, intense, delicately aquiline face with eyes of black opal. The hair of a woman thirty years younger cascaded in curls and ripples at its sides.

Shattuck sat motionless, listening to the frantic barking. The bedroom was warm and dark. A soft anvillike bang sounded from the old heater. He definitely did not want to go outside.

"What are those damn-fool dogs barking about now, J.W.?" his wife wondered in the darkness.

"I don't know, Mother," the rancher admitted as he slid his long legs out from under the quilts. He bent over, hunting for his socks. "Could be coyotes, maybe wolves. Too, it's cold enough and the pickings are thin enough for them to risk trying the henhouse again. Thought we'd cured 'em of that last winter, though." He pulled up the last sock, found his boots by the nightstand.

David rose, looked excited. "Should I get my gun, Dad?"

Shattuck nodded. "My twelve-gauge, too."

"And mine," said the woman, scrambling out of the other side of the bed.

"Don't you think you ought to stay here, Mother?"

A wry, delightful smile crossed her face, feminine lightning. "Go—" and she added a colorfully crass suggestion. Shattuck said nothing, merely smiled ever so slightly.

By the time David returned to look down at his tall father and his mother expectantly, they were already dressed and donning winter coats. The son passed out the armory. Husband and wife methodically checked their weapons. Four shells slid into four chambers.

Suitably attired for the cold and armed against whatever might be threatening their domain, the family started for the back of the rambling house.

The chill hit Shattuck the moment he opened the rear door. Dry, freezing air caressed his stubbled cheeks like steel wool, and his breath formed ghost patterns in the night.

Off to the south, nothing could be seen under the black clouds of the receding storm. The remainder of the night sky was clear. He regarded the nearly full moon and its tenebrous halo, a sign, perhaps, of more wetness to come.

"It wouldn't be a wolf, Dad, would it?" David theorized nearby. "Isn't it too light out for them to come in this close?"

"Could be a sick one, David," his father told him curtly. "Funny, the dogs have shut up. Quiet now."

The faintest whisper of a breeze stirred the cold air. From the henhouse came only a soft clucking, nervous and uncertain. That was to be expected from the way Cotton and Gin had been carrying on. But the cluckings weren't panicky, as they would have been if the scent of wolf were in the wind. The guineas, at least, would have sensed that, and they were quiet.

"Must be out back of the tank somewhere, J.W.," his

wife said. The rancher nodded slowly, and they started off past the coop.

Behind it the dogs were wandering back and forth, looking puzzled and anxious but not straining at their tethers, either. Cotton, the big Irish setter, whined as the family came up to him. The big weimaraner, Gin, abruptly turned, barked at the distance, and then turned whining to David.

"Never seen dogs act like this before," Shattuck mused. "Something out there's got 'em stirred, all right, but they don't seem anxious to be out after it."

He looked out toward the distant tank, the deep artificial pond that held the ranch's water supply. Overhead the sky was almost white with stars. The moon spread pale fingers across the still water. A light snow had sugared the ground, final testament of the retreating storm.

"See anything, Mother?"

His wife shook her head slowly, one finger resting easily on the trigger of the .30-30. "Not a thing, J.W. If there is something out there, we're going to have to let the dogs find it."

"Yep." He bent over Cotton, his hands working gently at the setter's collar. David was performing the same actions with Gin.

"All right, girl," he whispered into one russet ear, "go git it. Let him go, David."

Both dogs were set free at the same time. They started off toward the tank on the run. Twenty meters from the near shore they unexpectedly slowed, turned, and came trotting back toward the henhouse. Something appeared to pull at them. They whirled, ran at the tank once more. And once more came to a halt, reversed their direction, and headed back toward the astonished family.

"I swear, Mother," Shattuck muttered, "strangest behavior I ever saw." He gestured with the end of the shotgun. "Still, there's for sure something out back there. It may scare the dogs, but it doesn't scare me. It's on our property; better go find out whatever it is."

Nothing rose to confront them when they reached the rim of the tank or when they started around it. The tank backed up against a slight rise that had once housed a den of rattlers. They started up the slight slope.

Alternately barking and whining as though they couldn't make up their minds whether to be angry or afraid, the two dogs trotted alongside. They showed no inclination to charge ahead, as was the normal manner of dogs.

As they approached the rim of the rise, a brightness separate from that falling from the lambent moon seemed to come from just ahead.

"Something burning over there, J.W.," Beth Shattuck said huskily. The rancher considered, shook his head positively.

"We would smell smoke sure in this air, Mother. Could be a plane crash, maybe, but I think we would have heard it hit. Car or bike's a possibility, but I don't know any kid in town fool enough to be out playing at motorcross on a night like this."

"It might be something that's fallen from a plane, Dad," suggested his son helpfully. "You read lots of times about a piece of cargo or part of an engine that breaks loose."

His father didn't nod or smile, but quiet approval was in his words. "Could be."

They topped the little hill and looked down the other side at a wide plain. Wild wheat full of dead stalks clustered as if for warmth around the trunks of bushy mesquite trees, the latter's branches gnarled and grooved like the arms of old men.

But the thing that had fallen here wasn't burning. It had struck a section of dry broken slate, and there were no burn marks around it.

Shattuck, his wife, and his son stood staring at it. "Whatever it is, it don't look dangerous," he finally decided, setting the safety on his shotgun. He started down the slope.

"Sure is bright," David observed.

The thing lying amid dry rock and gravel was about the size of Mrs. Shattuck's washing machine. It was roughly spherical but with many smooth, flat surfaces. Many of those surfaces appeared to be inlaid with tiny squares and other geometric shapes that glowed like inlaid lights.

Several long, twisted projections not unlike antennae

rose from the top surfaces, and two stuck out from one side. They were the only interruptions in the otherwise uniform shape.

Closer inspection revealed that the tiny, multicolored lights were flush with the various flat surfaces. Crimson and deep purple predominated, though every color of the rainbow was present. Some remained steady and unwinking, while others pulsed light to dark to light again at seemingly random intervals.

Still regarding the object warily, Shattuck circled it once, staring admiringly at the display of brilliant lights. Exclusive of the inlaid many-shaded patterns, the rest of the thing shone brightly with a deep yellow the hue of old butter.

"What do you reckon it's made out of?" he asked his wife.

"It looks like metal, J.W., but it has no shiny surfaces."

It was true. The material itself, rather than something from within, seemed to emit the light. The slick sides did show a luster and sheen like metal, but the object was at least partly translucent, unlike any metal they had ever seen. Where the two largest projections vanished into the surface they could actually see them continue inside.

It was the intense mosaic of colored shapes—rhombohedrons, triangles, circles, and such—that prevented them from peering deeper into the thing. Cautiously, Mrs. Shattuck moved right up next to the device. Feeling no heat, she reached out a hand and touched it.

"It's not hot," she announced. "Looks like metal, but it feels like plastic." Her gaze went upward momentarily. "I don't think this fell out of some airliner, David." She ran her palm over it. "It's downright cold, in fact."

Quite unexpectedly, the object emitted a sound. All three took several hurried steps backward. Three muzzles rose in unison.

The drama didn't intensify, however, and they relaxed. Other than the new noises, the object remained sitting immobile, glowing as beautifully as ever. Only now it was softly saying *hmm-hmm-hmm, buzz-hmm-buzz . . . tick! Hmm-hmm-hmm, buzz-hmm-buzz . . . tick! . . .*

Over and over again.

"It must still be working," David mused. "But what is it, and what's it do?"

His father shrugged again. "Beats me." He moved down to the device again and commenced a nose-to-surface inspection.

"What are you looking for, Dad?"

"Something to identify it. Whoever lost this is going to want it back."

"I know!" the boy said, suddenly aglow with a sense of imminent importance. "It's a satellite! Maybe a Russian spacecraft that landed in the wrong place."

"No Old Glory," his father said. "No hammer and sickle, either, 'less they're underneath."

"I don't know," his wife murmured, her eyes never leaving J.W. "It doesn't look like a satellite, at least not any kind I ever read about, David—ours or theirs. And even spacecraft that are designed to come down in one piece usually have burn marks or signs of reentry beat into them.

"Look. There's not a streak anywhere on it or on the ground. It sure landed softly." She pointed to the base of the object. The gravel there was hardly disturbed, and bent grasses were raising their tousled heads through the snow once again. "Even the snow around it isn't melted. I don't think it so much as bounced."

"Nothing," came Shattuck's voice. They both turned to see him rising, brushing at his pants. "I can't find anything saying anything, let alone where it's from. Whoever built this is kind of closemouthed." He appeared to come to a decision, looked at his son.

"Yes, Dad?"

"Run back to the house and get the pickup, boy. Check out the winch and make sure it isn't froze up."

"Okay." The youth took two long strides toward the house, skidded to a halt, and looked back. "What are we gonna do with it?"

"Well, now," his father said appraisingly as he studied the fascinating whatever-it-was, "I'm not sure." Almost painfully rich colors flashed and blinked at him. "I don't know that it's good for anything, but it sure is pretty.''

"It sure is that, J.W.," his wife commented, staring at it. She put an arm around his waist. His went over her shoulder. They stood regarding the glowing thing in the night as David puffed and panted his way toward the ranch garage.

Eventually she looked up at her husband and smiled. "You know, J.W., I think I've got an interestin' idea . . ."

"Actually, Miss Goldberg," Joe Chester was saying as the late-model station wagon bounced along the sunny back road, "I'm convinced that if it did come down intact, it did so in such a place and fashion that we're never going to find it. We've been looking for a month now, and we haven't got a hint as to its whereabouts. Myself, I'm pretty sure it burned up at the last minute on entry."

"Science," the older woman told him in a voice buttressed by dedication, "requires patience even above brains, Major. I'm sorry we're inconveniencing you. Please feel free to go home any time."

"Oh, that's all right," Chester replied, a polite if false smile plastered across his face to conceal his irritation. "No trouble at all."

Turning away from the backseat, he stared out the front window again at the snow-covered wheat and corn fields they were passing through. He couldn't leave any more than they could, though his reasons were different, if no less compelling. His orders had directed him to accompany and watch over the little expedition for as long as the three scientists found it worthwhile to continue.

He wondered what Charlene was doing today.

A chance glance at his watch told him the date as well as the time. If the three musketeers in the backseat kept this up many more weeks, he would miss spending the holidays with his family. Somehow he had to convince them that further search was absurd.

Before this had started, he'd been more than half-convinced that the suspected UFO was more fictional than real. Failing that, it had certainly burned up, blown up, or otherwise scattered itself undetectably across a wide section of west Texas. Even if it *had* existed and *had* come down in one section, this part of the state was crisscrossed with uncountable deep creeks overgrown with cottonwood, live oak, and other thick vegetation. Or it could have fallen into a deep dirty lake.

A thousand people, he was positive, could scour the same territory and have no better luck than the five of them had had. A month of this was more than enough.

He was sick of the whole business—sick of small-town motels, sick of lonely beds, and sick of the scientists' subtle but certain air of condescension toward him. He was even getting sick of real country cooking, a sure sign it was time to quit and go home.

They still had some time left before the holidays. He resigned himself to continuing the hunt a while longer.

The day wore on, and they followed the by now monotonous procedure of interviewing farmer after farmer. If even one had seen something strange, anything out of the ordinary, he would have understood the scientists' insistence on going on.

But none of the puzzled men and women they talked with had noticed anything out of the ordinary. That was hardly surprising, considering the terrible storm that had raged that night. Everyone had sensibly been inside in bed or stretched out in front of a roaring fire.

Some of the looks they got suggested that many thought the peculiar group of five people had spent too many such nights wandering around exposed to the elements, with the result that their brains were slightly frozen in spots.

"It's getting dark," Sarah Goldberg noted. "We'd better be getting back to Albany." She was first back into the station wagon, oblivious to the curious stares of the cattleman they'd just interviewed.

"We've about covered all the farms and residences in this area," she said when the wagon was rolling again. "Tomorrow we'll move our base of operation to Breckenridge and commence a fresh spiral outward from there."

As the temperature outside dropped, Chester turned on the car's heater. To add to his discomfort, it had begun putting out a disagreeable odor lately, in addition to a steady grinding as if a bearing or something had broken loose and was rattling about inside it.

He couldn't find fault with it. It had been in constant use all day and night the past month. It was only sounding the frustration and irritation Chester felt himself.

In the rapidly growing darkness the driver, known to them all only as Pat, had switched the brights on. The extra illumination was welcome on the narrow back farm roads. Pat rarely had to dim them, as oncoming cars were infrequent.

This part of the county was especially thinly populated. Pat slowed, afraid of missing the Albany turnoff, and Goldberg began screaming like a high-schooler whose date had unexpectedly turned out to be the town wolf.

"Stop the car! Stop the car!"

The usually phlegmatic, imperturbable Pat slammed a size-thirteen shoe on the brake, and they were all thrown sharply forward. Chester pushed hair from his eyes and turned to look angrily into the backseat.

"What is it now, Miss Goldberg?" he asked, fighting to remain civil. The old woman's eyes ignored him as she stared out the window on her left.

"Look—look at that," she murmured.

Something in her tone made Chester turn quickly to gaze in the indicated direction; he had to peer around the considerable bulk of the driver to do so.

Disappointment was instant. Just off the road and ahead was yet another of the many isolated ranches they'd passed and stopped at during the past month. This one was a bit more modern, a little larger than the average, but otherwise unspectacular.

Befitting the season, it was lined around roof edge and windows with Christmas lights. Two plastic, meter-high candy canes flanked the entrance to the yard in front of the main house.

Chester felt a pang of homesickness at the sight, as he had at every such group of decorations they'd passed. He'd never get home in time to string his own lights. Charlene and Mary-Ellen would be heartbroken, and the things would sit up in the attic, unused, for another year.

"Not the house. Not the house," Goldberg stammered, noticing the direction of his gaze. "Off to the left of it, in the back."

Off to one side of the house and set farther back from the road was a large barn. The front edge of the barn's roof was also lined with lights. The cause of the staid scientist's sudden hysteria was located there.

As was common in such structures, a large square gap was set above the ground over the barn's entrance, opening into the hayloft. The opening was currently filled by an object of indeterminate size and dimensions.

It lit the whole front of the barn with an incandescent yellow glow as soft and intense as an Arizona sunset. Within the yellow dwelt a horde of colored pinpoints arranged in intricate and strange patterns to form a photonic mosaic. The lights shifted position as they watched.

"It's so bright, the smaller lights so deep and rich," Tut observed quietly. "LEDs, maybe?"

"No," objected Goldberg with assurance. "The color is too intense even for that. Pull in here, Pat; there's no gate."

Until now the stoic sergeant had responded with equanimity to requests from all his passengers. This time he glanced for confirmation from his real superior.

"By all means, Pat, let's see what it is," Chester declared, unable to take his fascinated gaze from the enigmatic object. So bright was its glow that it overwhelmed the sign that had been strung on wire just beneath it. The sign was cut from silver foil and consisted of four large letters—N-O-E-L, Chester read to himself.

Little bounces jostled the occupants of the station wagon as it turned left into the dirt driveway running toward the barn. As they stopped next to the house and the sergeant turned off the motor, the barking of two or more large dogs could be heard. Nothing rushed to meet them, however.

"I guess they're chained or in the house," Tut commented nervously. Chester wasn't surprised at the slight tremor in Tut's voice. Numerous stops had already shown that the huge engineer had a genuine fear of dogs.

Goldberg left the car and headed straight for the barn. The youngest of the three scientists put out a hand to restrain her before Chester could do so verbally.

"Better hold off a minute, Sarah."

She whirled, glared at him. "Why wait?"

Jean Calumet kept a hand on her even as he continued to regard the object set so temptingly near, up in the loft. The yellow glow was bright on olive, smooth skin. "I'm as curious to be into it as you are, Sarah, but remember where we are."

"So where are we?" she snapped, irritated at the delay.

"On another man's property," the diminutive Cajun told her. "This isn't Los Angeles or even Houston. People out here have archaic notions about things like property rights. We'd better wait till we have a chance to explain ourselves."

So while Goldberg and Tut groaned at the wait and Chester nodded gratefully to Calumet, they stood and fidgeted until several lights came on inside the house.

Two lean hairy shapes raced out of the front door, barking furiously. The cluster of visitors stood their ground, even Perham Tut, who would have returned to the safety of the car if it hadn't been for the disgusted look he received from Sarah Goldberg.

The dogs sniffed each of them in turn, then trotted quietly back toward the house, satisfied in the notable way of dogs that the newcomers presented no immediate threat to their masters.

A tall, clean-shaven man in his middle or late forties sallied forth to greet them. He was wearing a pair of threadbare blue jeans, a tired flannel shirt, and boots, all obviously donned in haste. He was even taller than Tut, though not nearly as massive. The thin adolescent who trailed slightly behind him was a couple of inches taller still.

"Evening," he said pleasantly. "I don't believe I know you all."

Chester stepped forward, identified himself and his companions with names only. The man shook hands with the men, nodded at Goldberg.

"I'm Jesse Shattuck; this is my son, David," he told them. "Can we help you folks with something? We don't get many visitors this time of night, strangers or otherwise."

A strong voice sounded from the door. "You gonna

all stand out there in the cold like a covey of paralyzed quail? Come on in and have some coffee and pie.''

"In a minute, Mother!'' the man yelled back at her. A screen door clattered shut by way of reply. The man looked back at Chester expectantly.

"We're up from Houston,'' the major told him, deciding that this man could tell truth from lie quicker than Chester could think up fresh deceptions. "I'm in the Air Force, attached to the National Aeronautics and Space Administration's Manned Space Center in Houston.'' He gestured behind him.

"My friends are all scientists. We've been out hunting around this part of the country for over a month.''

"We've been looking for that,'' Goldberg interrupted, pointing toward the barn, talking twice as fast as Chester. "Thank you for finding it for us. We'll see that you receive a suitable reward.''

That closed the matter as far as the scientists were concerned, and they started toward the barn. Chester started to say something but was interrupted by a disarming wave from Shattuck, who indicated that they should head toward the barn also.

Together they stood in the open space below the loft, staring mesmerized into its alien radiance.

"Is it safe there?'' Tut finally whispered, breaking the spell the object's beauty had cast over them. "It's right near the edge . . . it could fall out.''

"Huh uh,'' Shattuck assured him. "There's a couple of braces holding the base steady and a rope around its bottom under the hay. I don't reckon it would hurt it none if it did tumble out.'' Entranced by mere sight of the object, the three scientists failed to note the rancher's evaluation.

"What are you counting, Jean?'' Goldberg asked her young colleague, noticing that his mouth was moving silently as he stared at the object.

"The facets. I can't call them sides; the thing's too much like a jewel to me.'' He squinted into the soft glare. "If the rest of the artifact matches what's visible, I would estimate a total of twenty-four sides, not counting projections such as the apparent antennae.

"That suggests they could have a system based on two,

three, four, six, eight, twelve, or twenty-four, and that's only if their mathematics conform in any way to our own. Ten sides would have made things a lot simpler.''

"Not necessarily," countered Perham Tut through pursed lips. "The twenty-four sides might be merely decorative, having no mathematical significance whatsoever.''

"That's true," admitted Calumet reluctantly.

"We'll find out as soon as we can get it back to the lab and begin taking it apart," Goldberg informed them in her half-gentle, half-shrill tones. "How do we go about getting it down?" She faced the quiet Shattuck. "How did you get it up there in the first place?''

"Put it in a wire net and used the hay lift," the rancher explained easily.

"We might," suggested Tut, rubbing his chin, "fit it in the back of the wagon. That would save some time.''

"No, no," objected Goldberg, speaking as though correcting a child. "Look how bright it is already. Do you want to drive all the way back to Houston with it shining like a spotlight out the car windows? One reporter finds out, and we'll never be able to study this at the proper pace. No, we need a panel truck or a small van." She eyed Chester. "You can get this for us, Major?''

Chester found himself nodding. "But for now," she continued briskly, "we can at least get it down for a closer look. Mr. Shamuck—''

"Shattuck," the rancher corrected her.

"Yes, Mr. Shattuck . . . if you'll be good enough to bring it down the same way—and as gently—as you took it up, it will be a help to our preliminary examination.''

"Why should he?" inquired a new voice. "Is it yours?''

Everyone turned, saw Mrs. Shattuck walking toward them. She wore exactly the same attire as her husband.

"I guess if you're all goin' to stand out here in the cold and freeze, someone better be around to be ready to thaw you out.'' Startlingly youthful dark eyes focused on the older woman. "I asked you a question, honey.''

"Uh, no, not exactly, it doesn't," replied Goldberg, momentarily flustered by the abruptness of the question.

"What do you mean, 'not exactly'?"

"Well, while we didn't build it or . . . See here," Goldberg said, stiffening and trying to stay civil despite her mounting impatience at these irritating, continuing delays, "I don't think you realize quite what you have up in your hayloft."

"It should be clear to *anyone*," Tut added condescendingly, "that whatever it is, it is certainly not a Christmas decoration."

"No?" exclaimed Mrs. Shattuck, her gaze darting up to the softly humming semisphere. "How do you know? Don't you think it looks pretty up there, whatever kind of watchamacallit it really is?"

"Umm, actually, I suppose it does," confessed Tut, taken aback. He really hadn't pondered much on the artifact's aesthetic properties.

"You *admit* you don't own it," she pressed relentlessly, eyes flashing.

"We said we didn't *build* it," Tut argued, "but in the name of the United States government, as its representatives in the search for extraterrestrial life, we, uh, hereby claim it."

She looked away from him, her mouth twisted in a disdainful grimace. Her attention settled eventually on Chester as the one actually in charge.

"What about it, mister? Is that thing legally the property of the government?"

Chester started to reply, "I don't think there's any—" and he stopped, thoughtful.

"What is this, Major?" Goldberg wanted to know. "It does belong to us . . . and the government, doesn't it?"

After a considerable pause, Chester answered, "Frankly, I don't know. I'm a military man, Miss Goldberg, not a lawyer."

"That's what I thought," Mrs. Shattuck said, obviously satisfied. She glanced up at her husband. "Well, J.W.?"

The rancher turned and looked wordlessly at Chester.

" 'Watchamacallit,' she calls it!" sniffed Goldberg. "You actually don't know what it is, do you?"

"Oh, judgin' from who you say you are and what I can tell of it—" She jabbed a thumb toward the blinking

artifact. ''—I'd guess it's some kind of artificial un-
manned craft from off this world, probably from outside
our solar system. Just because we got television out here
doesn't mean we're ignorant, honey.''

''It doesn't look like it's government property, does
it?'' observed Shattuck softly. ''Not yet, anyway. Since
it come down on our property, I expect we'll hang on
to it for a bit.''

''Now, look here,'' Tut began heatedly, moving his
bulk forward. ''If you think for one minute that we're
going to let you hang on to the most important discovery
of the last five centuries just to satisfy your personal—
take your hand off me, Jean,'' he told his much smaller
associate.

''You bet your ass we're going to hang on to it, four-
eyes,'' Mrs. Shattuck informed him in no uncertain
terms.

''Excuse me,'' Chester said hurriedly to Shattuck.
''We don't mean to seem unfriendly. You must realize
you're going to have to give up the artifact eventually.
Why not make things simpler for us and yourselves and
let us take it away. Tomorrow, say.''

''I might just have let you do that an hour ago,'' the
rancher told him with a significant glance at the fuming
Tut and Goldberg. ''But at this point I'm feeling sort of
ornery. So, no offense, mind, but I think we'll hang on
to it for a while.'' He gazed up at the barn.

''It looks mighty pretty up there, in the middle of the
other lights. Right in keeping with the season.''

''No offense,'' agreed Chester amiably, though his
mind was churning unhappily at the turn events had
taken. ''You understand we'll have to take official action
to obtain the artifact.''

''I understand you've got to do what you think is
right,'' Shattuck concurred. ''Now, if you want to check
the legality of it all, I expect you'll want to talk to the
sheriff over in Breckenridge. Name's Amos Biggers. You
go talk to him and let me know what he says.''

''We'll do that, and thank you,'' Chester replied. He
turned to face the vivacious, defiant woman standing
nearby. Hands on hips, she stared evenly back at him.

''Thanks for the coffee and pie offer, ma'am. I hope I

can take you up on it under more pleasant circumstances." She softened somewhat, even smiled back at him.

"Maybe so. If you're goin' to Breckenridge, watch yourself. Some of the roads that way are still pretty icy. We don't want you happy folks to go pile up in a ditch somewhere the middle of this cold night." Her smile widened.

"No, we don't want that," agreed Chester. Turning, he shepherded the scientists back toward the station wagon. They protested every step of the way.

Goldberg was beside herself. "Who do these . . . these cattle people think they are? Who do you think you are, Major? Are you here as our aide, to help us, or not? I think maybe a few words to your superior officer—"

"We'll do what we can, Miss Goldberg," Chester announced, fighting to keep his temper in check, "but we'll do it legally. When you calm down, you'll see this is the best way. You might also recall that if any situation requires the use of force, then I'm wholly in charge. You may complain to General MacGregor if that's what you want."

"Well, I'll think about it," she grumbled, climbing into the car.

"Really, Major Chester," exclaimed Tut from the back of the wagon as the engine turned over, "how can we simply leave like this? They might do anything with the artifact after we're gone." He nodded toward the ranch house.

"They could bury it somewhere in one of these endless fields. If it doesn't generate sufficient radiation of a type we can detect, we might never locate it. Or he could be overcome by a bumpkin's curiosity and try to take it apart. He might ruin it completely. The importance, the knowledge at stake here . . ." He shook his head in disbelief.

"This situation is absolutely insane. This would never happen in Massachusetts."

"That's right, Mr. Tut," admitted Chester, turning to look back over the seat as they backed up and the sergeant sent the car toward the highway. "This isn't Massachusetts. And if you don't believe me—" He pointed toward the house receding to one side and behind them. "—look over there, toward the front door. You'll see a very big teenage boy standing there with a rifle about as big as he is. He's been there ever since we started toward the barn.

"You don't go around threatening people out here, Mr. Tut. They don't look kindly on it, and they have a strong sense of right and wrong. If you and Miss Goldberg could have been a little more polite and acted less like barons of the fief, we might have been spared all this. It's too late now, though. You challenged that man, and he reacted."

"More polite, he says," Goldberg finally sputtered violently. "In the face of that, he asks us to be polite!"

Chester sighed and settled himself back in his seat alongside the driver. "Now we're going to have to get proper legal confirmation of our claim. That means telling at least one new person about the craft's landing. And this was supposed to be kept quiet." He glanced sharply over his left shoulder. "Or have you all forgotten that in your haste to get at the thing?"

"All right, sir, so it's supposed to be kept quiet, sir," fumed Tut. "So let's do this quietly . . . *quietly* contact Fort Hood and have a couple of truckloads of troops brought in. Show the locals a bit of force. We'll show them that—"

Chester cut him off, shaking his head steadily. "You don't seem to understand, Mr. Tut. Not only isn't this Massachusetts, it's not Cam Ranh Bay or Saigon—or Moscow, either. We don't want these people talking to the media, now or later.

"Calm down and relax, and we'll salvage this business. Oh, I don't think you have to worry about this Shattuck burying or breaking into your precious UFO, either. Believe me, I'm just as anxious to get at its insides as you are."

"Why aren't you worried?" Goldberg asked challengingly.

"Because they *like* the craft up there in the hayloft, lighting up their little 'Noel' sign and showing off the rest of their Christmas decorations. They didn't chase us off because they're planning anything underhanded. They did it because they think they're in the right.''

Chester would have been interested in the family meeting the Shattucks were conducting as the station wagon skidded and bumped and bounced its frigid way toward distant Breckenridge. The result of that meeting was a long-distance phone call that Mrs. Shattuck placed to San Francisco.

Sheriff Biggers of Breckenridge was built like a tarnished fireplug. Enormous arms stuck out of his long white shirt, currently rolled up to his elbows. They were coated with a healthy crop of red curls, as was his head. He had the look of a man who'd worked hard all his life and would continue to do so until his body finally betrayed him.

His voice, however, was a surprise, as gentle and smooth as processed cheese. ''You say this thing landed on Shattuck's property, hmm? I know J.W. and his missus.'' Biggers chuckled at a private thought. ''The wrong people to get riled, Major.''

''But surely you can see the importance to us of this discovery, Sheriff,'' Goldberg broke in ingratiatingly from the back of the office. ''This represents our first contact with another intelligent civilization. We *must* be allowed to examine it.''

''Yes, I can see all that, ma'am,'' admitted Biggers, scratching a thick ear. ''Trouble is, as near as I can see, the Shattucks have a right to it, since it came down on their land.'' He spread his hands in an expansive gesture of helplessness.

''If J.W. wants to lay a claim to it, I don't see as how I can legally go in and take it away from them.''

''This is ridiculous,'' snorted Tut, turning away in mounting frustration. ''Utterly ridiculous!''

''That it may be,'' conceded the sheriff, ''but I've heard that about plenty of laws. Ridiculous or not, they all seem to stand up in court. Now, if you want me to go out to J.W.'s and take that spaceship or whatever it is away from him, you'd better find me some legal grounds to do it with.''

''There is, naturally, no precedent for such a matter,''

mused Calumet thoughtfully. "If we could obtain a writ from a high authority giving you permission, from the capital, say. An order from the governor of the state of Texas ought to suffice, don't you think?"

Biggers nodded very slowly, impressed. "If you can get me that, I'd certainly be bound to go in and enforce it, son."

Chester looked at the younger scientist with fresh respect. "Can you do that?"

"I think so." The Cajun physicist smiled shyly. "May I use your telephone, Sheriff?"

"I'd like to let you, Mr. Calumet, but," he said apologetically, "the county budget's been kind of tight lately. They keep a tight watch on how we spend our money. There's a pay phone just outside the station."

Calumet grinned. "That will do." The three scientists left the office, leaving Chester and the sheriff seated across from each other. The driver sat impassively nearby.

"I don't think I've ever seen three people quite as excited as that bunch of yours," Biggers said conversationally.

"They have reason to be excited, Sheriff. If I didn't have so many other things to worry about, I'd be just as excited and anxious as they are."

A moment's silence, then Biggers leaned forward suddenly and spoke in a fashion new to Chester. "You know, I've been a sheriff, deputy and chief, in this county for close on thirty-five years now, and not once in those thirty-five years did I have occasion to think I might be making the wrong decision." He looked across at the major.

"What do you think? Should I go take that thing from J.W. without waiting for proper authority?"

The honesty and forthrightness that would keep Joe Chester from ever making brigadier replied, "I wouldn't go against thirty-five years' judgment, Chief."

Biggers leaned back in his frayed swivel chair, pleased and relieved. "That's what I was hoping you'd say, Major." He drew a plug of tobacco from his shirt pocket, bit a hunk off, and offered the same to Chester.

The major waved it away with a smile. "No thanks, never tried the stuff."

"You should," Biggers told him, his mouth full of juice. "Helped me give up cigarettes thirty years ago." He smiled a wide, brown-stained smile. "Also helped me get rid of my first wife." And he leaned over and spit delicately into a cuspidor hidden behind the old desk.

Calumet hadn't been bragging. He knew the right people in Austin, but even so, the wheels of government creaked instead of spinning. It was several days before the formal document, dutifully signed by the governor, arrived at the post office in Breckenridge.

Thus armed, the little group set out again for the Shattuck ranch, accompanied by a second car that held a deputy and a reluctant Sheriff Biggers.

It also held Josiah Chester. The second car provided him with a way of avoiding the company of the three complaining scientists. They'd had him crawling the walls of the country motel the past few days while they waited for the state order to arrive. He enjoyed the chance to ride instead with the soft-spoken sheriff for a change.

"Do you think we'll have any trouble?" Chester was asking him.

Biggers didn't have to consider the question. "Naw. J.W.'s a good man. Stubborn, sure, and at that only half as stubborn as his missus, but they're good law-abiding folks. J.W. will read every word of that writ"—he gestured at the formal-looking envelope resting on the patrol car's dash—"and then his wife'll read it, and then he'll shrug and say, 'What's got to be will be.' And then he'll do his damnedest to help you get that thing out of his barn and loaded for you.

"A shame I have to do this. You folks shouldn't have tried to push them around."

"Not me," corrected Chester quickly. "My charges let their excitement run away with them."

"I guess I can understand that," declared the sheriff sympathetically. "I'm looking forward to seeing this visitor from Mars myself."

"Not Mars," Chester corrected gently. "We're fairly sure it's from much farther out than Mars."

"Is that God's truth?" Biggers murmured. "Me, I still can't believe in radio."

It was late afternoon hurrying toward evening when the two cars pulled into the open area before the sprawling Shattuck home. This time it was Mrs. Shattuck who was first out to greet them, wiping dirty hands on the seat of her jeans. They were surely the same ones, Chester reflected, that she'd been wearing days ago, only they'd been washed in the interval.

"Expected to see you back sooner than this," she said by way of hello.

"We moved as fast as we could," Goldberg assured her, the touch of frost in her voice nicely matching that in the air.

"I'll bet you did," said the younger woman. She turned, roared toward the house. "David! Go find your father. Tell him the eggheads from Houston are back!"

Chester repressed a smile even as Tut and Calumet winced, while Goldberg grew more superior than before.

"Hello, Amos," Mrs. Shattuck said to the sheriff.

He tapped the brim of his hat as he replied. "Afternoon, Beth. I'm sorry about this."

"Damn silly of you. We told these folks to look you up. Now, don't you worry about a thing, Amos. You just do what you have to do."

"I thought you'd say something like that, Beth."

She looked impatiently behind her, standing on tiptoe to see over a fence. "Now, where's J.W.—that tank inlet filter ought to be fixed by now."

"Is that it?" the sheriff asked Chester, pointing toward the barn. His voice was touched with awe.

The multiple-faced craft sat as before on the lip of the hayloft, still shining as brightly as before. Its multiple patterns of inlaid lights continued their steady, exotic blinking. Even this far away Chester could hear the faint mechanical beat from within.

Hmm-hmm-hmm . . . buzz-hmm-buzz . . . tick! Hmm-hmm-hmm . . . buzz-hmm-buzz . . . tick!

"Sure is pretty," was the sheriff's first and only comment.

"Ain't it, though?" agreed Beth Shattuck. "Fits in

right nice with the rest of the lights." Sarah Goldberg gave her a venomous glare.

"That J.W.?" asked the sheriff.

Beth Shattuck turned and looked. "That's him." Her extraordinary voice rent the air again. "Hurry up, dammit!"

Chester recognized the tall, lanky figure of Jesse Shattuck but not the man accompanying him. Both were dressed alike in flannel shirts, dirt-encrusted jeans, and well-used work shoes, although those worn by the stranger were not nearly as scuffed and battered as the rancher's. Something else didn't fit. The man's long white sideburns were too neatly clipped, his demeanor different even at a distance. His face was pink instead of earthenware-red like Shattuck's.

"Howdy," the rancher said, greeting Chester. He ignored the scientists, nodded once at the sheriff. "Hello, Amos."

"J.W.," the sheriff murmured. "Who's your friend?"

"Oh, this is an old acquaintance of the missus, Amos. Mr. Wheaton, meet Sheriff Biggers."

"I'm pleased," the smaller, softer man said, shaking hands. He had a voice like an off-tune organ, cracked but powerful. He shook hands with Chester, stepped back.

"Would your first name by any chance be Cable?" asked Jean Calumet uncertainly.

"By any chance I am unable to deny it," the man replied.

Chester revised his initial appraisal of the newcomer again. He was not, he decided firmly, a handyman.

Mentally he removed flannel shirt, dirty pants, and shoes from Wheaton, substituted a slightly loud three-hundred-dollar suit, and combed the white hair. Meanwhile Calumet had turned to speak to Beth Shattuck.

"How do you and Mr. Wheaton happen to know one another?"

She smiled magnificently at him. "Cable was my agent's lawyer. Still is, I think."

" 'Agent'?" echoed the young scientist awkwardly.

Chester studied the rancher's wife intently, noted the flashing black eyes, the elegant ebony mane, and the still striking figure.

"The Story of Joshua," he said abruptly, *"Idyllwild River."* She was smiling at him now, a smile he recognized fully. That film about sulky racing . . . He snapped his fingers in remembrance.

"Something Beauty," he murmured.

"American Beauty," she told him, nodding approval. "I quit acting when I turned fourteen, though. J.W. was working for a contractor in California. After the war we came back out here. His country—mine now." She gestured at the spacious ranch house, the sturdy old barn, and the land beyond.

"It's not Hollywood, thank God."

"This is all very interesting," broke in Goldberg impatiently. "While I'm certain we'd all *love* to listen to the details of Mrs. Shattuck's career, we have something rather more important to deal with." She looked expectantly at Biggers.

"Sheriff?"

"I know, ma'am, I know." He turned and walked back to the patrol car. When he returned, he had the fancy envelope in one hand. This he opened and handed the contents apologetically but firmly to Shattuck.

"J.W., this here's an order from the governor directing you to turn that alien satellite, extratres—" He stopped trying to recite the contents of the note and concluded, "Whatever it is, you're supposed to let these folks take it away with them."

"Let me see that, Jesse," murmured the church-organ voice of Wheaton. Shattuck handed the paper to the smaller man, watched as he skimmed through the long document.

Tut and Calumet grew restless as the study continued. Goldberg ignored the proceedings, her gaze fixed on the multisided, radiant object ensconced in the hayloft opening.

Eventually Wheaton looked up, smiled. "This is very interesting, Sheriff, Major Chester. As long as we're exchanging missives . . ." He reached into the back pocket of his pants and withdrew a thick roll of paper. Opening the roll up, he shook the dry Texas dust from it. Chester counted an impressive number of attached sheets.

"Let's see what we've got here," Wheaton began as he flipped one page after another. "This one here is a restraining order forbidding any representative of any agency of the United States government, or any other government, from removing any item whatsoever from the property henceforth called the Shattuck ranch. Attached is a map of said ranch and copy of the title deed, going back to 1874." Wheaton looked up at Shattuck. "Fine man, your grandfather, Jesse."

He continued turning pages, mumbling to himself just low enough so that Chester couldn't decipher his words. "Here," he continued, more lucidly, "is a court order granting temporary title to the object, or device, said object or device to be referred to in all proceedings henceforth as the 'extraterrestrial artifact,' jointly to Jesse William Shattuck and family. Permission is given for them to do with said extraterrestrial artifact as they please, understanding that they will do all in their power to maintain said artifact in good condition." Again his eyes met Chester's.

"That means they can turn it over to you if they so desire, or they can use it for a doorstop, a conversation piece, or even a Christmas ornament." He returned his attention to new pages.

"Any objection to the aforementioned order or orders shall be submitted for consideration by any individual or government agency to the proper legal authorities." Wheaton handed the sheaf of paper to a thoroughly awed Biggers.

"You can see there, Sheriff, that all included forms and orders are signed by Justices A. Hammond and D. G. Lamar of the Supreme Court of the State of Texas. I believe they take precedence even over an executive directive of the governor's.

"Of course," he added pleasantly, "the governor can always declare a state of emergency and call out the National Guard to come seize my client's property. He's welcome to do so. However—" He turned to face an increasingly nervous Chester. "—I believe that might result in a touch more publicity than any of us would like."

"Let's see," he mused speculatively, "the government rides in to steal legally claimed property from its discoverers. We could have some nice posed shots of the Shattucks standing on their front porch while Guard troops in helmets and full battle gear stand lined up across from them, machine guns and bazookas at the ready to deal with this massive threat to the American way of life. That would look impressive, say, on the front page of *The Washington Post*. What do you think, Major?''

All eyes focused on Chester, attention he could have done without. Hopefully he looked at Biggers, but the sheriff wanted nothing to do with that ream of legal documentation.

''As far as I can see, I've been overruled, Major. I'm willin' to do what you think best, though.''

Thanks a whole lot, Chester thought. ''I think,'' he ventured after a brief pause, ''we'd better go back to Breckenridge and consider this very carefully.''

Perham Tut made a noise Chester wouldn't have thought was in him. He held his temper in check, managing also to ignore the low stream of bitter curses falling from Goldberg's lips. Calumet said nothing. He was eyeing Wheaton respectfully.

''We'll be back, of course,'' Chester added, trying to salvage something from the meeting. Wheaton didn't appear fazed.

''I expect so. But if you'll excuse us—'' He glanced up at the rancher. ''—we'll have to hurry, Jesse, if we're going to get that new pipe put in before sundown.''

Shattuck nodded. Both men turned and headed for the rear of the house as the disgruntled scientists piled back into the station wagon.

''What now?'' Goldberg wanted to know as they chugged and bumped back toward Breckenridge. ''In the papers we don't want anything, or a long court fight, either.''

''United States of America versus J. W. Shattuck and family,'' Calumet added. Chester winced at the field day the papers would have with that one. ''Uncle Colossus and the Hitlerian physicists against just plain country folks. No, Major, we have to find another way.''

''I'm open to suggestions,'' admitted Chester tersely.

It was silent in the car for several minutes. ''Washington is still expecting to hear from us,'' the young chemist continued. "It occurs to me that we have preserved secrecy very well. No one knows yet that we've actually located the spacecraft."

Chester started. Calumet was right. Only the five of them—and Sheriff Biggers—knew that an alien craft had set down on the planet in one piece.

"I think it's time, Major, to bring larger forces to bear," Calumet went on briskly. "You'd best notify your General MacGregor and also the Pentagon. I'll want all three of us to speak with NASA headquarters. When more important people realize what we've found and convey it to *their* superiors, we should be able to persuade these people to give up the craft voluntarily."

"From what I've seen," Chester mused, "neither Shattuck nor his wife persuades too easily. Who'd you have in mind to try and persuade them?"

"The President," Calumet said, staring out the front windshield past Chester. "It will take several days for those other people I mentioned to convince him of the urgency of the matter. After he is convinced, I'm sure he'll rush to cooperate with us."

"What about Wheaton?"

Calumet frowned. "He's going to be a problem. He's just obstinate and smart enough to make trouble. But the President can be a pretty persuasive man. He might be able to convince even a maverick legal genius like Cable Wheaton that it would be in the best interests of his clients to allow matters to take their natural and inevitable course . . . quietly." He leaned back in the seat.

"For example, I've always heard that Wheaton aspires to sit on the Supreme Court some day. A President has a lot of options at his command. Who knows what pressures, benign and otherwise, he might bring to bear?"

What, indeed? wondered a benumbed Chester, feeling way out of his depth and wishing fervently he was back home before the family fireplace with Charlene and the kids.

Hmm-hmm-hmm . . . buzz-hmm-buzz . . . tick! sang the yellow blossom out of the galactic vastnesses from its snug perch in the barn loft.

High above, the moon had commenced its descent, but

the stars still shone bright and clear. Several hours remained until sunrise. Nothing stirred on the grounds of
the ranch.

On the farm road up from the ranch house a large
eighteen-wheeler slowed and stopped, pulling onto the
road shoulder. Its headlights dimmed. Back doors
opened, and a ramp slid out. A tight knot of men moved
quickly down the ramp, ran forward.

At the cab of the truck they were joined by a bigger,
older man. Plans were discussed in muted voices.
Clutching various instruments of a nonscientific nature, they began moving, crouched low but still running,
toward the ranch house.

Behind them activity continued as other men within
the truck struggled silently to rig a mobile winch and
sling in expectation of the others' return.

As was usual lately, Chester was having a difficult time
sleeping. The Korean and Vietnam wars had made light
sleepers out of many men. He woke as he found himself
reaching across the mattress for the woman who wasn't
there.

Rubbing his eyes, he rolled over and stared at the ceiling. Once again unarguably, helplessly awake, he slid his
legs to the side and sat up.

The three scientists, he knew, would be sound asleep
in their respective rooms. The budget for this kind of
endeavor provided for privacy for all concerned.

Disgusted with himself, envious of their ability to
sleep, and unhappy with the way events had gone the last
couple of days, he wrestled his fatigued form into his
clothes. A check of his watch showed the wrong side of
four A.M.—an insane hour.

Down the main street was a twenty-four-hour café fre-
quented by off-freeway truckers. He filled his pockets
with the usual paraphernalia without which a man felt
unbalanced: wallet, keys, pocketknife, and small flashlight.

He would, he decided, have a couple of cups of coffee,
stretch them out for as long as possible, read the morning
paper from Dallas, and then maybe eat some breakfast.

Hopefully he could at least prolong things until the sun came up.

He closed the motel-room door behind him, not bothering to lock it. That was one of the advantages of living outside a city. Partway through the motel lot he paused, thinking. This morning his loneliness was particularly strong. A little company would do him good.

The soft-spoken companionship of the sergeant was more to his liking that that of the scientists, who would be downright uncommunicative this time of the morning, even Calumet.

Turning, he walked two units past his own room and knocked on the door of number six. It was possible the sergeant was already awake. Chester had encountered him down at the truck stop several times, often before he arrived himself. He wondered if Pat had as much trouble sleeping as he did.

There was no response, and he knocked again, louder. One last time. It was just as well, he decided. Pat was probably down at the café already and would be glad to see him.

But when he arrived, a quick search of the small dining area showed no sign of the sergeant. Chester took a seat, thinking perhaps that Pat was in the men's room. Ten minutes of waiting dispelled the likelihood of that.

Chester was puzzled. No place else in town except the gas station across the street would be open for several hours, and he could see that the sergeant wasn't lingering there, chatting with the sleepy attendant.

Prompted by something stronger than just curiosity, he left his coffee half-finished and strolled back to the motel. Further knocks, verging on pounding, produced no response from within number six. The station wagon was still parked in front of the room.

Had the sergeant gone off on some errand of his own? That seemed unlikely, since he was under strict orders to be available to drive at any time.

Chester made a decision he regretted in advance. Probably he'd come out looking the fool, he thought as he walked toward the office. There he woke the groggy manager-owner of the motel and borrowed the duplicate key to room six.

He opened the room. The sergeant was not in bed. Nor was he in the bathroom, hiding in a closet, or elsewhere about. Chester checked the bed carefully, noted that it hadn't been slept in.

"Lookin' for your friend, the big fella?"

Chester spun, reaching for the pistol at his hip that wasn't there. It was only the bathrobe-clad form of the motel manager.

Chester forced himself to relax, startled at how tense he was. "Yes, of course," he explained.

"Could have told you 'bout him," the manager declared with an air of superiority. "Heard a noise out back a couple of hours ago . . . don't know exactly when. Didn't look at my clock. I'm used to engines wakin' me up. Get a lot of folks come in the middle of the night.

"There was this big rig pulled up behind the back rooms. It struck me funny, you know? Because there's no reason for a truck to pull in here. Truckers, they sleep in their cabs and park behind the night station 'cross the street. Never had a one take a room here.

"I saw a couple of fellas get out. They met somebody else . . . big fella, coulda been your friend. They yakked a minute or two, then all climbed in and drove off together. Didn't see nothin' to make noise about, so I went back to bed."

"You're sure it was my friend?" Chester asked tightly.

"Nope. Said it coulda been," the manager replied. "But I am sure of one thing."

"What's that?"

"I'm still tired." He turned and walked back toward his office, leaving Chester standing paralyzed with anxiety in front of an ominously deserted room number six.

He whirled finally, ran to the phone, and stopped with one hand about to pick up the receiver. Part of the conversation he'd had with the sheriff as he'd driven out to the ranch came back to him.

"They sure like their privacy," Biggers had told him. "They've got a TV, all right, and radio. But they pipe and filter their water out of their tank, and they've got their own generator for power. There are gas lines running all over that part of the county, and J.W. sneaks some of what they need from here and there. No telephone, though. No real contact with the outside world except for the mail.''

No telephone, Chester thought frantically. His hand left the receiver. The three scientists would have to be told eventually, of course. But not now, not yet.

He picked up the phone, firmly this time, and dialed. There was a pause and a click, and a voice said, "Post operator. May I help you, sir?"

"This is Major Josiah Chester. I have an emergency call for General MacGregor. He'll be at his home now, operator.''

About an hour to have troops here, MacGregor had told him. But that had been over a month before. Were the helicopter-borne special units still standing by?

They'd better be, he thought grimly.

The cluster of seven men had reached the entrance to the open, flat area in front of the house and barn. It was well lit by the steady glow from the alien device. Each man was clad entirely in black and had black streaked across cheeks, forehead, and other projecting parts of his face.

Turning, the big man in the lead caught the attention of his companions. "If possible, no killing," he instructed them. "If you must, do it fast.''

Someone in the back of the group spoke up. "What about using the guns? Should we—''

"It doesn't matter. There's no one near enough to hear, and even if there were, people here fire off guns all the time. That's one thing we don't have to worry about, but I'd prefer to avoid any killing.''

"Why?" a coldly casual voice asked.

"It's always better to be neat than sloppy," the leader explained. He pointed toward the house, moving his gaze from one man to another. "You, you, you, and you, form a semicircle from the front to the rear side of the house. I don't think there are any other doors.

"You two, get out the suppressant. I can see the dogs from here, sleeping on the front porch. Move fast. They might not wake up in time to do much barking. The rest of you come with me to the barn.''

Short nods all around. This group was not given much

to talking. Each was a professional, knew his job. They moved forward.

Cotton, the setter, raised his head at the rapid approach of the strange human. The scent was unfamiliar, and so was the face. As he started to growl softly, Gin also woke.

Something went *puff* in the setter's face. In his dog fashion he felt an overwhelming tiredness. Quickly and quietly, both animals fell asleep again.

Already the three men in the lead had reached the base of the barn. Like a sphere full of jewels, the alien craft shone above the foil sign, tiny, far duller decorative lights strung to either side of it.

Hmm-hmm-hmm . . . buzz-hmm-buzz . . . tick! Hmm-hmm-hmm . . . buzz-hmm-buzz . . . tick! it murmured mechanically.

"Got the roll?" the leader inquired. One of the two men with him smiled, patted the pack on his back. It contained a fine, superstrong mesh net and equally strong cables. The rancher had clearly used the hay winch and pulley arrangement to raise the craft into the loft. It would serve conveniently for getting it down again. The other man started to assemble the tiny collapsing cart strapped to his back.

If all went well, they would have the precious device down and set on the cart in a few minutes. The family would sleep on peacefully, hearing and seeing nothing. In the morning they would miss it, but by then it would be on its way out of the country.

They opened the barn door quietly, with a minimum of squeaks, thanks to the judicious use of the oilcan brought for just that purpose. Everything had been thought of and carefully planned out.

There was movement inside, and the two men froze, but it was only the uneasy shuffling of the two horses and the cows inside.

They mounted the metal ladder leading to the hayloft, were joined soon by the third man. The leader watched as they worked, looking with satisfaction out toward the road, where the truck sat waiting.

One man used a convenient rake to pull the hay cable into the loft. He started to arrange the net over the device while his companion sought to slip the net underneath it where possible. This finished, he hung by his arms from the stout support beam and oiled the pulley.

The net was attached by cables to the pulley hook, much as a bale of hay would be. The leader leaned out and beckoned. Leaving his position in front of the house, the nearest of four guards ran over to the barn. The leader met him in front of the doors. Together they took up the slack in the thick rope running through the pulley.

A signal to the men above produced a wave in response. In the loft, both men sought to make sure the device was well encased in the net. It remained only to slide it a little to the right and then to lock the net shut beneath.

The larger of the two put both hands against the side of the glowing yellow artifact and shoved gently to fit it perfectly in the net. It wasn't terribly heavy and started to move without trouble.

Unexpectedly, the yellow glow intensified to a brightness that drowned out the hundreds of lights set inside. Both men were tossed aside as if by a giant hand. Neither let out a squeal, a yell, or so much as a deep breath. But each lay unconscious, one in a very unnatural position. They continued to breathe softly, but they did not move.

Below, the leader had let go of the rope at the moment of the flash. He'd seen at least one of the men in the loft thrown backward, and now he cursed silently to himself. A muttered order to his companion sent the other man toward the barn door.

Hmm-hmm-hmm . . . buzz-hmm-buzz . . . tick! Tick! Ticka-mmmmmmmm . . .

The yellow glow increased further, and the steady song of the device changed to a steady, rich whine. As he put a hand on the barn door, something that looked like a thick yellow wire reached down from the device. It was not metal, however. It wasn't even solid. If it was light, it did not behave in the manner of light. It curved and bent at odd angles.

It touched the man on the chest. He stood frozen for a moment as the light ran halolike over his body. When the light went away, he collapsed, making a slight noise as though a bit of carrot or chicken bone had become caught in his throat.

His eyes never moving from the alien object, although by now the yellow glow was almost too strong to look at, the leader began backing slowly away from the barn. The yellow cable had not vanished. It continued to twist and turn like wire, though he could see through it easily.

The tenuous tentacle started to move along the ground in front of the barn, occasionally touching the ground like a dog hunting for a scent. When it touched earth, little puffs of dirt would jump explosively though silently into the air, as if a bullet had struck ground.

Backing away faster, the leader called to his men, not caring now if those in the house heard him. The thread abruptly swung over his head and touched one of the men guarding the house. He dropped his gun, and his hands went to his neck where the yellow light had touched him as he fell forward.

Now the leader had turned and was running, running, his heart pounding with fear of the unknown. He wanted to scream but couldn't spare the wind. The light continued moving over his head.

At last he reached the truck. Someone leaned out of the cab, waving wildly at him. As he did so, the yellow light passed through the glass windshield and touched him. He slumped, his upper body, head, and arms dangling over the door.

Like a live thing, the thread moved to the back of the truck and touched the man who stood paralyzed there. Then it curled around and began probing inside the open trailer.

Changing his course, the leader found himself sprinting through the dark brush. Prickly pear and Spanish sword tore at his neat black coveralls, and he felt blood running down his legs. Something heavy yet not oppressive tickled the middle of his back. It felt uncannily like a smooth finger rubbing his spine. He smelled marzipan and felt himself falling before he started to fall.

Nothing stirred outside the Shattuck house.

Mmmmmmm-ticka, tick! tick! Hmm-hmm-hmm . . . buzz-hmm-buzz . . . tick!

* * *

Chester ignored the noise in the seat behind him as he piloted the station wagon recklessly along the familiar road out of Breckenridge. They should arrive at the same time as the copters from Fort Hood. He underestimated the commotion his early-morning call to the general had caused.

Considerable confusion reigned when they drove up to the ranch. The units had already arrived. More people than the land there had ever felt at one time were roaming around the ranch buildings and surrounding ground.

Two big transport helicopters were settled like monster beetles on the road ahead. Armed men with many-patched uniforms and funny hats milled about in confusion.

Chester was the last out of the station wagon as he cut the engine before the ranch house. All three scientists were already heading at their respective top speeds for the barn. Their worries, and Chester's, turned out to be groundless.

Even from here he could see the alien device resting in its former position high up in the hayloft; despite the noise, he could hear it humming its atonal hymn. Gem lights winked on and off within a globe of moon.

His first thought satisfied, he turned his attention to the house, headed toward it.

A smartly clad ranger blocked his path with a slim M-18. "Sorry, sir, no one permitted past this point without authorization."

Chester fumbled for identification, trying to locate the proper cards and peer past the bulk of the soldier as well. "I'm Major Josiah Chester," he explained, "Air Force Intelligence. I'm the one who placed the emergency call that brought you all out here."

The soldier listened impassively, noncommittally. It was the printed identification that pleased him. After a careful study, he stepped aside. "Go on in, Major."

The first thing he saw in the big living room was a very alive Beth Shattuck and a long row of bodies. They were of indeterminate nationality and size, alike only in their clothing. Some lay frozen in odd positions. They looked like a family of ravens worked on by a not-too-steady-handed taxidermist.

"Mornin', Major," Beth Shattuck greeted him brightly. "Seems we've been invaded twice tonight." She indicated the row of near corpses. "First by these. Then by your friends. They are your friends, aren't they?" He nodded ruefully. "Then they come swooping down with the most god-awful yelling and hollering you can imagine. Like to scared the chickens plumb to death.

"Cotton and Gin woke up woozy right when it happened. They're both in David's room hiding under his bed, and nothing can get them out. I got tired of shoutin' at those two bitches, so I came out here. What's goin' on? Who are these ugly catatonics—" She gestured again at the row of bodies. "—and why the invasion? You folks tryin' to make a comedy picture or somethin'?"

"There's no comedy to it, Mrs. Shattuck," Chester told her softly as he moved from one softly breathing, motionless form to the next. He stopped at the one he was hunting for, turned it over. Frightened, angry eyes glared back at him helplessly.

"Excuse me, sir?"

Chester looked up from the limp form into the face of an earnest captain of special forces. He repeated his identification, verbal and written, for the officer's benefit.

The captain stood back while Chester went through the sergeant's pockets, acutely aware of those eyes following him. Other than that, the big man didn't twitch a muscle, though Chester could feel as well as hear the man breathing.

There was nothing in the man's pockets that proved particularly instructive, unless it was the exceedingly large amount of cash. He fondled a bent, smudged card on which numbers were listed for girlfriends, bowling alleys, and restaurants. Odd, but all the numbers were out of state.

It might have been his imagination, but it seemed to Chester that when he handled that particular item the sergeant's eyes widened slightly. He handed the card to the captain, along with the cash and the rest of the items.

"While Intelligence is running checks on these people and their identities, have them research the numbers on that card, delicately. They might turn up some interesting people at the other end of each of them."

"Yes, sir," acknowledged the captain, saluting respectfully.

"Now, what happened here?" Chester asked him.

"Nothing, sir. We flew out as fast as we could, putting on our boots on board ship. Someone got somebody big awfully excited."

"That was me," Chester told him.

"We'd been standing by for weeks," the captain went on, "told to be ready for an unspecified emergency. When we got the call, we were ordered to prepare to land shooting. But when we came in, no one challenged us.

"We found these—" He indicated the bodies, a couple of which were beginning to twitch. "—scattered between that barn, all along the road up to a big semi—I don't know if you can see it in the darkness, sir."

"We passed it coming in," Chester said.

"There's a fancy sling and winch arrangement inside the rear trailer of it, sir, along with a pile of legitimate cargo—cover, we presume. We were informed on the way about the satellite."

Chester did not enlighten the captain further. "It seems pretty obvious they came here to steal it, sir. We've spent most of our time waiting for someone to give us new orders." He looked hopefully at Chester.

"Load up your men, go home, and forget about this morning," the major instructed him. "You've done your job." He gestured with a thumb at the now stirring, moaning bodies nearby. "Make sure these are turned over to base intelligence for 'debriefing.' " His stress on the last word was peculiar.

"If they *can* be debriefed. What happened to them?"

"Just a minute, sir." The captain turned, shouted to a man bent over one of the forms. He rose, walked over to join them. Chester noted the captain's bars and medical insignia on his field uniform.

"Never saw anything quite like it," was his response to Chester's questions. "Full paralysis of every voluntary muscle. Those necessary to maintain the life functions are operating normally."

"Any idea what caused it?"

"None." The doctor shook his head slowly. "I can't imagine what happened."

"I can," said a soft voice. All three officers turned, looked out the front door.

Shattuck, obviously bored and annoyed with the whole business, was standing and watching the milling soldiers. His son sat curled nearby on a swing bench. There was a kitten in his lap.

Chester had noticed the abundance of half-wild cats swarming about the ranch on his first arrival. Now, though, it occurred to him to wonder how the cats and farm fowl coexisted. He mentioned it to the rancher.

"That's what I'm talking about," Shattuck said, pleased. "It's just like the coyote."

"What coyote?" Chester asked.

"Normally the dogs keep them well clear of the hen-house," the rancher explained. "But when it gets as cold as it's been lately, we let them sleep on the porch. I wouldn't put a good dog out in the snow any more than I would a good man.

"Those damn coyotes are smart enough to know when the dogs are tied up here instead of out back. That's when they come in quick and quiet, and I end up losing a hen a week. I'd rather do that than lose Cotton or Gin. They're part of the family."

"I understand," a new voice said. Chester saw that Jean Calumet had left the barn to join the little group on the porch. "I've got three dogs myself, back home. Don't have the temperature problems you do, though."

Shattuck examined the younger man with a fresh eye. "Where you from, son?"

"Little town near Baton Rouge," came the reply. Shattuck nodded as if that explained everything.

"About the coyote," Chester reminded the rancher curiously.

"Yeah. We came out one morning, a couple of days ago, and found two of them, a male and his bitch, lying side by side just outside the henhouse. They'd dug under the fence I'd put up around it. So I guess they'd already been inside and were coming out again, with one bird between them.

"When they come out, something had stopped them clean. They just lay there in the yard. I thought they were dead at first, but you could see their eyes move and that they were still breathing. So David and I took them way out behind the tank. When we checked them yesterday evening, we saw where they'd gotten up and run off. I don't expect them to come back again. Something shook them up pretty bad.

"Now, this doctor here has been saying that something knocked these fellows down and frazzled them good without killing them. They look just like those two coyotes."

"Make a note, Captain," Chester told the special forces officer, "of when we can expect them to come around again."

"Yes, sir."

Under the captain's direction, stretchers were used to ferry the motionless black-clad shapes to the waiting helicopters. When the *whup-whup* of many blades had faded to the south, Calumet spoke quietly to the rancher.

"You realize what this means, don't you, Mr. Shattuck?"

"Always did hate rhetorical questions," came the piercing voice of Beth Shattuck. "They're what pass for smarts in Hollywood. Ask a lot of questions that you can make other folk give the answers to and they think you're downright brilliant. Suppose you tell us what it means, good-lookin'."

Slightly unsettled at the compliment, Calumet wrestled with a reply. "It means," he finally burst out, "that that thing up in your hayloft is dangerous. It paralyzed a couple of animals, and now it's apparently done the same thing to a large group of armed men. I saw guns in the room. Did any of you hear a shot?"

"Can't say as we did," Shattuck confessed. Calumet smiled grimly.

"That means that the craft—" He pointed toward the glowing object up in the barn. "—incapacitated nearly a dozen experienced, no doubt ruthless individuals, whether they were directly in front of it or out on the road, before any of them could resist in any way. I believe any reasonable legal authority, on learning that, would classify the device as dangerous and order it removed by the proper supervisory personnel.

"What will your Mr. Wheaton have to say about that?" he finished.

"Don't know," Shattuck admitted.

"He was called back to San Francisco on business," his wife informed them, "but he'll be back if we need him, don't you worry. All we have to do is give him a call."

"Give him a call?" Chester looked confused. "I thought you didn't have a telephone out here."

"We don't. We got a lady in Cisco takes phone calls for us and relays them to the ranch via CB radio. We can get messages out the same way. One of them sent Cable hotfooting out of here two days ago. Took the plane from Abilene to Dallas and then out to the coast." Her expression turned angry.

"Now, that thing up there hasn't killed a soul. It didn't kill those coyotes, and I don't expect it really injured those men. But I can see how you could jumble it up in a court to where you'd make it look like the thing was dangerous."

"Please believe me, Mrs. Shattuck," Calumet pleaded, "we don't want to take anything that's rightfully yours. You'll be suitably reimbursed just for finding it, I promise in the name of the government. In fact, in a few days you should be hearing from—"

"The President?" David blurted from the swing. "Ah, he called two nights ago. It was something!"

"I see," murmured Calumet, clearly surprised. "Uh, what did he say?"

"Pretty much what you all have told us, Mr. Calumet," Shattuck informed them. "Went on about how important the proper study of that thing would be to the country. How I ought to do my patriotic duty and turn it over to you without causing anyone any trouble and about how, like you just said, the government would make things right by us." He paused.

"I told him that if he wanted to make things right by us, he ought to take a look at how our taxes have gone up here for the past eight years."

"What did he say?" inquired a fascinated Chester.

"Said he'd look into it. Sounded like he meant it, too." The rancher pulled a pipe from a shirt pocket, commenced stuffing it with tobacco. At least, Chester was fairly sure it was tobacco.

"Reckon he's no better and no worse than any other Washington politician. They all sound sincere. Anyhow," Shattuck finished, lighting up, "I told him we'd cooperate."

"You did!" Calumet seemed to rise off the ground, turned to shout toward the barn. "Sarah, Perry—we can have it."

"In four days time," Beth Shattuck put in. Calumet turned back, blinking.

"In four days? Why four days?"

"Well," she went on, since her husband was puffing away, "we don't believe like some folks do in keepin' the lights up until New Year's. It's Christmas we celebrate. People think it's kind of funny of us to take them down so early, but then, they think we're kind of funny, too."

"That's for sure," David put in, evidently relishing his family's notoriety.

"And they're right, for the most part," his mother went on. "For hereabouts, we *are* somethin' out of the ordinary. Of course, we think everybody *else* around is a bit crazy, so there's a nice balance struck."

"Four days," Calumet grumbled. "I suppose we can wait, but—" He indicated the empty living room. "—what if more of their types show up?"

"Now, I have to admit, that's a problem," agreed Shattuck, speaking around the stem of his pipe. "Soviets, you think?"

"Possibly," replied Chester guardedly. "One of them, their leader, was our driver. They knew exactly what was going on all the time, through him. But we've nothing so far to indicate who they were working for." He indicated the fluorescent alien craft.

"That would have been worth anybody's trouble. Sure, it might have been the Soviets, maybe the Chinese." To his surprise, he found he was chuckling. "Or perhaps the French, or the Rockefeller Foundation, I don't know. Whoever it was will find out how monumentally unsuccessful they were.

"So if you don't mind, just as a precaution, we'll post a suitable guard around the ranch for the next four days."

"You don't mean you're going to let them keep it up there?" a startled Calumet broke in.

"What difference will four days make, Mr. Calumet?" Chester wanted to know, speaking in a sharp military manner for the first time. He was feeling a little lightheaded. "Remember the unfavorable publicity we could generate. We don't want Mr. Wheaton flying back from San Francisco with a planeload of panting photographers drooling at his heels.

"When the proper time comes, I want to see the public informed of our discoveries through scientific journals and channels, as I'm certain you do—not through the *National Enquirer*. Besides, it appears that the device likes it here. Any attempt to move it before we understand what motivates it and we could all be lying like logs out in the yard there.

"Anyhow," he added at the crestfallen expression on the young scientist's face, "I don't see why we couldn't set up a few trailers here where you could study the device without having to move it . . . if the Shattucks will give us permission." He faced the rancher.

"Long as they don't go breaking it apart until after the twenty-fifth," Shattuck finally agreed. He knocked his pipe against a post, worked to refresh it. "After that they can take it apart to their heart's content." He turned and stared at the subject of the discussion.

"It sure seems a shame, though, as pretty as it is." He let out a deep sigh, then turned back to Chester. "Not that we object to being protected, you understand, but be sure your people stay outside our fence. I don't want them scaring the cows and tramping through the winter garden."

"Don't worry, Mr. Shattuck," Chester reassured him, glad to be on familiar ground again. "They'll be stationed well away from the house. Remember, we don't want to draw attention to you."

"That's okay, then," Shattuck agreed. "You can put your trailers over there, behind the greenhouse."

Chester turned, squinted into the darkness at a dull

white building across from the house. He hadn't paid much attention to it before.

"There are water outlets back there," Beth Shattuck told him. "You can hook your trailers up to them if you like. Tank's plenty full."

"Thank you. That's very hospitable of you," confessed Calumet, inclined to be friendly now. "What do you grow in your greenhouse, Mrs. Shattuck?" he asked politely. "Tomatoes, house plants?"

She shook her head once, pulled out a pipe that matched her husband's, and began filling it. "Nope. Tropical orchids. You'd be surprised what the market for fresh-grown orchids is in Dallas–Fort Worth. I've been experimentin' with some intriguing cross-pollination. I'll show you later if you're curious. Right now I'd better go catch up on my beauty sleep. I need all I can get these days." She turned and walked away, leaving the suave chemist standing open-mouthed.

The past several days Joe Chester had slept soundly. Tonight his sleep was especially deep, since he could rest secure in the knowledge that tomorrow the troublesome, fascinating alien device would be safely on its way via military helicopter to the Manned Space Center in Houston, allowing him to spend at least a portion of the holiday with his family.

So the shattering roar and subsequent rolling concussion came as even more of a shock than it would have in the weeks previous. Chester, wartime reactions still active, threw himself out of bed. He was on his feet and stumbling outside before the trailer cot had ceased trembling.

Freezing air formed a weathery gauntlet that stunned his still-warm skin even through the long woolen underwear. The numbness gradually gave way to a steady pounding.

A soft susurration rose from the surrounding knot of trailers as others came awake, uncertain queries volleying from trailer to trailer. A glance up and down the road showed distant lights winking on. There were two battalions of crack but nonetheless trigger-ready troops stationed around the ranch, and they would need to know soon what was going on.

"Oh, my God, no!" an agonized voice sounded nearby. Then Calumet was rushing past him, clad in pajamas and robe, his bare feet kicking up dirt and gravel behind him as he ran toward the barn.

Goldberg and Tut appeared shortly thereafter, the big physicist struggling to clear his eyes and adjust his glasses simultaneously. Goldberg simply stared, her mouth moving slowly. She shivered a little and looked her age.

A light had gone out of the barnyard.

In its explosive departure the spacecraft had taken the front half of the barn roof with it. Bits and pieces of wood were still raining down on them, clattering like hail on the metal roofs of the trailers and bouncing off the sprawling ranch house nearby. From the front porch the two dogs were barking and whining piteously.

Looking toward the house, he saw that all three Shattucks were standing there, gazing at the barn. At least, he reflected with stunned relief, they'd elected to display the device on the barn instead of their home.

"Due west," a shrill-soft tone sounded behind him. Following Goldberg's instructions, he turned his eyes to the western sky. A bright star was rising heavenward there, shrinking in intensity as he watched. It was gone quickly.

Goldberg sat down on the hard earth, her old flannel nightgown crumpling devotedly around her, and sobbed. Chester had no words to assuage the loss of a lifetime's opportunity.

Tut was trying to comfort her, but Chester could sense that the younger man was having difficulty holding back tears himself.

As was often true of people in shock, Chester was unaware of his own paralysis. With the clarity of the stunned he noted how only wisps of hay were falling now. He noticed as well that there was no fire in the combustible loft and that none of the fallen fragments of wood were so much as scorched. Their mechanical visitor's method of propulsion was as infinitely cold as the reaches it was once again traversing—cold and silent.

There'd been no muted roar of pitiful, primitive rockets, no whine of energy building. The initial *crack* had been the sound of barn wood and metal giving way. The subsequent booming had been produced by air rushing in to fill the path displaced by the craft's departure. Again he looked at the vast hole in the barn and marveled at the acceleration achieved so rapidly.

A dejected figure was walking toward him, head staring dully at the ground. Calumet had both hands in the pockets of his robe, a picture of dejection too severe for the cold to affect. He stopped, noticing that the Shattucks had moved to stand midway between their home and the barn. Chester strolled over to join them all.

"Well," said Beth Shattuck to the distraught Calumet, "it appears like you were right, after all."

"Right?" he muttered, seeming to only half hear her.

"Yep. About it bein' dangerous." She pointed forward. "Look what it went and did to our barn. Come on, J.W.," she urged her husband, "we'd better go reassure those fool cows or they'll give nothin' but Bulgarian buttermilk for a month."

The three Shattucks started for the remains of their barn. At least three and maybe four small gray-black cats of dubious pedigree trailed in their wake.

Again Chester stared upward in the direction taken by the vanished visitor from another world, another system. He found that he had to look away. The stars beneath that cloudless big country sky were pressing unbearably close all of a sudden.

"What do you think happened, Mr. Calumet—Jean?"

Somehow the chemist heard him and gave an indifferent shrug. "It was a robotic lander, probably similar in function to our advanced Viking landers. It set down here, gathered the information it was designed to, and left. Now it's on its way home, that's all." His gaze turned starward, unafraid.

"The operative question is, How long did it take in coming? If it was ten years or something equally reasonable, we may finally meet some of those beings we've always told ourselves are running around bumping into each other like crazy out there. If it took a thousand, then neither you nor I will be around to see it."

"I wonder if it set down here accidentally," Chester

murmured. "In a way they might be as disappointed as we were after the first couple of Mars landings." He nodded at the barn. "It couldn't have learned very much sitting up there."

"That all depends on what you want to study," countered Calumet. "I'm not so sure its touchdown here was as random as we might think. It was an incredibly sophisticated device. Can you conceive of an average family reacting to it as the Shattucks did? Their one reaction to it was that it was beautiful.

"Then we have the matter of the chicken-stealing coyotes which the device paralyzed, not to mention those thugs on their way to your base. I'd give twenty years of my life to have a look at the sensing equipment inside that thing.

"Somehow it must have made up its mind that it liked the Shattucks and this location and that it wasn't going to be moved. Furthermore, it was apparently intelligent enough to decide that the theft of chickens was detrimental to the family. Or that might just have been some sort of experiment. We'll never know. Not now."

"It's gone," noted Chester perfunctorily, "and there's nothing we can do about it. I'll make a report, calm the troops guarding the ranch, and then we can all go home, I guess. It's finished."

"I wonder," Calumet murmured, gazing heavenward.

"What?"

"Oh, nothing, really. It's just that it's not every night you see a new star recede into the firmament—funny coincidence."

"What is?" a puzzled Chester wanted to know.

Calumet looked at his watch. "That in a couple of hours dawn will break on the morning of the twenty-fifth." His smile was crooked. "Maybe we weren't meant to have too close a look at our guest this time around. Merry Christmas, Major."

Calumet wrapped his robe a little tighter around him and walked toward the big trailer that held sleeping quarters for the three scientists. Chester headed for his own and the field telephone inside.

He hesitated with the door half-open, even though he knew that the heat from the little electric heater was being sucked voraciously into the open air. His eyes went for the last time to the empty path the departed device had taken on its homeward course to no one knew where.

"And to all a good night," he whispered softly as he closed the door quietly behind him, shutting out the sky.

COLLECTIBLE

It's hard to see horror in bright sunshine, when it's warm and all you're wearing are shorts, a tank top, and sandals. It's hard to see horror when everyone around you seems to be having a great time, laughing and taking life easy. But it's always present. Even at its nicest, the world isn't necessarily an inherently benign place. The best we can do is try to shut out the bad and concentrate on the nice. Because if we don't, we end up turning ourselves over to an uncaring reality, to madness or hopelessness or worse.

There's plenty of terror amid the sunlight. It's just that most of us manage to shut it out. Occasionally, though, it impinges on our consciousness whether we want it to or not. The old drunk shambling across the street in front of the car. The bag lady sifting through garbage in hopes of finding something salable. The husband who goes berserk and murders eighteen family members in Arkansas. The teacher who finally has had too much and shoots a tormenting student.

That's true horror. Not bloodsucking aristocrats who turn into picturesque flying mammals or vast shapeless eminences from imaginary universes.

The line that separates the real world from unreality is thin and easily snapped, like cheap elastic. What is real and what is hallucination is not a matter of physics but of perception. Darkness is not always the catalyst for dreams. Life is as real as an individual desires it to be, or as insubstantial.

SHE SAW EHAHM-NA-EULAE CLEARLY FOR THE first time when she discovered Frank and her best friend,

231

Maureen, in bed together. It was a nebulous, leering aquamarine smudge on the wall above and behind the water bed. Its long snout hung over the custom headboard, the sinuous body plastered against the woodwork and wall and ceiling like a huge, torpid spider. Clawed forelegs cupped the matching built-in bookcase at either side of the bed. Membranous wings scratched by livid arterial lines covered the ceiling from wall to wall.

Clearest of all the dimly perceived features were the dragon's eyes, bulbous citrine orbs cut by deep crimson slits: whip-scar pupils. Vitreous yellow bulbs, they seemed to float freely in their sockets like quicksilver on glass, mocking her. The triforked red tongue flicked nervously at her, and the armored tail caressed the ceiling.

Neither Frank nor Maureen noticed Ehahm-na-eulae. They had neither the inclination nor the sensitivity to see him. Pearl had seen him several times lately, but never before in such detail.

Wrinkled covers and sheets fell away from Frank's naked torso as he sat up fast. He brushed long black hair away from his eyes and forehead, stared at her, and mumbled.

"Well, shit . . ."

How eloquent you are, Pearl thought wildly. How predictable. He was no prize . . . but Pearl was no prizewinner. Frank had been far better than nothing, a great deal better than the men she'd become used to. She'd had silly, little-girl hopes, fast fading now.

And Maureen . . . helpful, friendly Maureen . . . lay lazily alongside traitorous dreams and smiled slyly, her grin a mixture of innocence and snollygostery.

To lose Frank was bad. To lose him to the one woman Pearl thought she could trust was worse. Emotional critical mass. Critical mess, she corrected herself hysterically. You read too goddamn much. She whirled and fled down the hall.

"Pearl . . . wait! Pearl, honey!"

Putting a restraining hand on his chest, the slim girl next to him ran her fingers through the curls there. "Forget it, Frank. There's nothing you can do now. Nothing I can do." She shrugged indifferently. "You can try to

help someone like Pearl all you want, but some people
are just born sorry.''

''Yeah, but I . . .''

''There's nothing we can do,'' she repeated firmly. He
allowed himself to be pulled down.

Halfway back to her own apartment Pearl stopped running. It was a foggy morning, and the beach on her left
was still deserted. Stooped and jacketed against the Pacific chill, the lonely figure of some retired man stood
silhouetted against the early morning light. He held a
metal detector, moving the dish-shaped end back and
forth across the bronze sand. Back and forth, back and
forth, looking more insect than human, he formed a solitary icon of the elderly beach culture.

Waves massaged the tide line, sucking out and digest-
ing the detritus of the weekend: beer cans, lost rubber
sandals on their way back to Taiwan, forgotten toys, ba-
nana peels, thousands of fading cigarette butts, Popsicle
sticks, sticky paper cones that had once held miniature
cumulus shapes of cotton candy.

Her apartment did not face the ocean, but from her
single window she could smell the distinctive sour sea-
weed odor. She mounted the two flights of stairs, pushed
against the recalcitrant door, and stumbled inside. The
secondhand alarm clock on the dresser insisted it was
seven in the morning. She had thirty minutes to get to
work. No time for breakfast, even if she had been hungry. Just coffee.

A switch and several minutes turned the coils of the
hot plate red; she, it, and the clock were the only alive
occupants of the apartment. The hot plate and the ancient
refrigerator filled what would have been the closet. There
was a tiny bathroom nearby with a stall shower, john,
and sink. The white porcelain was badly wounded, ugly
black streaks and circles showing through.

Filling a cup with hot water from the pot on the hot
plate, she added instant coffee and a little sugar, moved
to the chair facing the window. Cream was a luxury not
to be thought of.

She sipped tiredly. The water purchased by the beach

city was highly mineralized. It gave the coffee a strong alkaline taste she could never get used to.

The window looked out on the apartment building across the alley. Yellow roll-up shades walled off the window directly opposite her own. She'd never seen them open. If humanity resided anywhere beyond that impenetrable barrier of faded yellow paper, she had no idea what it might look like.

Nor would she ever inquire. Prerequisites for communication in the megalopolis of Los Angeles were a willingness to initiate conversation and a car. Pearl had neither.

To her surprise, she found her hand was shaking. She'd thought Frank and she had it all together, and that had been helping *her* get it all together. Now her life was back where it had been last year, one of a karma kind with the broken windows in the back of the building that the garbage men consistently refused to pick up and that the building's manager obstinately refused to break up and place in cans.

She surveyed her collection slowly, savoring each item so painfully paid for, and managed to smile. Her hand stopped shaking. A hobby was good for the soul, she'd been told. It also gave her something else to think about besides her life, which had taken on all the aspects of permanent residence in a dentist's chair. A friend had suggested the hobby. That friend was dead, killed a year ago by a drunk driver, her body and mind shattered like the windows back of the building's garage.

Bad year, Pearl thought, sipping. Worse than the year before.

But the collection helped soothe her, took her mind off the comic-opera confrontation earlier.

The glass dragons stood neatly aligned on top of the dresser, guarding the steady tick of the old clock. Four dragon planters scattered around the room held plants in various stages of decomposition or health. The two coleuses were doing well, but they were notoriously tough. The dieffenbachia was not as strong, and the purple velvet was nearly dead. But the planters alternately grinned or growled or pouted back at her, unchanged and frozenly enthusiastic.

Wings and teeth, claws and tails, scales and eyes of various size and composition and color filled the tiny room. They hinted at unknown lands and times, strange worlds where grace and power were the norm instead of the exception and wonderful magics made life a kaleidoscope of unending delight.

At night a dragon light lit the room, its horned head supporting the torn shade, a forty-watt bulb embedded neatly in its upcurving spine. From the ceiling hung a dragon kite, vast paper wings hiding the worst of the peeling plaster. Everywhere dragons concealed, brightened, or served some useful function.

Her thoughts drifted on the smell of decaying kelp and salt. Eventually they came around to consider the mist shape she'd thought she'd seen on the ceiling, wall, and backboard of the bed this morning. A fine dragon shape that had been!

She recalled the vein marks in the wings, the powerful talons, and the floating, limpid eyes. For a vision it had been very well defined. She could imagine herself seeing something like it in a moment of great mental stress. It resembled none of the dragons in her collection, nor any she'd seen but been unable to afford.

Surely it had been staring back at her. Its expression puzzled her. At first she'd imagined it to be a leer, but that could have been due to her own unfortunate position at the time and the circumstances of the moment. It could have been expectation, she thought deliciously. Or perhaps indifference, or contemplation.

Another puzzle came from the name. Ehahm-na-eulae. All of her dragons had pet names, but nothing like that. It had been there, in her head, simultaneous with the vision. Where had it come from? It sounded faintly biblical, but many strange names sounded "faintly biblical." That's a product of your upbringing, she told herself. Life had been more solid in Oklahoma. And colder.

Ehahm-na-eulae. eHAHM-na-eulae. Oriental, maybe? She'd certainly read enough about Oriental dragons, everything that was available in the local library. Always she had the books to herself. Usually she had the library to herself. In her neighborhood literacy was not considered a prime ingredient for survival.

If not Oriental, not biblical, how about Hindu? She resolved to research the lineage as soon as she had the chance. It would be fun. Anything that involved dragons, even imaginary ones, was pleasurable. It was research in the real world that was difficult. Like trying to locate a real friend or true lover (and forget such fantasies as true love).

She washed the dragon spoon carefully, then the dragon mug. Its tail formed the mug handle. She moved to the dresser and brushed back her hair, the dragon framing the top of the mirror, holding the mirror firmly for her.

The face that looked back at her out of the mirror was used. Lines formed in her forehead like ripples in the sand, and there were sandbags beneath each eye. No time or need for makeup now. She tucked the blouse back into her skirt and secured her hair in back with a rubber band.

Next to the dresser was a small cabinet. A dragon of Mexican onyx rested on top. Inside the cabinet were additional clothes, other personal effects, and old movie magazines. The top drawer released a couple of bottles, thick-walled and squat, with seductive mouths now sealed tight by pungent corks. She hesitated, chose one.

She sipped ladylike from it. Honey-colored liquid burned her throat. She stared at the bottle, muttered a silent "what the hell," and downed a full, gut-scouring swallow. She recorked the bottle then, inordinately proud of not choking, and forced herself to put it back in the cabinet and close the doors.

Two tiny china dragons flanked the black hulk of the telephone. She stared at it for several minutes before dialing. The click-click ricocheted inside her head. Cigarette. I wish to God I had a cigarette.

The phone made some peculiar, unfamiliar noises. A strange voice came on.

"Is this . . . ?" and the voice repeated Pearl's number.

"Yes . . . operator? What's the trouble?"

"I'm terribly sorry, Miss, uh . . . Sommer. This is the United Telephone business office. There seems to be some discrepancy in our records. You appear to be two

months behind in your account? I'm afraid until at least
the oldest bill is paid . . . you understand.''

"But I—'' She stopped herself. She was a lousy liar.
"Look, please, can I make one collect call?''

"I don't . . .'' The voice turned unexpectantly human.
"Collect? I suppose that would be all right. What number would you like, please? I'll try and connect you
through this exchange.''

"Thank you, operator, really. I promise I'll get those
back payments in right away, right away.'' She gave the
number. Dialing noises came back at her. Fearsomely
beautiful, a dragon on the far wall snarled down at her
from a poster and gave her courage.

Faint noises, then: "I have a collect call for Frank
from Pearl. Will you accept the charges?''

Mumbling . . . two mumblings, one female. A single
click, final in the room, like the opening of a switch-
blade. Then the operator's voice, embarrassed.

"I'm sorry, Miss Sommer. The—''

Pearl hung up. On the operator, on Frank, on that incredible little bitch Maureen, on that part of her soiled
world. Golden haze clouded her thoughts, and she
thought again of the bottles in the cabinet. The onyx
dragon guarding it sat expressionless, solid.

No . . . no, dammit.

She happened to glance at the clock. It was nearly
eight. Oh, God.

She splurged on bus fare. Normally she walked to
work, but she happened to reach the stop just as the bus
was pulling up. It would save her twenty-five minutes.

The precious quarter clanked forlornly as it tumbled
out of sight into the collection box. She walked unsteadily toward the back of the bus. People turned nervous or
curious stares on her. She felt like shouting, screaming
back at them. There wasn't a damn thing wrong with her.
Not a damn thing! She was as good as any of 'em—
better, even. Just some bad luck lately. That didn't affect
the way a person looked, did it? Then what were they all
staring at? Mind your own goddamn business, she yelled
silently at them.

Poor commuters crowded the bus, those unable to afford a car, the Untouchables of the freeway society.

Brakes screeched a shrill about-to-stop warning, and she found herself stumbling forward, oddly fascinated at her inability to keep her balance. A vapid-faced youth in glasses and jeans caught her, kept her from falling. She almost said thank you, until she felt one hand fumbling beneath her skirt.

He smirked at her, the oily grin making her angrier than the cheap feel. He exited the bus before she could curse him.

Her face burning, she slumped into a seat. His hand was branded into her flesh. Down the aisle, an old black leaned on his cane and chuckled at her. She turned away, pressed her forehead against the window. In the chill of early morning it was comfortingly cool. By noon the fog would have burned off and the coast would be sweltering, unusually humid and hot for southern California.

A streamlined, writhing shape cavorted through the air outside the bus and glared with enormous yellow eyes back into her own. She sat up straighter on the worn seat. Ehahm-na-eulae, she thought excitedly. Again, here, outside the sanctum of her collection.

He was very clear now, the outline sharp and precise, each individual scale outlined in sunlight. This morning's horror, the sallow-faced pervert who'd accosted her, all faded at the sight of the glorious bewinged apparition paralleling the bus.

He kept pace easily, skittering across the tops of cars and trucks. One time he settled himself on the hood of a big semi like the king of all hood ornaments, gleaming talons clutching the engine cover while the triple tongue flicked tantalizingly at her.

He launched himself ahead to perch nimbly on a stoplight, balancing himself with translucent wings that filtered the fire from the morning sun, an eagle atop a metal broomstick.

For the first time she saw true colors, scales of metallic iridescent green and blue shot through with slivers of silver. Once he opened his mouth wide and emitted a flash of pure dragon flame and smiled haughtily at her as if to say: I am pure, I am clean, I am a dragon of a lineage unbroken back ten thousand years through time and space, and this is but the barest hint of what I, Ehahm-na-eulae, can do!

She almost missed her stop, and when she stepped onto the sidewalk, the dragon-wraith was gone.

Howard Johnson's lay two blocks north, a threatening tower of twelve stories that lay athwart two of the town's main streets like a vision out of Piranesi. Within lay twelve stories of soot-filled ashtrays to be emptied, spilled sodas to be mopped up, torn paper to be collected by hand, and a Hades of missing towels that she would have to pay for. Worst of all were the hectares of unmade beds that she would painfully have to remake, only to find on the morrow that, like Tantalus, she would have to begin again from the bottom.

A vast presence confronted her in the building's first sublevel. It stood by the clock that held the card that recorded the substance of her life. Miss Perkins was a towering harpy, a violent, gutter-mouthed giant of a woman with shoulders like a fullback and a voice like a Neanderthal.

Actually, Emma Perkins was a smallish middle-aged woman of pleasant disposition and firm but fair inclinations. She was the supervising housekeeper, and she looked sadly at Pearl as she came tottering in, breathless from running the two blocks from the bus stop.

"You're forty minutes late, Pearl," she said more pityingly than accusatorially. "That's three times in two weeks." She eyed the floor uncomfortably. "Last time it was over an hour."

"I—I know, Miss Perkins. I'm sorry. I've had some trouble and—"

"Everyone in this world has trouble, Pearl. I have trouble, my sister Jane has trouble, China has trouble. The world's full of troubles."

"Yes, ma'am."

"The trick is not to bring your troubles to work, isn't it?"

"Yes, ma'am, but I—"

"Some of us are better at doing that than others. That's a sad fact, but still it's a fact." She stared at Pearl, shocked by her appearance and trying hard not to show it.

"I'll . . . try to do better, ma'am. Really I will. I won't be late ag—"

"I understand, dear. You look terribly tired." Miss Perkins forced a smile. "Why don't you take a few days off? There's a three-day weekend coming up week after next, and we'll need everyone at full strength then." She took one of Pearl's hands, patted it in grandmotherly fashion.

"I'm sure with a little genuine rest and some time to think about what you really want, you'll find yourself feeling much better." She used the hand she was patting to guide Pearl toward the door leading out to the subterranean garage.

"Yes," Pearl began desperately, "but I need the—"

"I understand, dear." The door was closing behind Pearl. "In two weeks, when you're feeling better. If you still want the job." The door closed.

Pearl stood, swaying slightly. Then the import of what had just happened penetrated the fog in her brain. "Goddamn you, you rotten old whore! You can take your job and shove it! You hear me? SHOVE IT!"

The door did not reply. Pearl turned, started toward the distant exit of the dark garage. Something made a noise behind her. She stopped. The sound came again, louder this time. It sounded like garbage cans being moved around on the level below hers. It echoed through the otherwise deserted garage, bounced off shiny new Chevys and Fords. She turned.

A head was emerging from between a Corvette and a big muraled van. Vast globular eyes stared at her, stared through her own eyes into the brain beyond. The red slash of a pupil expanded in the left, then the right one, contracted lazily as the eyes rolled independently, like a chameleon's.

Teeth of all sizes and shapes were revealed by the hungry, half-opened mouth. Some were curved and outthrust like tusks. Others were slim as needles and just as straight. A few curved backward like the fangs of a snake.

Orange flame came in hot puffs from the dark gullet, the fire shining on the crystal cave inside those jaws. The dragon padded toward her on massive cushioned feet, the only sounds the faint roar of its breath and the regular tick-click its claws made on the concrete.

Pearl was backing instinctively away from this very real, very uncuddly monster. She was alone in the garage. "M-M-Miss Perkins . . . Miss Per-*KINS*!"

She spun and ran, feeling the hot breath closing on her back, expecting her skin to shrivel and crisp or hot fire of another kind to shoot through her as long teeth sank into her back and legs.

Then she was out in shockingly bright daylight. She slowed to a reluctant walk. A glance over her shoulder showed nothing emerging from the cave of the garage behind her. People stopped staring at her when she ceased running. A mother inconspicuously shooed her two children across the street, away from an encounter with Pearl.

She lifted her head, lengthened her stride, and assumed a confident air. I see dragons all the time, she told herself firmly. Real ones. In my apartment. When I'm under pressure, I sometimes conjure up imaginary ones, that's all. It happens when I nightdream, sometimes when I daydream, and occasionally, like today, when I'm not thinking intentionally about them at all. They're my refuge, and it's good to have a refuge, she told herself.

Idly, she examined the faces around her, the awkward bodies flowing past. Dragons are always perfect, she noted disdainfully. Fat ones, thin ones, big or small, they're always perfectly proportioned and exquisite of design. Their wings are never too big, their heads never at the end of necks too long, their tails constantly producing just the proper counterbalance for weight and length. Not like clumsy, inelegant human beings."

That night she finished the bottle of the morning and part of another. It was dark outside now, cooling off rapidly as the fog trundled in to cloak the beach communities.

Somewhere nearby a stereo was playing a scratched copy of a song she thought she recognized, full of electric guitars and challenging moans. A stubborn car was grinding dully on the street below, refusing its impotent owner's fervent demands to turn over.

She tried the phone again. It was possible the business

office hadn't disconnected her yet. Surprisingly, there was a dial tone. She fingered the numbers.

The voice that answered was not Frank's. She could even have coped with Maureen's, anyone's, just someone familiar to talk at, if not to. But the voice was perfunctory and mechanically unsympathetic; a recording.

"I'm sorry, but the number you have reached has been disconnected, and there is no new number."

The phone hummed patiently at her until she placed the receiver back in its cradle. She lay back on the bed, hearing the springs creak in the room's remaining heat, and began to shake.

Jesus, got to stop this. C'mon, woman, get ahold of yourself. Cigarette . . . got to have a cigarette.

She fumbled unsuccessfully through the drawer in the phone stand, then had a thought and looked beneath the bed. A crumpled white rectangle lay there. Exhausted from the effort of placing her swimming head lower than her torso but feeling triumphant, she picked it up. Two white cylinders remained in the pack.

Selecting the unbroken one, she located matches and lit up, leaning back contentedly against the stained pillow. The smoke's usual acridness was smothered by the residue of the liquor in her throat. She puffed deeply. Then she began to cry.

A scratching penetrated the room. It came from the open window. Her eyes turned, tried to focus through the smoke in front of her face and behind it. In the cabinet the brown lines of the onyx dragon seemed to shimmy. A faint breeze stirred the wings of the dragon kite, set it turning slowly overhead.

Clean and sharp as a chef's cutlery, the talons slipped over the sill and into the room. Bottomless eye pools of yellow-gold stared at her. She was not afraid this time. Maybe it was the dragon's deliberate pace, maybe the familiar surroundings of her own apartment, but she wasn't afraid.

All the dragons in the room—planters of clay, miniatures of china, poster paper and ceramic cup—seemed to expand slightly, turn slightly. She felt their eyes on her.

Silent as a cat, the adamantine, shimmering body slid through the window. Once inside, it filled much of the single room. Wings unfurled, strong and wind-defying, bumping against the ceiling.

Enthralled, she watched as it moved toward her on powerful legs. Foreclaws gripped the metal end of the bed. The magnificent head moved from side to side on the muscular iridescence of the long neck, hypnotizing her, those cabochon eyes pulling her up and into the dragon soul.

It moved slowly forward. Somehow the bed held its great weight without collapsing. Wings fluttered, irritable in the confined space. They blotted out the ceiling and obscured any hint of the pale, sickly plaster or the weak incandescent light.

Then Ehahm-na-eulae was over her, and she could have reached up and run her fingers over the thousand teeth, some curved, some straight, some hooked fanglike backward. The great eyes no longer moved independently. Both stared down into hers. Ehahm-na-eulae moved a little nearer, only its tail dragging on the floor as a mesmerized Pearl listlessly dropped the cigarette. The dragon opened its mouth, and she felt fire wash over her, clean dragon flame, light at first but rising in intensity. It didn't hurt at all. She'd known it wouldn't. It cleansed and didn't hurt at all.

She embraced the flame and Ehahm-na-eulae of the dragons and line of dragons that was ten thousand years old, as old as the forever freeing flame that engulfed her for the first and final time, purified and cleansed Pearl who was only seventeen . . .

ABOUT THE AUTHOR

Born in New York City in 1946, Alan Dean Foster was raised in Los Angeles, California. After receiving a bachelor's degree in political science and a Master of Fine Arts in motion pictures from UCLA in 1968–1969, he worked for two years as a public relations copywriter in a small Studio City, California, firm.

His writing career began in 1968 when August Derleth bought a long letter of Foster's and published it as a short story in his biannual *Arkham Collector Magazine*. Sales of short fiction to other magazines followed. His first try at a novel, *The Tar-Aiym Krang*, was published by Ballantine Books in 1972.

Foster has toured extensively around the world. Besides traveling, he enjoys classical and rock music, old films, basketball, body surfing, and weight lifting. He has taught screenwriting, literature, and film history at UCLA and Los Angeles City College.

Currently, he resides in Arizona.